ISBN:978-0-6487687-0-8

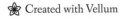 Created with Vellum

BLACKBIRD CROWNED

KERI ARTHUR

KA PUBLISHING PTY LTD

With thanks to:

The Lulus
Indigo Chick Designs
Hot Tree Editing
Debbie from DP+
Robyn E.
Jake from J Caleb Designs for the amazing cover

CHAPTER ONE

A soft but insistent beeping dragged me from the depths of sleep. I rolled onto my side and hugged my pillow over my ears, doing my best to ignore the noise.

It took several minutes and half a dozen more beeps for the realization to hit: it was my phone.

I swore and groped for it on the bedside table, then cracked an eye open. Multiple messages, sender unknown. I turned down the sound and then shoved the thing under the pillow. It was three in the goddamn morning and it had been a very long day. The last thing I needed was random texts at this hour.

The phone started vibrating instead.

I swore again, grabbed it, and hit the messages button. Twenty of them had come in the last five minutes, and all had the exact same wording—*you need to get out of the apartment. Now.*

My pulse skipped several beats and then galloped on. While it was possible these texts were misdirected, I wasn't about to ignore them. Not after all the shit that had gone down lately.

I pushed into a sitting position, then sent back, *who is this?*

There was no immediate response, and the stirring unease grew stronger. My gaze rose from the brightness of the screen to the deep shadows crowding the room. Nothing stirred, and the two knives that lay unsheathed on the spare pillow were inert. Those knives—which had been handed down to the firstborn female in the De Montfort line of witches from time immemorial—were a gift from the goddess Vivienne and born of magic as much as steel. While traditionally they held the power of life and death, they were now reacting to the presence of demons and dark elves, whether they were full or half blood.

That the knives currently *weren't* glowing didn't ease the tension slithering through me.

I scanned the darkness again. I was sleeping in my brother's room because mine still had a great gaping hole in the roof thanks to the demon-spawned witchling who'd tried to bring the entire building down on top of me. Max wouldn't object, as he was never likely to come back here.

My brother—my twin—was a traitor.

He was working with Darkside—the dark reflection of Earth that existed on a different plane, a place where demons, dark elves, and multiple other nasties lived—to bring down the current royal family in order to claim the throne and reinstall witch rule.

Just how far he'd go—and whether he was truly willing to sacrifice me in order to achieve his dream—was a question that had yet to be answered. I might be his blood price —a payment extracted by dark elves for services rendered— but, as yet, that payment had not been called in.

I wanted to believe that it wouldn't be. That Max

would, in the end, value me more than his dreams of domination.

The saner part of my soul—the part that ran on practicality rather than emotion—said it was a vague hope, at best.

Tears stung my eyes. I scraped a hand across them, then glanced at the screen as it beeped again.

Who the hell do you think?

A smile tugged at my lips. I could almost hear the annoyance running through Max's reply. *Then why are you texting from an unknown number?*

So I can't be traced. By you or by others.

Meaning he suspected we were aware of his duplicity. But did he know about Winter? I had a sudden suspicion no one had as yet told him about his lover's death—or that I was the one responsible for it. I had no doubt his responses would be a whole lot more emotional if he was aware.

Others being Darkside?

Again, there were several beats before his reply came in. *Yes.*

Why would you be worried about them tracing you when you're working with them, brother?

Mo—our grandmother, though in truth she was centuries older than that—might have wanted to string him along on the chance we could grab him and then force information out of him, but the fact he was texting from an unknown number suggested that was an unlikely hope.

Not now that he'd claimed the sword in the stone, at any rate. That sword had for centuries chosen countless witch kings before the last of them had handed human royalty both the crown *and* the means of stifling any magical assault. Max might not be aware the sword he held wasn't the true king's sword, but it was nevertheless a powerful symbol to all those who believed witch rule needed to be restored, no matter what the price or the cost. There was certainly a scarily high number of them out there—and they were in all levels of the government, given just how many of our attempts to track down and question those involved in this mad plot had gone sideways.

Of course, I wasn't about to directly confront him about the sword, but I had no intention of letting him entirely off the hook, either.

Because Darkside is not a united place, and there are a number of factions at work here. Some are friendlier than others when it comes to agreements made.

At least he was no longer affronting my intelligence by denying he was working with them.

Well color me surprised, I sent back and added a couple of shocked emojis. *It's fucking Darkside. They'll eat you up and spit you out when they're finished with you, brother.*

Gwen, you don't understand what I'm trying to achieve.

Oh, I believe I do.

Look, I haven't the time to explain right now, but there are reasons. Good reasons. But for now, you need to get out.

Why?

They're coming for you. You have five minutes, if that.

My gaze darted to the knives. Nex and Vita remained inert, but that didn't mean trouble wasn't about to hit. It just meant this time it wasn't demons.

But even as that thought crossed my mind, a faint flicker of lightning ran down Nex's blade.

I swore and quickly typed, *then call them off!*

Not my faction. Move. Leave.

Max!

No response.

I tossed the blankets off and scrambled out of bed. A storm raged outside, and the night was chilly. I shivered my way into jeans and a sweater before shoving on socks and boots.

The flickers down Nex's side grew brighter.

I raced over to the window and slid it open. The wind whipped in, full of ice. The shivers got stronger, but I leaned out. No one moved in the small courtyard below; no shadows lurked near the metal bin or moved down the lane beyond the fence line.

I had no idea what was coming at us, but it wasn't doing so from this direction. Which was good, as it at least gave us a safe escape route.

I moved back to the bed and shoved my hand under the pillow to retrieve the simple leather pouch I'd hidden there earlier. Though its weight told me its contents were safe, I nevertheless wasted several valuable seconds undoing the drawstrings then upending the pouch. The ring that tumbled into my hand was dominated by a huge red ruby onto which a cross and a rose had been carved. This was no ordinary ring, but rather, the Witch King's coronation ring. If Vivienne were to be believed—and, in all honesty, who in their right mind would ignore the words of a very old goddess? —it was the only way to find Elysian, the Witch King's real sword.

As stone met skin, a bloody fire pulsed to life deep in the ruby's heart and quickly fell into a rhythm that matched the rapid beating of my heart.

That pulse was recognition. Acceptance. Proof that I was the true heir despite the fact that never before in the history of our people had a woman claimed either the sword or the crown.

It was a fate I certainly wished had passed me by, but one I had no choice but to accept. Elysian was the only means of truly defeating and containing the dark army's might.

I shoved the ring back into the pouch, then carefully tucked it into my bra, under my left breast. It was a little uncomfortable, but as hiding places went, it was one of the better ones. A strip search would of course find it, but a regular pat down or emptying of pockets would not.

Why instinct thought such an action might happen in my near future was something I didn't dwell on.

I shoved my phone into my pocket, strapped on the knife belt, then grabbed Nex and Vita and left the room. The wind tugged at the tarps covering the roof in my bedroom, and the flapping echoed through the stillness. I stepped into the room and raised Nex. Her bright light pushed away the shadows, highlighting both the hole in the floor and the one above. Nothing cut through the heavy canvas, and there was no sign of magic other than the multiple spells protecting this place.

Which left only one option for an attack—the front door.

I padded down the stairs, wincing a little as the floorboards creaked. Like most of the buildings in this section of old Ainslyn, ours was a three-story, fairly narrow brick terrace. Our book and healing store took up most of the ground floor, and the first floor held the kitchen and living area as well as Mo's bedroom.

I paused near her door and once again studied the shadows. Nothing stirred, and yet Nex's pulsing grew stronger.

I gripped the door handle; energy immediately caressed my fingers, probing my touch but providing no threat. That Mo had implemented a locking spell suggested she might have been expecting trouble. That she hadn't passed the suspicion on to me wasn't really surprising, given her already stated intention of drawing their attacks away from me.

The door clicked open, and I stepped inside.

"What's happened?" she immediately asked.

"Got a text from Max. He said we needed to leave ASAP."

She jumped out of bed and started pulling on clothes. She was very much a De Montfort in appearance—tall and lean, with brown skin and plaited gray hair that hung down to her butt. Her eyes were a merry blue, with irises that were ringed with gold and shone with power. I was almost the total opposite. Max might have inherited the De Montfort looks, but I'd taken after my mother's side of the family —white skin, blonde hair, and dark eyes. And lean was something I'd never be.

"I'm betting he didn't actually say 'we.'" Her warm, mellow voice held an edge of annoyance. "That boy has absolutely no consideration for the old woman who raised him."

A smile twitched my lips, despite the fact it was nothing but a bitter truth. "Hey, he hasn't exactly called his dogs off me, either."

"Which makes me wonder why he's giving you a warning now." She threw on a rather colorful patchwork coat and then scooped up her purse and slung it over her shoulder. "It might well be a trap."

"Might be." In truth, it was a possibility that hadn't occurred to me. I still trusted him, still believed him, despite everything. "But he said it was a faction he didn't control, and I'm thinking he'd rather his forces get me than the opposition."

She shot me a surprised glance. "He told you that?"

"He told me it was an opposing faction, yes." I hesitated. "But only after I said we knew he was working alongside them."

"Something he'd no doubt have guessed anyway." She grimaced. "I damn well knew it was a mistake to come back here but—"

"I wasn't up to the longer flight back to Southport."

And for a very good reason—only forty-eight hours had passed since our battle at the dark altar, and I'd barely survived. That I *had* was due almost entirely to Mo's healing abilities. But weariness still rode me, and there was a drifting "fogginess" in my brain that I rather suspected was due to my temporary incursion into the gray space—the unseen, uninhabited, energy-filled dimension between our world and Darkside.

The only way to lock or unlock the main gate into Darkside was via the gray space, using Elysian. That was why my brother had been desperate to claim the sword in the stone, and why Mo had set up what I now knew to be a multidimensional wall of magic to warn us if any attempt was made to open that gate. What we'd do if that happened sooner rather than later, I couldn't say, especially as we'd yet to find the real sword.

"Yes, but we could have easily stayed overnight in a hotel." Mo slipped on her boots. "Did you open Max's window in case we need to escape?"

"I did."

"Then let's go lay a little trap and see what our attackers have to say for themselves."

I raised an eyebrow. "Wouldn't it be safer to just leave?"

"Undoubtedly, but I'm getting a little tired of these bastards constantly attacking us. Time to find out why."

"We already know why—they want you dead and me captured."

"Well, yes, but it's also an undeniable truth that the best way to kill any hydra is to sever its heads one by one."

I blinked. "Hydras are real?"

"They were." A smile tugged at her lips. "Too many got their heads severed, though, and the race died out."

I stepped back, allowing her to get past. "Could Winter have been one of those heads?"

"It's possible he was playing both sides, but I doubt it. It's more likely he was the inducement and errand boy." She strode across to the old sash window that looked out onto the street below.

"From what I saw at the dark altar, he was a whole lot more than that. Errand boys don't have the control over demons that he had."

"Except this one was also consort to a would-be king, and that would undoubtedly give him power. But he was in the end just a half-breed. Dark elves would never have rallied around one such as he."

I stopped beside her. The rain lashed the road below and raced along the gutters, but there was no sign of movement. That didn't necessarily mean anything, given concealment spells were easy enough to access. I wasn't spotting any of the usual tells of such magic, however.

"If they're already up on the roof," I said, "they're not yet attempting to cut through the tarp."

"Given their lack of success in previous attacks on us here, it'd be logical for their next attempt to be a two-pronged one." She let the curtain drop and stepped back. "I'll head upstairs and place a snare across the roof. You keep an eye on the front door."

I sheathed both knives and headed for the stairs. While I felt decidedly safer with them in my hands, the growing intensity of the lightning flickering down Nex's sides would quickly give the game away to any intruders who lurked below.

I paused at the landing and squatted close to the wall. Nothing appeared out of place below, and there were no shadowy figures to be seen, either within the store, in the section of street visible through the windows, or the inset entrance.

The heated flickers of Nex's power, now pulsing through the leather sheath and warming my thigh, very much suggested that appearance was a lie.

I silently padded down the stairs and paused again on the bottom step, my gaze sweeping the service counter and the three lines of shelving that dominated the main shop area.

There was nothing out of place and no evidence that anyone or anything had entered. The front door remained locked and bolted.

Whatever Nex sensed, it wasn't as yet in the building.

I walked down the nearest shelving aisle and stopped just behind the small T at the end. By removing a couple of ornaments and books, I'd be able to see the front door while still remaining hidden.

Magic touched the air, a familiar caress of power. Mo, creating her net underneath the hole in the roof. I couldn't help but hope it wouldn't be necessary. The last thing we needed with a storm in full fury was a sliced-open tarp incapable of keeping the weather out.

A hulking, half-shadowed figure moved across the front window and stopped close to the inset doorway. My heart leapt into high gear, beating so fast it felt ready to tear out of my chest. I knew exactly what that figure was. Knew the damage he could inflict. And I certainly knew from bitter experience just how easily the energy whip coiled in his left hand—a hand that was the size of a shovel—burned through metal, wood, and flesh. I still bore the scars of my encounter with the last one.

I sucked in a breath and resisted the urge to draw the knives and cinder his ass. Until I was sure there wasn't anyone else out there, I had to be patient.

Patience had never been one of my strong points.

I shifted from one foot to the other, then stilled as a faint sparkle formed around the door's sliding bolt; a heartbeat later, it was open. A similar sparkle assaulted the deadlock, then the handle turned and the door opened to reveal ... no one.

Which was impossible, of course. The giant hadn't moved and certainly couldn't have been responsible for unlocking the door. He was a half-demon and incapable of magic.

I narrowed my gaze and gripped Nex's hilt. That was when I saw it—a faint shift in shadows.

A Blackbird.

The giant was with a fucking *Blackbird*.

While I was well aware that Darkside had their hooks into witches right across the spectrum, I hadn't expected the Durants to be amongst their number. They were the ancient protectors of witch kings and still offered their services to the current royal family, even if that duty had technically ended when the crown had passed from witch to human. Their main skill set was the ability to manipulate both light and shadow, and it made them dangerous enemies, especially when many of them were also spell capable.

But it did at least explain why the spells protecting *this* place hadn't reacted—Mo had recently redefined who could and couldn't enter the building after hours, and in that process had added an exception for Blackbirds.

For several seconds, those shadows neither moved into the store nor back out of the giant's way. Then they parted, and a woman stepped out. She was tall, curvaceous, and dressed from head to toe in black. What surprised me was the sword strapped across her back. As far as I'd been aware, only the male members of the Durant line of witches could wield the spirit blades. There were twelve in existence—one for each of the Blackbirds who stood at the round table— and each sword contained the soul of a witch whose penance on death was to destroy the dark forces whose power they'd coveted in life.

Of course, that didn't mean more swords couldn't have been made in recent years, or that the males of the Durant line were in fact the only ones with the power or the ability to wield them.

It also didn't mean *this* sword was a spirit sword. It might simply be regular old body-slicing steel.

The Durant glanced around, her gaze sweeping across the three shelving aisles before returning to the one hiding me. My breath caught in my throat, and I froze, mentally crossing all things that she wasn't sensing Nex's continuing pulse. While her energy was more an electrical discharge along the same lines of lightning than magic, it was now so damn strong that the faint smell of sulfur touched the air. Which was yet another new development when it came to these knives and one I could do without at this particular moment.

After several more seconds, the Durant turned and began to weave an exception into Mo's magic—something that absolutely should *not* have been possible. Not by anyone unfamiliar with her magic, at any rate. Mo wasn't just an ordinary witch—she was an old-fashioned mage, proficient in both elemental magic *and* spellcraft. She basically held more power in her pinkie finger than most witches had in their entire being.

The only person who could have told her how to safely alter Mo's spells was Max—but why would he do that if the Durant worked for a different faction?

It made no sense.

But then, few things did these days.

I tightened my grip on Nex's hilt, then stepped clear of the shelving and silently walked forward.

"I'd rather you didn't weave a door into our magic for your hulking friend," I said, voice flat. "The last time one of those bastards got in here, he half destroyed the place."

She made no sound or response; she didn't even look around. She simply wrapped the shadows back around her body and disappeared from sight.

Or so she thought.

While I couldn't physically see her, I could still see the blur of her shadows as she came at me. I had no idea whether this was due to my death grip on Nex or a result of my deepening connection with Luc Durant—a Blackbird who *did* hold a seat at the round table—but either way, it was a useful development.

Particularly in a situation like this.

I pretended to look around, as if confused by her sudden disappearance, but every sense I had was attuned to her silent approach. When the breeze of her incoming sword blow was close enough to wash across my skin, I dove away, rolled back up, then spun and lashed out with one booted foot, attempting to kick her legs out from underneath her.

She didn't fall. Not entirely.

Once again, the air gave warning. I drew Nex and Vita, then thrust upright to meet the blow. Sparks flew as the crossed blades caught and held invisible steel. Nex's lightning flared brighter and, just for an instant, I heard a scream —one that was high-pitched and not of this world.

I frowned but sent Nex's lightning up the sword onto its hilt, and then across the hand that held it. The stench of burning skin filled the air, and the woman hissed, quickly releasing her weapon. But as the sword clattered to the floor near my feet, the shadows moved, giving me a brief glimpse of the knuckle-duster coming straight at my face. I leaned back but not fast enough. Metal scraped across my chin, drawing blood.

I lashed out with Vita, slicing through flesh and bone as easily as shadow. Blood sprayed, and the woman howled, a sound of agony and fury combined. I didn't give her time to react—I stepped back, raised a booted foot, and kicked at the deep center of her shadowed form. There was a grunt, followed by a crash. The shelving shook as books and a body fell to the floor. I rebalanced and watched as the shadows unraveled around my attacker.

She didn't get up. There was blood on her face, a deep cut on her left arm, and part of her hand was gone. I glanced down and saw the missing digits still wrapped around the sword's grip.

An odd whistling had my head snapping around. The mutant man-mountain now stood in the doorway, and the energy whip lit the air as it cracked toward me.

I cursed and dropped low. The blow that would have taken off my head sheered instead through the shelf behind me, destroying the long line of potions stacked there and sending glass and liquid flying.

As the whip recoiled, I leapt up and followed it, Nex

and Vita gripped tight in readiness. Lightning rolled down their sides and filled the darkness with their eagerness to kill.

The man-mountain turned and ran.

My footsteps were loud on the old flagstones as I chased after him. Both blades were afire, the lightning deadly snakes ready to strike.

I dashed out onto the pavement and skidded to a halt. The man-mountain was a dozen buildings away already. For a big man, he was fast.

But not fast enough.

I crossed the knives and smoked his ass.

As his ashes washed down the drain, I went back into our store and locked the door behind me. I had no idea if there were more Durants or demons out there, but it never hurt to be careful.

The stairs creaked, and I glanced up, my grip briefly tightening on Nex's hilt.

It was Mo, not more bad guys.

"What happened up there?" I sheathed the knives and walked across the room. The Durant's breathing was rapid and thready, but her eyelids fluttered, suggesting she was on the cusp of consciousness. Which was good, because we definitely needed to question the bitch.

"A couple of minor demons attempted to get through, but it was nothing I couldn't handle." Mo followed me through the room. "Who's this?"

"The Durant who was attempting to install a gateway in your magic so a man-mountain with an energy whip could enter."

She frowned. "Most Durants aren't capable of magic—"

"Luc and two of his sisters are, and they surely can't be the only ones." I squatted next to my captive and started going through her pockets. They contained her car keys but nothing else of importance.

"Yes, but Luc is also a knight of the round table."

I frowned up at her. "Becoming one of the twelve gives them magic?"

"In a sense, yes. When they're matched with the soul blade, they gain the knowledge and power of the witch within. And his sisters inherited their magic from their Lancaster grandmother, did they not?"

"Yes, but that only adds weight to my initial comment."

She grunted—though whether that meant she agreed or not I couldn't say—then knelt beside me and lightly pressed her hands either side of the woman's temple. Her fingers lit with a golden glow as she probed the woman's injuries and then began the healing process. After several minutes, both the cut on the woman's arm and the skin where her fingers had been severed healed over. Which I suspected wouldn't please our captive, but missing fingers were a small price to pay for working with Darkside.

Despite Mo's healing touch, the woman didn't wake. In fact, she seemed to slip into deeper unconsciousness. I frowned at Mo as she withdrew her touch. "You're not going to wake her so we can question her?"

"No, I'm not. As I said, I'm a little peeved over these constant attacks. Besides, she's a Durant. They don't crack easily."

"Speaking from experience, I take it?"

I unzipped the woman's jacket and patted her down, but there was no ID or anything else that might provide a clue as to who she was. I guess that wasn't really surprising; she obviously knew the danger of attacking us and had no doubt divested herself of any means of identification beforehand.

"I came across a couple of them back in the day when I was working as an interrogator for the High Council," Mo was saying, "Not all Durants followed legal lines."

"Which I guess could be expected given their skill set. They'd make excellent thieves."

"It was more the assassination business that called them to our attention." She frowned. "It's rather an odd move for Darkside to send a Durant here, though."

"Not really. Not if their goal was simply to kill you and capture me."

"But in failing, they've very much revealed the depth of their infiltration into witch families. I wouldn't have thought they'd be so sure of their position and strength at this point to risk it."

I motioned to the sword. "She was bearing what I think is a revamped version of the soul swords. Maybe they intended to sow confusion and doubt."

"Unlikely, given no one who knows anything at all about soul blades would ever mistake that thing for one. Whatever the hell it contained, it certainly didn't follow the light."

"Most of those in soul blades didn't either. They were placed in the sword as penance for fraternizing with Darkside."

A smile twitched her lips. "I think it safe to say they were doing a whole lot more than merely fraternizing. But still I don't believe a soul inhabited this blade. I think it was a demon."

My gaze darted to the sword. "An actual demon? How in the hell is that possible?"

"Anything is possible when it comes to the right spell, and dark elves do have a history of subjugating others to their will."

No doubt. "But what use would an actual demon be? It's not like that can impart any sort of magical energy to help with a kill."

"No, but it's not beyond the realm of feasibility that they could imbue the user with physical strength. There were plenty of such items in ancient times."

I frowned. "I was under the impression that the means of creating soul blades—and whatever this thing is—had been forgotten."

"We did. They obviously didn't." She rose. "I'll keep an eye on our captive. You might want to grab her keys and go see if you can find her car. And call Luc on your way. He can organize for the preternatural boys to come and pick her up."

The Preternatural Division was a part of the National Crime Agency and had both witches and psi talents on their books to help investigate supernatural and magical crimes. They'd gotten involved in this whole mess after a number of possible heirs for the Witch King's crown had turned up dead.

Max, eliminating the competition and ensuring he was the only one able to draw Elysian.

My eyebrows rose. "And you can't call him because ...?"

"Because I'm an interfering old bird who has a vested interest in seeing you and him hook up."

"Do I want to know what this vested interest might be— aside from the satisfaction of proving you were right about him being my destiny, that is? Or should I just ignore the whole thing as per usual?"

She grinned. "Luc knows. I've gone into great detail with the man."

I gave her a long look. "About what?"

"Grandbairns, of course. I want lots of them."

I rolled my eyes. "Don't be expecting babies from me anytime soon—especially when we haven't even had sex yet. And, besides, you already have two."

Which had been an utterly surprising revelation and no real cause for celebration. Max's only intention in having kids had been to secure his line of succession. His twins—a boy and a girl—were currently under our guard, and while Max had made no attempt as yet to get them back, I had no doubt he would.

Mo's amusement faded. "Yes, and I suspect it's going to take years for us to unpick the damage Darkside has done to them both."

I frowned. "Riona seemed relatively untouched by darkness."

"Reign is not. But that's a problem for after we've stopped your brother and Darkside. Go."

I picked up the keys, dragged on a coat, and then headed out. The wind whipped around me and the rain hit hard, blowing me back a step or two before I caught my balance and trudged on.

There were double yellow lines down most of the street, so unless you had off-street parking—we did, thanks to the old blacksmith building Mo had bought quite a few years ago—there was no legitimate place to stop. Not that those in league with Darksiders would be all that worried about rules. I headed in the same direction the man-mountain had been running. There might be no parking this side of the old bridge but the other side did have several out-of-hours sections. I couldn't imagine the Blackbird would have risked allowing man-mountain to walk too far, dead of night or not. His size and shape made him not only easy to spot but also signaled to anyone who knew anything about demons and Darkside exactly what he was.

I ran over the bridge and spotted a Ford Transit van sitting in front of the small café just down from the corner intersection. I clicked the remote, and the lights flashed in response. My hand drifted to Nex's hilt, but her steel remained silent. No demons waited within the van's dark confines. Whether anything else did was a question that could only be answered the hard way.

I moved around to the back of the van, gripped the handles, then opened the doors and jumped back.

Nothing attacked. The inside of the van was as empty as the front. I closed the doors, then walked around to the driver side and climbed in. The cab reeked of demon, and I half gagged, trying to breathe through my nose but nevertheless feeling the creature's foul scent coat the back of my throat.

After a cursory look around the cabin, finding nothing of note, I flipped open the center console. Inside was a shitload of rubbish. Whoever owned this van really liked his or her jelly babies, because there were multiple packets of them, most empty. I dumped them all onto the passenger seat and found, at the very bottom, a pink diamanté-decorated phone case. I unlatched it; there were four pockets inside, one containing cash and the other three cards. The first was a credit card, the second her license. Our Blackbird's name was Noelle Durant, she was twenty-five years old, and she lived in Taunton, which if I remembered correctly was somewhere in Somerset. The third ... My stomach dropped. The third was an ID. Our Blackbird worked for the Preternatural Division.

And *that*, no doubt, explained how the damn demons had so easily uncovered the hospital where the preternatural team had been keeping my cousin Gareth, and why they'd unleashed such a strong force against the team's defenses there. They'd been well informed of exactly what to expect by our traitorous witch.

I shoved the ID back into its pocket and then hit the power button on the phone. It was one of the newer models with facial recognition, and immediately asked for a pin when mine was naturally rejected. As the keypad flashed up, my gaze was drawn to the shaded image behind it. It was of a smiling family—four men and five women—and they all shared the same facial structure, jade green eyes, and black hair. In the photo the Blackbird currently unconscious on our shop's floor had her arm around the waist of a man I knew very, very well.

If this photo was anything to go by, Noelle Durant was Luc's sister.

CHAPTER TWO

I swore and scrubbed a hand across my eyes. While I'd never actually met any of Luc's siblings, I knew from the few bits and pieces he'd said about them that they were a close-knit family. This was going to hit him hard.

I stared down at the picture for several more seconds, wondering why on earth Luc's sister would betray her family like this when she obviously—if this lock-screen picture was anything to go by—cared about them.

I took a deep breath and released it slowly. I couldn't call the preternatural boys. Not without warning Luc first.

I got out my phone and rang him. The call almost immediately flipped over to voicemail and asked me to leave a message.

"Luc, it's Gwen. I need you to ring me as soon as you get this. It's—"

"I'm here," he said, his deep, velvety voice sounding somewhat harassed. "Sorry, I was in a late-night meeting. Everything okay?"

No, it isn't. I briefly closed my eyes, gathering courage. "I need you to come to our store right away."

"That's impossible, because I'm in London and it'll take me hours to get to Ainslyn. What's happened?"

I hesitated, still reluctant to hurt him with the news his sister was working for the other side. And yet, was it not better he hear it from me first rather than anyone else? "Our store was broken into again—"

"Why the hell are you there, rather than the safe house?"

"Because I didn't have the energy to fly all the way back—"

"There's a multitude of other accommodation possibilities between King Island and Southport that would have been—"

"Will you just shut up and let me finish?"

"Seeing you asked so nicely, please do proceed." There was an edge of amusement in his tone—one that would sadly disappear all too soon.

"A couple demons and another of those giant half-bloods wielding an energy whip broke in, but this time they were accompanied by a sword-bearing Durant."

He sucked in a breath. "It can't be one of the twelve. They're all here."

"It wasn't. It's a woman."

"The sword wasn't soul-gifted, then?"

"Unfortunately, it was, though it was a demon rather than a witch."

"But that's—"

"Don't say impossible, because there's been a ton of recent events that have proven there's no such thing as impossible when it comes to this sort of shit."

He half laughed. "True enough. Is the woman still alive?"

"Yes, and the sword is now inactive. Nex and Vita burned the demon from the blade."

"I didn't know that was possible."

"Neither did I until it happened."

"Have you called Jason yet?"

Jason was the man in charge of the preternatural team working the case, and a good friend of Luc's. "Not yet. I thought I'd better give you the heads-up first."

"Thanks, but there're plenty of Durants out there, and not all of them play on the right side of the tracks. There's nothing I can do that Jason can't."

"That's not why I called you first."

"Then why?" He paused. "You have her name?"

"I do." I hesitated again. "It's Noelle Durant."

"My *sister*? No, it can't be. She wouldn't—"

"Luc," I cut in softly, "there's a picture of you and a group I presume to be your family on her phone."

The silence seemed to stretch on forever. I climbed out of the van, shoved Noelle's phone into my pocket, and walked back toward the shop. The rain ran like tears down my face.

"Is the phone in a case that's pink and decorated with diamantés?" he asked eventually.

"Yes."

He swore. "I gave her that for Christmas last year."

"I'm sorry, Luc." Which seemed a totally inadequate statement, but I knew he'd understand the intent behind it.

"So am I." Footsteps echoed down the phone line—he was on the move. "Look, I don't care how, keep her at the shop. I've a friend with a helicopter who owes me a favor, so it won't take me much longer than the preternatural boys to get there."

"Okay."

"Thanks."

The line went dead. I took another of those deep breaths that didn't do much to ease the churning in my gut, and pushed open the shop's door.

Mo was behind the service counter making a pot of tea. She'd obviously swept up the broken glass but Noelle remained where she'd fallen, though a rolled-up coat now lay under her head and a blanket had been draped over her body. Obviously, Mo had decided she wasn't going to wake any time soon.

Mo briefly glanced at me as she poured tea into her cup and my mug. "Anything?"

I leaned against the counter and tugged off my sodden boots and socks. The flagstones under my feet were unexpectedly warm. It was almost as if heat was rising up from the earth. "Her name's Noelle. She's Luc's sister."

Mo's eyebrows rose. "Seriously?"

I nodded. "He's currently on his way here via helicopter. He wants us to hold her until he arrives, even if the preternatural team want to whisk her away."

"And you've rung them?"

"Not yet. I figured he had the right to talk to her first."

"I'm not sure Jason and his crew would agree with that. Biscuit?"

She held out the opened packet of Chocolate Hobnobs, and I plucked out a couple. Given it was unlikely we'd get back to sleep anytime soon, the crunchy, oaty goodness at least made a vague pass at being breakfast food.

"I'll call them in half an hour. That way, they should arrive the same time as Luc, depending on where exactly they are at the moment." I accepted the mug she pushed my way with a nod of thanks.

Mo leaned back against the counter. "I'm thinking once

25

this particular mess is sorted out, we should make an effort to find the king's sword."

I wrinkled my nose. "And how exactly are we going to do that? Fly around England with the ring in our claws, waiting for it to spotlight where it lies?"

A smile tugged at her lips. "Not a bad idea but one that will take altogether too long."

"We could go ask Vivienne for clarification. I mean, she's the Lady of the Lake and she made the goddamn sword. She has to know where it is."

"If Vivienne had been inclined to tell us, she most certainly would have already."

"Old goddesses," I noted, "are very annoying."

Mo laughed. "Always. But I was thinking there might be a more ready reference to hand."

I frowned. "Like what?"

She raised her eyebrows. "Are you forgetting the old book of fables you bought back from Jackie's after she was attacked?"

Jackie was a longtime friend of Mo's, and a witch who'd been studying and documenting the Witch King's line for almost as long as she'd been alive. She was also one of the two people guarding Max's twins.

"Yes, but it didn't give any indication of where the sword was. It's just lots of lovely pictures of three witch kings and multiple others."

"And what of the backgrounds? There's a reason your instincts centered on that book—you need to trust them more."

"I do trust them. I'm standing here right now because I trusted the damn things. But when it comes to information, they're often as recalcitrant as old goddesses."

She laughed again. "Go get the book."

I put my mug down, snagged another Hobnob, and munched on it as I ran upstairs. The book of fables was still sitting on the coffee table, hidden in the middle of a number of other tomes, all of which smelled older than Methuselah. I pulled it out and lifted it. The title on the front was written in Latin, which I couldn't read, but the handwritten transcription on the inside cover said its full title was *The Fables of Kings from the Time of Swords*. It was an absolute work of art—even the leather cover was an intricately carved and beautiful piece of work.

I headed back downstairs and placed it on the counter. Mo carefully opened it up and began to look through the vellum pages. Each one was exquisitely and lavishly decorated, the colorful illustrations still vibrant, beautiful, and in many cases, inked with gold.

The three witch kings were all in there, along with many others whose names I didn't recognize. Interestingly, on second viewing, I realized the sword the three witch kings carried was far plainer than the ones held aloft by the others.

I mentioned it to Mo, and she smiled. "Because when a sword holds true power, there is no need for ornamentation."

"We're talking about kings here." My voice was dry. "And have you ever met a man who wasn't into the whole 'mine is bigger and better than yours' thing? Even Uhtric wasn't immune to that propensity, if the somewhat elaborate design of the sword he left in the stone was anything to go by."

A smile twitched her lips. "There *were* two who didn't care for ostentatious displays of wealth, but for the most part, you're right."

She stopped at Uhtric's image, which also happened to

27

be the final one in the book, even though he wasn't the last of the witch kings. Like many of the other illustrations, he sat astride a warhorse with his sword raised. Unlike the others, lightning burned from the sword's tip and raced across storm-clad skies that answered in kind.

"Did Uhtric call down lightning to kill the demons?" I asked.

"Many times. But as you've discovered with the blades, it's neither easy nor without risk."

"At least he lived to tell the tale. Cedric didn't." The second king to bear the sword to war had apparently been vaporized by the forces that had run through him—though thankfully not before he'd managed to contain Darkside and relock the main gateway.

"Cedric was a moron who was warned multiple times not to raise Elysian's full power when he wasn't in the gray." She tapped the page lightly with one finger. "The background in this is rather odd—it's not a battleground or victory procession like most of the others."

I leaned forward and studied the image. I hadn't really noticed it the last time I'd looked, but Mo was right—the gently rolling hills were a rather odd choice for a king not only portrayed in full battle armor but who'd won a major battle and saved all of England.

"What background have Cedric's and Aldred's pictures got?"

She carefully turned the pages back until she found Cedric's. "Different angle but that's definitely the same hill."

The hill in question vaguely resembled a man lying down, with a stony, beak-like nose. "And Aldred's?"

His image was close to the beginning of the tome, and

the odd-looking hill made another appearance, albeit from yet another different angle.

"It can't be a coincidence," I said. "Not given all the other images have very different backgrounds."

"I wouldn't think so." She took a drink of tea and contemplated the image for several seconds. "I have to say, it looks vaguely familiar, but for the life of me, I can't place where it is."

I got my phone out. "I'll Google 'hills that look like people lying down'—there can't be that many of them."

She raised her eyebrows. "It surely couldn't be that easy."

"Why not? It's about time *something* was."

"True enough." She pushed away from the counter. "I'd better go check on our captive. It feels like she's stirring."

I glanced across the room but couldn't see any sign of movement. But then, I was neither a mage nor a healer attuned to the human body. "Where's her sword?"

"On the shelf above the hand creams. I thought the Blackbirds might want to examine it."

"To what purpose? It's not like they can replicate the spell to force a soul into servitude, and besides, they've lost the skill to mold steel into swords capable of holding souls, haven't they?"

"As I said earlier, yes, but in truth, nothing is ever lost if you know where to look for it." She bent to examine Noelle and after a few seconds, grunted. "Consciousness is definitely surfacing; these damn Durants can never be trusted to react as expected."

"Tell me about it," I muttered as I typed in the search parameters.

"I suspect that's frustration with one particular Durant speaking."

She suspected right. The damn man had determined nothing would happen between us until the threat of a war with Darkside was over. He was also utterly ignoring my sensible response that given we might not survive said war, it would be far better to grab satisfaction now while we still could. He might not be made of stone, but he certainly had a core of steel. Nothing I'd said or done so far had changed his mind.

I glanced down at my phone as the search results popped up. "Apparently there're eight natural structures that resemble people. Four are sleeping giants, one that supposedly resembles the profile of a queen, and three are standing stones."

"Where are the four?"

"Bute, Arran, Powys, and Bodmin Moor."

"Bodmin?" She rose and walked back. "That's a definite possibility."

"Any particular reason why?"

"Vivienne had a penchant for a couple of the lakes out that way. It was a long time ago—way before Uhtric's time—but it's worth checking."

"You think the sword's in a lake? Wouldn't that have a detrimental effect on the steel?"

She gave me the look—one that said "don't be daft." "You're talking about a weapon made by a woman who lives in water."

"Which doesn't mean anything given the old gods did like mixing things up when it came to humanity."

"True, but Vivienne for the most part has a soft spot for us."

"A soft spot that has in the past killed thousands." I held up a hand to forestall Mo's response. "And yes, I know she had her reasons."

Her mouth twitched. "In truth, they weren't always good ones. Something as simple as an unsatisfactory tithe could have dire consequences."

"Thank god we don't have to tithe her these days, then." I glanced at the time. "I'd better ring Jason."

She poured us both another cup of tea while I did so and then asked, "How long?"

"Half an hour." I leaned a hip against the counter and plucked another biscuit out of the packet. To hell with calories or the waistline. "We driving or flying to Bodmin Moor?"

"Flying would be safer given what happened at the bridge." She studied me for a second. "Why?"

I shrugged. "The ring only reacts when it touches my skin, which means I'll probably have to be in human form to use it."

"We can hire a car once we get there. No biggie." She pursed her lips. "I might ring Barney and let him know we probably won't make it back to Southport tonight."

Barney was her current lover and head of Ainslyn's witch council. "Ask him if his nephew has enhanced those photos you took of the King's Stone yet. It might be handy to know what the inscription actually says."

"I will." She picked up her cup and headed for the stairs. "Keep an eye on her, just in case."

I nodded, waited until she'd made it up to the landing, and then pulled the pink phone out of my pocket and padded across to our captive. It took a couple of tries, but I eventually positioned it correctly to recognize her face and got the phone unlocked. I rose, then hesitated. Mo might have deepened her slumber, but I doubted we could take the chance it would hold. Not given what she'd said about Durants. I shoved the phone on a nearby shelf then walked to the storage area at the rear of the shop and grabbed a long length of packing twine. She might still be able to magic her way of it, but her doing so would at least give me warning that she was awake and active.

I lashed the twine several times around her ankles and then tied it off on the nearby shelving. Once she was secured, I grabbed her phone and moved back to the counter, sipping my tea as I went through her device.

There was the usual assortment of photos, but nothing very recent, which was odd. She wasn't a lot younger than me, and I sure as hell took plenty of pics when I was out partying with Mia and Ginny—or had, before the world had decided to go crazy. And I guess she did have the same excuse, even if she was working with the other side.

I flicked over to her contacts and started scrolling through them. One number in the C section immediately jumped out at me. Not only because it was an unusual name—Charna, which meant dark, and had in the past been used as a nickname for Darkside—but because the last five digits matched the partial number we'd found in a carryall that belong to Tris—a former boyfriend who'd not only used me to get information for Darkside, but who'd recently been murdered in order to stop us questioning him.

That a similar number was stored in Noelle's phone could have been nothing more than a coincidence, of course, but in honesty, it was also highly unlikely.

I called the number. It rang a couple of times then flipped over to voicemail. The voice that answered was electronic rather than Max's, as I'd been half expecting. Which, given he'd used a concealed number this morning, didn't actually mean anything.

I jotted the number down in the notes tab of my phone

and then continued scrolling through the list. Nothing else jumped out at me.

I shoved the phone back into my pocket, checked my captive was still asleep, then propped my butt on the counter and scrolled through social media to see what was happening on the other side of the world.

Luc arrived twenty minutes later. He was a gorgeous man with lovely wide shoulders, well-muscled arms, and the build of an athlete. His short hair was as black as sin, his eyes the most startling shade of jade, and his face as close to angelic as any mere mortal was ever likely to get.

As I let him in, an indefinable force fizzed between us. It was more than mere awareness and deeper than simple desire—it was a connection that whispered of destiny and age, of a bond not just weeks in the making, but decades.

It was, according to Mo, *anima nexum*, which basically meant soul connection. Apparently there were three different types—one that was little more than a meeting of gazes and a recognition of fate, one where souls are doomed to battle each other through time eternal, or a final version where two souls were destined to meet through multiple lifetimes until whatever had gone wrong in their initial relationship was rectified.

Luc and I were the third type, and our connection ran back to the soon-to-be wife of the very first Witch King and the Blackbird who'd abandoned her when their affair had become known. And it had been Vivienne—incensed that the Blackbird had walked away from love rather than overturn duty and confront the king—who'd laid this curse on us.

"You got here fast."

"Kit was already prepping for another trip, and it wasn't much of a detour. Where is she?"

I motioned to the still form on the floor. "Mo spelled her asleep, but she didn't escape without permanent injury, I'm afraid."

"How bad?" It was flatly said but the air burned with the force of the emotions he was suppressing.

"She's missing a part of her left hand, including her last two fingers."

Just for a moment, anger flared deep in his eyes. Anger at me for my actions, and anger at himself for not being able to protect—or at least shield—his younger sister from something like this.

"I'm sorry, Luc," I said softly. "I really had no other choice. I also had no idea is was your sister until after it was all over."

He drew in a deep breath and released it slowly. The anger disappeared from his eyes, and a somewhat wan smile twisted his lips. "This is not your fault."

"It's not yours, either."

"No." But the edge in his voice suggested he didn't actually believe that. "Have you talked to her?"

I shook my head. "And if you want to, I'll need to call Mo down to wake her."

"Already here," Mo said, as she came down the stairs. "Heard the copter fly in a few minutes ago. How are you, dear boy?"

"Disbelieving." He grimaced. "It seems the tendrils of darkness are far wider than any of us presumed."

"I'm afraid Darkside has never risen without first ensuring they had a solid base from which to launch their attacks."

She squatted behind Noelle and placed her fingers on either temple. Luc stopped at his sister's feet, his face expressionless but his eyes glowing with the fury he was somehow restraining.

Noelle's eyes snapped open, but for several seconds there was nothing more than vague incomprehension showing. Mo remained behind her, and faint tendrils of her healing magic continued to spin around the younger woman's body. Something obviously wasn't quite right—something that hadn't been apparent when she'd been unconscious. I rather suspected it had something to do with the odd sort of energy pushing back against Mo's healing power.

Noelle took a deep breath and looked around. There was no fear or confusion in her expression, just a vague sort of remoteness. It was almost as if she was only partially present.

"Luc, why are you here?" Her voice held a note of surprise that didn't quite seem real for some reason. "And where are we?"

"How about you stop with questions and start answering them." He crossed his arms. "For a start, why the fuck are you working with Darkside?"

"I'm not—"

"Then why did you break into this store accompanied by a half-blood demon?"

"I didn't—"

"I suppose you also weren't wielding a sword imbued with the soul of a demon?"

She frowned, though it was a half-hearted attempt at best. "A soul blade? We both know that's impossible—"

"Apparently not, given we have the blade and your fingerprints are all over it."

"Luc, I honestly have no clue what you're going on about." As she struggled to sit up, her gaze fell on her hand,

and the faintest glimmer of confusion stirred in her bright eyes. "Why am I missing fingers?"

Her reaction—or lack thereof—very much suggested she either had a will of iron when it came to controlling herself —which was very possible if Luc was anything to go by—or there was something else going on.

"I'm afraid that happened when I was defending myself against your sword attack." My voice was as cool as Luc's, despite the gathering suspicion there was more to her betrayal than we'd initially thought. "Your hand was healed to stop you bleeding out."

"But ... my fingers? You couldn't reattach them?"

"We're in a shop, not a hospital, dear woman," Mo said. "And you tried to kill my granddaughter. Think yourself lucky you're alive and coherent."

Noelle glanced around. Just for an instant, something flickered through her green eyes. Something that spoke of hunger, darkness, and inhumanity.

A chill ran through me, though I wasn't entirely sure why. My gaze met Mo's and she shook her head, silently telling me not to ask the questions now crowding my mind.

"Why did you come here, then?" Luc said. "Was it to kill Mo and Gwen? Or did you have other orders?"

"Why on earth would Kendrick send me here to kill either of these ladies? They're obviously not demons—"

"Noelle—"

"Damn it, Luc, I have *no* idea how I got here or what the hell is going on. You have to believe me!"

He obviously wanted to. Desperately. "I'd love to, but the evidence—"

"Can be manufactured. We both know *that*."

"Not in this case. Not with these ladies." He thrust a

hand through his hair. "What's the last thing you *do* remember, then?"

The shadows rolled through her eyes again, and she paused long enough that I thought she wasn't going to answer.

Her reply, when it did come, was oddly disjointed—as if she was struggling to remember. Or struggling to speak.

"I was sent to ... to Euston ... to investigate a disturbance."

"Alone?"

"No. Katie was with me."

"Katie being a fellow operative," Luc said with a quick glance my way. "What sort of disturbance?"

"I ... I can't remember."

He frowned. "What happened when you got there, then?"

"We went inside." This time, her reply was so faint it was barely audible, but the shadows in her eyes spoke of a trauma she either couldn't or wouldn't confront. A trauma that didn't bode well for Katie. "Everything beyond that is blurry."

"When did all this happen?"

"Today."

"You mean yesterday?"

"Today—Friday."

Alarm ran through Luc's expression. "*Last* Friday? Are you telling me you can't remember anything at *all* since then?"

Another flicker of confusion broke past the remoteness. "Why do you say that like it was ages ago?"

"Because Friday was three days ago."

"What? No. That's impossible."

"Apparently not." He scraped a hand across his bristly chin. "What about Katie? Do you know where she is?"

"No," she said quickly.

Too quickly, I thought, as that darkness surged in her eyes again.

Luc obviously agreed with me. "Are you *sure*?"

"Yes. Why would I lie about something like that?"

"That's what we're trying to uncover." He pursed his lips. "What's the address of the place in Euston you were sent to?"

Once again she struggled to reply. I wasn't entirely surprised to discover it was the same address that Gianna— the mother of Max's twins—had given us. Winter apparently ordered her to drop the kids off there a number of times.

"And what was the disturbance reported?"

"Screams and the stench of death."

"So why was a preternatural team sent in rather than regular cops?"

She shrugged. "I got my orders and obeyed them. Ask Kendrick if you want to know more than that."

Mo reached out and touched the top of Noelle's head. The tendrils of healing energy swirled upwards, and a few seconds later, Noelle's eyes closed and her head dropped. Mo gently lowered her back to the floor.

Luc frowned. "Why did you do that? We're not going to get any answers when she's unconscious."

"You're not going to get any real answers when she's awake. Trust me on that."

"Why?" I asked. "Has there been some sort of tele-pathic or spell-based interference in her mind?"

"I can't speak to the former, and there's definitely none

38

of the latter. But magic is only one of many means of controlling someone's thoughts or actions."

"Preternatural operatives are regularly screened for telepathic, medical, or magical interference," Luc said.

"And I would have thought an operative couldn't go missing for three days without someone noticing," she bit back. "Apparently, that's not the case at *all*."

He sucked in a breath, but a loud and somewhat urgent rapping on the door cut off anything he might have said. I automatically reached for Nex's hilt but relaxed when I realized it was Jason and two other men. I flexed my fingers in a vague attempt to ease the tension, then rose and walked over to let them in.

"You'd think Darkside would have learned their lesson when it came to attacking you two," Jason said. He was a tall but slender man with brown skin, silver hair, and bright green eyes. "What have we got this time?"

"One of your own," I said, even as Luc added, "My damn sister."

"What?" Jason immediately strode over. "Noelle? What the hell is she doing here?"

"That is very much the question of the moment," Mo said evenly. "And it is, unfortunately, one I suspect will take time and careful unpicking to answer."

Luc's gaze shot to her. "Unpicking? Why? I thought you said there was no magic on her?"

"There's not, but I've been monitoring her responses alongside her physical condition, and there's something odd happening with the electric output of her brain—something that only became evident on awakening."

"Would that be the odd shimmer reacting against your healing magic?" I asked.

Mo's gaze shot to mine. "You saw that?"

My smile was wry. "Obviously."

"Ladies," Jason said, voice sharp. "Can we please concentrate?"

Mo sighed. "I've seen this before, but it's nevertheless a very rare occurrence."

"Mo," Luc growled. "I'm really not in the mood for games right now. Whatever it is, just spit it out."

"Fine," Mo said. "But you're not going to like it."

"Mo—"

She raised her hand, stopping him. "I don't believe your sister is spelled or under telepathic influence. I believe she's absorbed a wraith demon."

CHAPTER THREE

"*A what?*" the three of us said together.

"A wraith demon. They're a rare find outside of Darkside, as they generally can't exist within the structure of our world."

"Meaning our atmosphere, or something else?" I asked.

"Our atmosphere is not all that different from Darkside —we couldn't exist in each other's worlds if that were not the case."

"Then why are wraiths rare here?"

"Because they're creatures of chaos. They cannot exist without it."

"Chaos as in disorder and confusion? Because I would have said the current state of the world would be perfect for them," I said.

"The chaos they crave is more along the lines of mass destruction and war. Indeed, the last time wraith demons emerged was during the Second World War. They infected a number of high-ranking government and military personal."

"To kill or control?" Jason asked. "And to what point?"

"If they control those who are in charge, they've more chance of creating the perfect situation in which to feed and grow." She grimaced. "That they're emerging again now is not a good sign."

"Why would it inhabit Noelle, though? It's not like she can help create the chaos they crave—she's not high enough in the pecking order."

"Perhaps not," Mo said, "but the Preternatural Division will play a part in any upcoming war with Darkside, and infecting her might be nothing more than a safe means of keeping track of what her division is doing."

"Then why not infect her boss? Or someone else in charge?" Jason asked.

Mo glanced at him. "It's very possible they already *have* infected others, especially when you consider how often our joint investigations have gone south. But the preternatural team will not be their only targets. They will try to infect as many as possible across the full spectrum of government."

"Well, fuck," Jason muttered.

"Understatement of the year," Luc said. "How the hell do we stop them? And can we get it out of Noelle?"

"I am by no means an expert on these things. I *was* working for the High Council at the time of the First World War, but wraith displacement was never something I was involved in—"

"Then who—"

"*However*," Mo continued, cutting Luc off. "I know the theory behind it all well enough. Wraiths are, essentially, gaseous creatures that seep into the body through the skin and become one with the neurological centers. Removal involves a mix of careful magical unpicking and the use of what we now call thermal imaging."

Which was why she'd been monitoring Noelle's brain

activity. Her electrical and maybe even biochemical outputs would have been very different with a wraith inside of her. That I'd also seen it was, as she'd said, interesting, though I had no idea what it meant.

"Can you do that?" Luc asked. "How dangerous will removal be?"

Mo grimaced. "I'm nowhere near skilled enough to perform such an operation, but the High Witch Council will certainly have a team who can. As to how dangerous the process is, that has always depended on not only how long and how deep the immersion is, but also on how old the wraith is. I've seen people infected with minor wraiths who came out intact mentally and physically while others lost their sanity."

Luc swore again and thrust a hand through his hair. "Then we need to act now."

Mo nodded and rose. "I'll go ring the council and get the process moving."

"Before you do," Jason said, "do we know *where* she was infected? I'll have to seal the area off until we can get it checked."

"You won't be checking it, the council will," Mo said. "Wraiths are tricky critters to deal with."

Jason hesitated and then nodded. "I'll still need the location."

Luc gave him the address then added, "She was sent there to investigate a possible Darkside disturbance."

"What sort of disturbance?" Jason said. "I wasn't informed about an attack in that area, and I should have been."

"Residents reported screams and a thick smell of death in the apartment above them," Luc said. "Noelle and Katie were sent to investigate—"

"Where's Katie then?" Jason cut in sharply.

"Noelle couldn't say. She can't remember anything more than arriving there."

Jason swore and turned to one of the men behind him. "Contact Kendrick and see if he's got any further information."

"Noelle was obviously infected within that apartment," Mo said. "Wraiths cannot move around easily in our world —there's far too much light pollution for them to survive more than a few minutes—and *that* means there has to be an active gateway present there."

Jason frowned. "I didn't think it was possible to create new gateways."

"The dark elves are capable of creating minor gateways but for the most part don't, as it generally costs their life. It's more likely that if there *is* a gateway there, it's simply a reformed one, especially given how old that part of London is."

"My education is obviously lacking," he said. "I had no idea gates could reform."

"Gateways have never been static nor entirely stable. Whatever external force caused the gates to form between our two planes also likes to tear them apart."

"Can we stop getting sidetracked?" Luc said, an edge in his voice. He waved a hand at his sister. "I need her fixed, Mo."

She touched his arm lightly. "They'll try their best, dear boy. I promise you that."

She stepped past him and headed upstairs to make her calls. Luc took a deep breath, though it did little to calm his inner emotional turbulence because it continued to wash across my senses. He glanced at me. "What happened to the sword Noelle was carrying?"

"We moved it out of her reach." I walked down to the shelf holding the pretty array of handmade soaps then reached up to the one above and grabbed the sword. The grip no longer held the charred remnants of Noelle's fingers —Mo had obviously removed them when she'd placed the sword up here—but it was icy to the touch and made my skin itch unpleasantly. The edges of the black blade were frosted, and the steel had an odd, almost greasy sheen to it.

I shivered and hurried back. Luc accepted the sword with a frown. "We've a couple of examples of these blades in our archives, but they're not soul swords, as such. As far as I'm aware, they were only ever used as conduits to channel whatever elemental force the dark elves were controlling."

Which was basically what the two king swords did, even if Elysian also granted its user the ability to step fully into the gray.

"Given the coldness emanating from the metal, I take it the power this sword channeled is ice?" And if it *did*, why hadn't Noelle used it on me?

Was it simply a matter of the infusion not being complete enough for her to fully control that portion of the blade's power? Or did she have orders not to kill me? Considering what Max had said, that was possible, though her sword blow could have cleaved me in two had I missed catching it with the knives. And the man-mountain certainly hadn't been playing around.

Luc nodded, his gaze still on the blade. "Dark elves used them to freeze and shatter opponents."

"Which, when it comes to the many varied ways in which they like to kill, sounds a lot quicker and cleaner than most," Jason commented.

"The archives suggest the opposite." Luc turned the

sword around and studied the top of the pommel.

"Mo said the sword was probably inhabited by an actual demon," I commented.

Luc nodded again. "But I don't think it was fused into the metal during smithing—which is what happened with our soul swords—but rather forced into the blade afterward."

I frowned. "What makes you think that?"

He turned the sword around. There was a small hole on top of the pommel where the button usually sat. "The entire hilt is hollow."

"What benefit would forcing a demon into the sword have, though?" Jason asked.

I glanced at him. "It's possible it might have imbued the user with a demon's speed or strength."

"And did it?" Luc's gaze jumped to mine. The jade depths were turbulent and deeply worried. He knew well enough that his sister might not come out of this alive.

I hesitated. "She *was* very strong, but I couldn't say whether that was her natural strength or demon infused. I was too busy concentrating on surviving."

His gaze dropped back to the sword, but not before I'd caught not only another flash of anger but also guilt. It was then I realized why—he'd failed once already to save someone he loved. He didn't want to repeat that failure with his sister, even if this situation was entirely different and utterly beyond his control.

I clenched my fingers and resisted the urge to wrap my arms around him and comfort him. Tell him that she'd be all right, even if I suspected that was a lie.

But this was neither the time nor the place, and I doubted he'd have appreciated it anyway. If I'd learned anything about this man, it was the fact that he was determined to keep his emotions—and me—at arm's length until this was all over and we were safe.

"One thing I don't understand," I said, "is why give Noelle the sword? If they wanted to use her to get at either Mo or me, why not do so openly? She's preternatural and your sister—I would have trusted her."

"I suspect they didn't intend for her to be seen or captured," Mo said as she clattered down the stairs. "They probably meant her to do nothing more than weave a doorway into my magic so that the half-blood giant could enter. But when you confronted her, the wraith's natural instinct for destruction and death kicked in."

"Meaning it wanted them *both* to die?" Luc said incredulously. "How does killing its host when it's not in its own environment even make sense?"

"Demonic actions don't always make sense," Mo said. "You should know that well enough."

Luc's answering grunt was not a happy sound. "Any luck with the High Council?"

She nodded and handed him a piece of paper. "The displacement team will meet you both here—it's a secure if old facility designed to cater for infestations such as this."

Luc glanced at the paper and then shoved it into his pocket. "You're not coming with us?"

"There's nothing either of us can do there." She motioned to Noelle. "She'll remain asleep until you reach your destination. It's safer for all of you."

Luc handed Jason the black sword, then bent, undid the twine, and carefully scooped up his sister. When he turned, our gazes met. Those vivid depths were still filled with concern, but this time, it was for me. "Whatever you're planning to do next, be careful. I don't need the additional worry right now."

A smile twitched my lips. "Careful is my middle name."

He snorted. "Which is like saying reserved is Mo's."

"I'll have you know I certainly can be, young man." Her voice was severe, but her blue eyes twinkled.

"Hmm" was all he said to *that*.

I smiled and followed them over to the door, locking it behind them.

"Will she survive the extraction process?" I crossed my arms and watched them walk down to the illegally parked black van.

"In all honesty, I don't know. Many didn't." She sighed and moved back to the stairs. "Even if she does, there's no guarantee she'll ever be the same. No one can be so intimately touched by darkness without side effects."

Then I could only hope that for Luc's—and his family's —sake, she was an exception to the rule.

I followed her up the stairs. "Did you tell the High Council about the apartment and the possible gateway?"

"Yes. They're sending a team over to deal with both."

"They've still got teams that deal with this sort of thing?" I said, surprised. "I thought wraiths hadn't been active since the last war?"

"For the most part, that's true. But the High Council learned the foolishness of disbanding such a specialist unit after a situation that developed eons ago—one that almost wiped out the entire council." She motioned to the next set of stairs. "You might want to go change into something warmer. I checked the forecast for Bodmin Moor, and it's going to be a perfectly shitty day."

"Fabulous," I muttered. "There's nothing nicer than flying in foul weather."

She grinned. "You're young. You'll survive."

"Yes, but that doesn't mean I have to freaking like it."

She laughed and disappeared into her room. Once I was in full waterproof gear, I pulled the ring out from under my breast and tucked it safely into the bottom of Vita's scabbard. Like the knives, the ring was made of silver, which was one of the few substances immune to the shifting magic. Then I lashed the two knives together so that they were easier to pick up with my claws.

Mo walked in. The backpack slung over her shoulders had two sets of wellies roughly tied onto it. "Thought I'd better bring along some proper footwear *and* some food. I know how grouchy you get if you don't have breakfast."

I grinned, although it was true enough. "There *are* villages in and around the Moor, you know, and they do have such things as cafés."

"Yes, but I'm thinking it might be better not to be seen in too many locations within the area. It's possible they're keeping a watchful eye on all the ancient sites."

"Why would they be doing that? Max has drawn the sword from the King's Stone, and they have no idea it's not the real one."

"Perhaps, but there are plenty of other god-gifted artifacts lost to the mists of time I bet they wouldn't mind getting their hands on."

I frowned and waved her to the window. "Like what? And why is this the first time you've mentioned such things?"

"Because in the current situation, it's hardly worth getting all het up trying to find them. Besides, I actually have *no* idea where to even start looking for them. Ready?"

"Yes. And you didn't answer the first part of that question."

"No, I didn't, did I?"

She laughed, changed shape, and flew out the

49

window. I shook my head and called to the magic that allowed us to shift. It rose swiftly, a thick wave of heat that swept through muscle, sinew, and bone, altering and miniaturizing all that I was in human form and shifting it across to my bird persona. As the power reached a peak, there was a moment of nothingness—a moment where I was neither human nor blackbird but held in unfeeling suspension somewhere between the two—and then I was winged, and the freedom and the glory of the skies was mine.

I scooped up the knives and flew out the window, following the brown speck that was Mo. The night was crisp and cold, and despite the ominous-looking clouds that curtained the sky and blocked the moon from sight, the storm had ceased. Dawn came and went in a glorious blaze of color, and it wasn't until we neared Launceston that the wind truly picked up and the rain began to fall again.

We regained human form in a rather scruffy-looking parking area in the grounds of an even scruffier-looking car rental place.

"I arranged for the use of a smallish all-wheel drive," she said, striding toward the small collection of transportable office units and sheds, one of which had Office emblazoned across the front. "I figured it would be safer on the off chance we have to go off-road."

I tucked my knives under my coat and followed. I wasn't seeing anything resembling a small SUV in the immediate area, just a ton of cars and trucks.

Mo took the steps two at a time and pressed the buzzer. There was no immediate response, but the internal lights were on, so someone was obviously around. Mo tried again; this time, an internal door slammed, then footsteps echoed.

"Sorry," a rather red-faced man in his mid-fifties said. "I

was giving the SUV a final once-over. I take it you're Mo De Montfort?"

When she nodded, he opened the door and ushered us inside. The interior space was the opposite of the rather grungy outside—modern, clean, and tidy. Once he'd gone through the details and we'd signed the paperwork, we headed outside to check the SUV for dents, scratches, and whatnot and then hit the road. I pulled my knives out and retrieved the ring. It pulsed warmly against my finger, but there was nothing to suggest it was in any way directional. Not yet anyway.

"There might not be," Mo commented when I mentioned it. "Not until we get closer. You want to open the sandwiches? I'm feeling a mite peckish."

I handed her one and munched on the other. The storm that had been threatening for most of the morning finally unleashed as we entered the hamlet of Bolventor, forcing Mo to slow to a crawl lest she miss the turnoff for Dozmary Pool.

As we crested the first hill of the old road, the left edge of the ruby at the heart of the coronation ring began to glow. A few seconds later, the road swept around to the left.

The ring *was* indicating direction.

We continued on. A triangular sign eventually appeared to indicate a small side road to the right, and the light within the ruby's heart indicated we needed to follow it.

Mo swung onto the narrow sidetrack and then slowed even further. The wipers weren't doing a whole lot to clear the force of the storm right now, and visibility was poor. I was *not* looking forward to stepping out into it, though if the sword *was* in the lake itself, the storm would be the least of my problems.

We crawled past a series of barely visible buildings and continued on, following what had become little more than a single farm lane. The ring's glow intensified to the point where the whole stone shone. We were obviously getting close.

The lane ended at a lovely old farmhouse and, opposite it, barely visible in the gloom, was the dark and choppy water of a lake.

"I gather that's Dozmary Pool?"

Mo nodded. "It's a singularly depressing-looking place for a good part of the year. I never really understood what Vivienne saw in it; many in medieval times had considered it to be bottomless, but in truth it is little deeper than a couple of meters."

"Is it connected to any of the larger lakes in the area?"

"I believe the marshy western edge feeds into Colliford Lake, though Vivienne doesn't need a direct above-ground connection to move from lake to lake. There are plenty of underground watercourses she can use. Ready?"

"As I'll ever be."

I shoved my phone into the glove compartment, changed my shoes for my wellies, then pulled the hood over my head and climbed out. The wind hit with the force of a hammer, driving me back a step or two before I caught my balance.

"Fuck," I shouted to the black blur that was Mo. "Can't we sit in the car until the storm is over?"

"The storm is the best cover we could have," she shouted back. "Even if someone *is* watching the lake, they're not going to see anything in this."

I couldn't see anything in this. Nothing beyond the pulsing red glow of the ring, at any rate.

I swore again and headed across to the rough old path that led down to the lake. The ground on either side of us rose, blocking at least some of the wind even if the rain still pelted my body and assaulted my face. I trudged on, peering through the gloom, waiting for a response from the lake to the ring's presence, but not seeing anything other than an old post-and-wire fence that ran out into the stormy waters and disappeared.

I was beginning to suspect I might have to do the same thing.

I stopped at the water's edge. Waves struck at my feet and splashed up my legs, but there was no sense of welcome. No sense of power. Which wasn't unexpected, given Vivienne no longer resided in this lake, but if the sword *did*, why was there no response?

I glanced at Mo. "What the hell do we do now?"

"A connection to the water has always been needed when interacting with the Lady of the Lake," she replied. "It may well be the same when it comes to her artifacts."

I squatted and pressed my hand into the icy water. For several heartbeats, nothing happened, then a ribbon of light burst from the heart of the ring and arced across the lake. It hit the surface at a point beyond the old fence and dove under.

Nothing else happened. Not for several minutes. Then an odd rumbling filled the air, and the ground shook. A heartbeat later, a larger than normal wave crashed into my body and drove me back onto my butt. I grunted and scanned the choppy lake, looking for whatever had displaced such a large volume of water.

There was nothing out there—nothing visible anyway.

Even the arc of light was being fragmented and blown away by the wind.

The ring, however, now pointed to the spot where its light ribbon had plunged into the water.

I glanced up at Mo. "I'm guessing I'll have to wade out."

"Vivienne never did like to make things easy, but do please be careful. I'm too old to be swimming out into icy water to rescue you."

"You're a mage—I imagine you could simply command the water to spit me out." I paused thoughtfully. "In fact, why can't you just make the water part so I can just walk out there?"

"Because my name is Mo not Moses. Besides, control over large bodies of water such as this was never my forte. Earth and storms are my comfort zones."

Which *didn't* mean she couldn't command the elements of water or even fire if the need rose. "What about the other two mages? Do they have specialties?"

"Gwendydd is the botanist of the group—she can draw on and manipulate the energy of the living world. Mryddin is the spell caster, with a sideline in refashioning rocks and metal." She pointed to the slate-gray sky. "The storm is only going to get worse, you know."

I took off my wellies and socks, handed her my knives, then rose and cautiously stepped into the water, inching my way forward in an effort to avoid tripping over whatever rubbish might lie on the lake's floor.

Slowly but surely I walked deeper into the choppy water. I did my best to ignore the ice leaching ever further up the inside of my pants, but a gasp nevertheless escaped when the water hit my nether regions.

I alternated between cursing the water, the weather, and the old goddess, and continued on, following the old fence line until it dove under the water. The water was just over chest-deep now, and I really wasn't seeing anything more than the choppy white-topped waves that crashed over my head with monotonous regularity.

And yet ... something was out there.

It was a presence that felt vaguely familiar and yet totally alien. It held no life and yet spoke of thunder and lightning, of the sky and the earth, and the energy that soared between them.

My heart began beating a whole lot faster, and an odd mix of trepidation and excitement ran through me. I raised the hand on which the ring sat; a beam of light shot from the ruby and plunged into the water just over ten feet ahead.

The sword was close.

So damn close.

I took a deep breath and then pushed on, only to discover the hard way that the ground dropped sharply. I unbalanced and went under, momentarily panicking as water rushed up my nose and down my throat. I kicked back to the ledge, coughing and spluttering as I tried to regain my composure.

The sword might be down there, but I'd have to dive to grab it—not something I'd ever been good at. I was definitely a floater more than a swimmer.

But that wasn't an option here. I sucked in another of those deep breaths that did little to ease the furious pounding of my pulse, and then dove under.

The water was black ink. I pushed out a hand, vaguely hoping the ring would again help me locate the sword. Red light pulsed briefly from the ruby and, in the dark depths far below, lightning responded, cutting through the darkness and briefly highlighting a vaguely cross-like shape. I kicked like crazy toward it, battling the turbulent water and my own instinctive need to rise back to the surface.

The closer I got, the fiercer the lightning became, until

the water fairly glowed with its force. It wasn't coming from the sword—which, like the one on King Island, had been sheathed deep in stone—but rather the crown that had been slung over the hilt.

That crown was Uhtric's, which we'd given to Vivienne for safekeeping. Obviously, we *had* needed it to find the sword.

The water's depth seemed to be far more than the few meters Mo had suggested. It wasn't until my lungs began to burn and the need to breathe became more urgent that I was finally close enough to reach out for the sword. But as my fingers wrapped around the hilt, an otherworldly wave surged from the metal, rushing through every part of my being, a fierce and brutal power that seemed to be seeking.

Or *assessing*.

The exposed portion of the blade's fuller—the beveled groove that ran down the center of the steel—began to glow with a strange, blue-white light, but the need to breathe was now all-consuming. I had to raise the sword—now—and get back to the surface. I did *not* want to make a second dive down.

I shifted the crown, gripped the hilt with both hands, then placed my feet on the stone and pulled back with all my might.

For an instant, the sword resisted.

Then that otherworldly power surged once more. This time, it spoke of earth and air, fire and water, life and death. It seemed to peel away flesh, muscle, and bone, leaving nothing behind except a being of pure energy.

It was that being the sword responded to.

The sword came free, and with such force it sent me flying backward. Out of the water and into the air.

Taking consciousness with it.

CHAPTER FOUR

Consciousness returned with the sharp awareness of both ice and fire. My body ached with cold, and yet flames burned underneath me. Flames that weren't in fact real, and whose source lay deep underground, in the molten heart of the earth itself.

They were mine to use if I so wished.

Just as the turbulent water only feet away from where I lay and the thunderous might of the skies above was.

It wasn't *just* the sword still gripped in my right hand providing the connection. Those elemental forces were now a part of me, an inner pulse as strong as my heart.

Fear surged, and my eyes sprang open. The storm still raged, but I could now see the ebb and flow of the currents that ran across the ominous sky, feel the force of electricity building behind the clouds, waiting to be unleashed.

I released the sword, and the sensations eased, though the pulse of ready power remained deep within. All I had to do was reach down and grasp ...

"Easy," Mo murmured. "Don't move just yet. Take your time, catch your breath."

My gaze flicked to her. She sat on the ground next to me, her knees drawn up close to her chest and her arms wrapped around them. Her grip was so fierce, her knuckles glowed in the gloom.

Because she was afraid. For me.

Which didn't do one thing to calm my inner turmoil.

"What the fuck just happened?" My voice was hoarse, and my throat felt raw. "Why didn't you warn me?"

"Because I didn't know it would be like that for you. It wasn't for either Cedric or Uhtric."

"But it *was* for Aldred?"

She hesitated. "To an extent. He said it was as if he'd been stripped down and examined by every force that ever existed within the universe. But it was only for a few brief minutes and did not occur again."

Being stripped down was definitely a no-frills description of what had just occurred. "So why would it happen to him and me and not to the other two witch kings?"

"Elysian was raw when Vivienne handed it to Aldred. Its power has been tempered and refined over the years."

"By the goddess?"

"And by the kings who have since drawn on its power."

"Which means I shouldn't have felt what I did—so why did I?" I pushed into a sitting position, but it was an effort that left me wheezing.

"It would suggest the De Montfort line has a direct connection back to Aldred." She shifted onto her knees and placed a hand over my forehead. Warmth pulsed from her fingertips, chasing away the inner chill but not the fear.

"*All* the witch kings can be traced back to Aldred." His line was the only one that could use the damn sword, after all. "And I thought the De Montfort connection ran back to Luis? I didn't think it went any further than that?"

Luis was the first-born son of Rodella Aquitaine, Uhtric's older sister. She'd been widowed soon after Luis had been born and subsequently married a second cousin—Phillip Aquitaine. Their union produced three more sons and two daughters, and that bloodline still existed today.

"We were obviously wrong about that." She rose and held out a hand. "Come on, let's get you out of the weather *and* those wet clothes."

I let her pull me upright. "Into what?"

"Once we're in the SUV, you can have my sweater. It'll keep you warm enough until we get back to Launceston and can buy something else."

I nodded and bent to pick up the sword, my fingers brushing the crown that remained hooked around the hilt. Lightning leapt from the oval-shaped, blue-gray stone at the heart of the crown and raced down the sword's fuller. I hesitated, fearing to touch either, lest that surge of otherworldly power repeated. Which was stupid. If I was to have any hope of defeating my brother and keeping the main gate locked, I'd have to learn to confront and control both this blade and the powers it could raise.

I unhooked the crown and handed it to Mo, and then, somewhat warily, gripped the sword's hilt. The fury of the storm intensified, and slender forks of unleashed lightning briefly danced around me. Then the sensation faded, as did the glow in the fuller, and Elysian was nothing more than a sword.

My gaze met Mo's. The fear remained in hers. "You sensed that surge."

"Yes."

"Why?"

She picked up my wellies and socks then turned and led the way back to the old path. As the ground rose around us

59

again, the wind eased, but not the rain. If anything, it seemed worse.

But maybe that was simply a matter of me being more attuned to it.

"Mo?" I prompted when she didn't immediately answer.

She sighed—a barely audible whisper of sound. "I'm a mage with power over earth and storms, remember. It's natural I'd feel the response of those elements when you grip Elysian's hilt."

Which made sense, I guess. "That doesn't explain why you're afraid."

She glanced briefly over her shoulder. "I know what those forces can do to the unprepared, Gwen."

I frowned. "But Aldred faced the same force and survived."

"He never had full access. Elysian might have been designed as both a gateway into the gray space and a means of gathering the power of all four elements, but the latter had been tempered after that initial burst of acceptance. No mere mortal could withstand the sheer power of the collective."

"You can."

"I'm a mage. We cannot be killed by that which we control."

Which didn't mean they *couldn't* be killed—a well-placed knife or bullet would certainly end their lives as easily as any mortal's.

"What I truly fear," she continued softly, "is that it's *my* bloodline enhancing the connection between you and the sword."

I stared at her back for several moments, not so much mulling over what she had said but what she hadn't, then said, somewhat incredulously, "Does that mean what I think it does?"

"Yes."

"But ... but I'm aging normally. Doesn't that fact alone mean I *couldn't* have inherited the DNA adaption that give mages their mega-long lifespans?"

"No, because it wasn't until I had my first child that the mutation kicked into gear for me."

I swore and thrust a hand through my sodden hair. "In a day filled with revelations, this is probably the shittiest."

She pulled the keys out of her pocket and opened the SUV. "Yes, and I'm so very sorry, Gwen."

I glanced at her sharply over the hood of the SUV. "For what?"

"For the heartbreak that lies in your future if indeed you have inherited that gene."

Just for an instant, I saw the echo of that heartbreak in her eyes. For century after century, she'd watched all those she cared about grow old and die—her lovers, her children, her grandchildren, and her great-grandchildren, on and on through the long centuries of her life as she aged only fractionally.

Tears stung my eyes and pain filled my heart. Not for me, not even for the future that might well await me, but for her. For everything she'd faced and the sacrifices she'd made as a guardian of this land.

She blinked and the echo was gone, even if it lingered within me. I took a deep, calming breath and then hurriedly stripped off. After emptying my wellies, I tossed the sword and my clothes into the footwell on top of the crown, then jumped in and pulled on the sweater Mo handed me. She'd knitted it out of chunky wool and it wasn't only warm, but smelled of a mix of cinnamon and citrus. It was the smell of my childhood; the smell of safety. I put on the seat belt and then drew my knees up close to my chest and tugged the sweater over them in an effort to warm up more quickly.

Mo started the SUV, turned the heater up to full, and then drove back down the lane.

"When did you start to suspect?" I asked. "It wasn't just now, was it?"

"No. It was in the shop, when you saw the shimmer of the wraith's energy."

I frowned. "Why would *that* make you suspect?"

"Because you were barefoot, and it was the earth's reaction to the weight of darkness that allowed you to sense the wraith, even if you weren't aware of it."

"Why didn't you say anything, then?"

"Because I hoped I was wrong."

I scrubbed a hand across my eyes. "So if I *have* inherited the mage gene, what does that actually mean? Other than a life spanning centuries, that is?"

"Well, for one thing, it'd explain why you can now access Nex and Vita's power without actually holding either knife. In fully accepting you, they must have unlocked that which was always within you."

Given how utterly drained accessing that ability left me, there was at least a small part of me that wished it had remained locked.

"Could that be why I recovered faster after what happened at the dark altar? I mean, I should have been out of it for days, at the very least."

"Probably. And if that *is* the case, then it is something of a relief. At least I don't have to worry so much about you being torn apart by the lightning."

"No, you just have to worry about me being erased by dark elves, demons, Elysian, and my brother."

"I'll ask you not to destroy my brief moment of respite, young lady."

I smiled, though my heart wasn't really in it. "So is it just your blood that's making the connection with Elysian stronger?"

"I suspect not, as this is the first time since the sword's creation that another important factor has come into being."

"I take it you mean Vivienne's declaration that Gwen-hwyfar's fate was tied to the sword, and that blood and destiny had converged in this timeline."

She nodded. "Gwenhwyfar bore Aldred one son before she killed herself. That son had five daughters, all of whom went on to bear daughters. I have no idea if that continued down through the centuries, but I now suspect it might have. It wouldn't be the first time an old god or goddess has interfered in the fertility of humans."

"I hope she's not playing that game these days," I muttered. "I rather suspect Luc wants both daughters *and* sons."

She smiled, though it was a rather pale imitation of its usual robust self. "If you *are* the culmination of Vivienne's plans, then I daresay her interference will end here."

"Unless of course, Luc follows the same path he has in countless other rebirths and chooses duty over love."

"I can't see that happening—not when all the various threads of Vivienne's plans seem to be converging in *this* lifetime." She grimaced. "Of course, it's now pretty obvious there are quite a number of things I haven't foreseen over the long years of my life."

I reached across and gripped her thigh. "You're a mage, not a goddess. You can't be expected to see the invisible threads of destiny woven through time and multiple genera-tions." A smile tugged at my lips. "I will, however, admit that I *did* go through a phase of believing you *were* actually a goddess when I was younger."

She laughed and placed her hand over mine, squeezing lightly. "You are a darling girl."

"One who loves you dearly, just in case I haven't said it often enough in the past."

Her gaze briefly met mine, her eyes alight with warmth and love. "You sure you're not just saying that to butter me up for babysitting duty in a few years' time?"

I grinned. "Given you've been telling Luc just how many grandkids you're expecting, could you blame me?"

She laughed again. "Definitely not."

I watched the wipers sweep across the windshield for a minute, knowing that despite the deluge of water, the storm's force was beginning to ease. That knowledge was damnably scary, and it made me wonder if I'd now go through the rest of my life being intimately aware of nature's every little pulse and beat.

"So where does all this leave me and the sword?" I asked eventually. "Are you able to teach me to use it?"

She hesitated. "With time, I can certainly teach you to control the powers that come with my bloodline. That, in turn, will help with the forces the sword can raise. But when it comes to the gray space? No. Only Aldred's line and the gods themselves can inhabit that dimension, and I'm afraid it's a case of learning on the job."

Which seemed pretty consistent with the haphazard manner the gods used to approach these things. "Time is something we might not have much of."

"I know." She paused to let some cars go past, then turned onto the road that led back to Launceston. "I'm actually surprised Max hasn't yet tested his sword against the gateway."

"We have his kids. He may not make a major move until he gets them back."

"There could be a multitude of reasons for his delay, but I doubt that's one of them."

I raised my eyebrows. "Why?"

"Because he's canny enough to realize his kids are safe with us—after all, if he can't find them, Darkside can't either. That might even have been what this morning's call was about—he didn't want to risk their whereabouts becoming known to the other factions if you were taken."

"Except I don't know where they are."

"He doesn't know that, remember."

"True." The threads of the storm's power were now visibly easing as the wind swept them on toward the sea. There was blue behind the gray, although the promise of warmth remained at least a day away.

I sucked in another of those deep breaths. These snippets of knowing were going to take some getting used to.

"Do you think Max is aware he needs to step onto the gray fields to open the main gate?"

"That would depend entirely on what old tomes he's managed to get his hands on."

"Was it mentioned in many of them?"

"I think there was one from Cedric's time that did, but it was likely destroyed when the monastery in which it was kept was demolished during Henry's dissolution."

"We thought the same thing about the De Montfort family bible, remember, but Max has apparently gotten his mitts on that."

"Yes, but the bible's presence was well known. The documents detailing what Cedric called 'The Battle on Gray' were not."

"And we're absolutely sure Mryddin's replica can't help its wielder to step onto the gray?"

"Yes." Her gaze narrowed. "Though he didn't actually clarify if it had the power to break the seals on the other gates."

Horror rose at the thought. "As in one mass destructive event, you mean?"

She glanced at me. "Yes."

"Well, fuck." I thrust a hand through my still wet hair. "Surely if *that* was possible, he'd have said something. I mean, it's more than a little important!"

"Mryddin can be a little vague on details at times. He's far older than either Gwendydd or myself, and his memory is not what it once was."

"Then maybe we need to go back and ask him."

"I'll see if Mary can contact him via the ancient council."

Mary was a soul soldier—an ancient warrior reborn into a newly dead body in order to fight darkness. Part of her skill was the ability to talk to the ancient—and very dead— druidic council. "If that were possible, why didn't we do that instead of trundling all the way down to his cave?"

"Because I felt the need to go down there. And it's just as well we did, given what happened."

What had happened was a full-on Darkside attack. "Well, if she does manage to contact him, she can ask when he's going to get his lazy butt into gear and join the fray."

"His lazy butt will only move if he feels his presence is necessary. And his definition of necessary has always been quite different to everyone else's."

"Meaning the old bastard might just remain locked in his cave?"

"Very possibly."

I swore and rubbed my forehead. "If Max does attempt to break open multiple minor gates, what are we going to do?"

"What we've always done—fight."

Such a simple answer to what would be a calamitous and world-changing event. "Meaning we do nothing except sit around and wait for the outpouring of evil? That doesn't seem like a sensible option to me."

"Because it isn't, and you know damn well I didn't mean that." She gave me a stern look, though it was somewhat spoiled by the twinkle in her eyes. "Max *will* try to open the main gate—he has no other choice, because the minor gates are by their very nature restrictive—"

"Yes, but does that actually matter if he manages to bust them all open at the same time?"

"I personally doubt that's possible, if only because Elysian herself was never designed for such a task. Besides, rebuilding the main gate destroyed one king and almost killed the other two. I'd imagine trying to open multiple minor gateways at the same time would have a similar outcome. And your brother is no Uhtric, no matter what he might believe."

"The only thing Max believes is the fact that witch king rule needs to be reinstated—and that he, by right of blood, is the one destined to do it."

"He always was an arrogant little sod—got that from his grandfather, I suspect."

I glanced at her. "Really?"

She nodded, her expression briefly dissolving into sadness. "Not that I knew him personally—it's just an impression I got from the many comments Fiona made over the years I helped her raise your father and uncle."

As she'd raised Max and me when the car crash took the

lives of both our parents. "So what will happen when he does attempt to open the main gate? Is the spell just an alarm? Because we're a good flight away from the gate at the best of times."

"If the spell does what it's designed to do, it should ensnare him."

"The one flaw being that he knows it's there. What are the chances of him finding someone to dissolve your spell?"

"In this world? Unlikely."

"And in the other?"

She hesitated. "A possibility. There are dark elves who hold the equivalent power of mages, and they're more than capable of unpicking any spell we create—as evidenced by what happened at Mryddin's cave. But the moment they make such an attempt, I'll know."

Knowing wasn't stopping, and the latter was more important than anything else right now. But she was well aware of that—after all, she'd been around to witness all three Darkside assaults.

"How did they break the seal the other times? It's not like they had the help of an heir then."

"As I said, the dark elves are the magical equivalent of mages. But they've never been without help from our side, either, even if those they turned weren't so intimately linked to the sword and the King's line." She grimaced. "There've always been humans and witches who are easily led astray by false promises of money and power."

Max had always hungered for both. Even from a very young age, he'd planned ever grander and more complicated schemes to improve his position, be it in money or in standing. Those needs had no doubt been amplified by his relationship with Winter.

"That doesn't explain how they broke open the gate, given Elysian is the key and only the king can wield her."

"The main gate—like the minor—is not entirely stable, despite what many believe. The same forces that stretch and break the minor gates sometimes attack the major. It has never entirely shattered, but two of the three Darkside attacks happened when the main gate cracked under the stress of such an event."

"And the third?"

"Was opened by a direct attack of dark elf magic."

I frowned. "If they've done it successfully before, why haven't they tried it again?"

"We believe the effort wiped out a good portion of their royal lines." She shrugged. "Hard to be sure, of course, but it was certainly centuries before we saw them in any great numbers again."

My gaze dropped to the items hidden under the wet bundle of clothes. "What are we going to do with Elysian and the crown? It's not safe to take either home, and I don't think we can risk taking them to the safe house."

"We can't risk hiding the sword out of easy reach, either. I think our best option would be the one the Blackbirds use on the soul blades."

"Make her invisible? Can you do that?"

"I can certainly spell her invisible, but it would mean you'd have to get used to moving around with an unwieldy sword strapped to your back. Whatever spell the Blackbirds use seems to erase that inconvenience."

"And you don't know it? That surprises me."

"It shouldn't. The Blackbirds are a closed-mouth lot at the best of times."

That was certainly true. "What about the crown? Do we similarly hide that?"

She hesitated. "While I doubt it will be necessary to shadow it, I do think we need to keep it and the ring close."

"Why? They'll be of no use to either Max or Darkside now that I've claimed the sword."

"I know but—" She shrugged. "I've a gut feeling they'll be of some use yet."

And Mo's gut feelings were best not ignored. "We'll need to contact one of the other Blackbirds to do the shadowing, then, as Luc's going to be busy with his sister for a few days."

"No, he won't. The process is long and delicate, and no one other than the council's specialists will be allowed anywhere near her while it's happening. Call him. If nothing else, it'll give him something to do other than worry."

I pulled my phone out of the glove compartment and made the call. It went to voicemail, so I left a message asking him to contact me as soon as possible.

"Even if we do manage to wrap an invisibility spell around Elysian, what happens when we need to change shape? I can't carry a sword *and* the two knives."

"Why not? You've carried the knives and that big old book home from Jackie's."

"In a backpack, not in my claws."

"You can lash the sword and the knives together easily enough, and it certainly wouldn't be any heavier." She cast an amused look my way. "You're just looking for excuses not to carry her about."

"Until I actually know how to use her, is there any actual point to me carrying her about?"

"Think of her as just a more powerful version of Nex and Vita," Mo said. "That will at least give you a good place to start."

"Nex and Vita can't pull the sheer range of power that Elysian can." I ran my gaze across the storm-clad skies, once again seeing the threads of energy. My gaze dropped. A similar energy ran up the trunks of the barely visible trees to my left. "Is it always like this for you?"

Mo glanced at me briefly. "Like what?"

I waved a hand toward the trees. "The lifeblood of the earth and the sky being so visible?"

"Ah." A smile twisted her lips. "It's really only evident in open spaces and in land unaltered by human hand."

"Human hands haven't altered the sky."

"Pollution has, especially over the cities." She shrugged. "You might notice it more at the moment, because the ability is very raw in you, but it will quickly tone down to a point where you won't notice it unless you're actively looking for it."

My phone rang, the tone telling me it was Ginny—who was not only my best friend but also my cousin. She normally worked as a specialist detective for the Major Crimes Unit, but had recently been forced to take leave. She'd helped us hide Max's twins, and that had led to Darkside becoming aware of her involvement. Max might not go after her, but the same couldn't be said about his Darkside cronies. In fact, it might not have even been Max behind the multiple attempts on both Mo's and my life, but rather those opposing factions he'd spoken of.

I hit the answer button and then said, "Hey, what's up?"

"I'm not sure." Her usually unruffled tone held an edge of worry. "Have you heard from Mia recently?"

Mia was the third member of our "inseparable gang of three," as Max had often called us when we'd all been younger. "Didn't she go back to Ainslyn for her mother's seventieth?"

"Yes, but I haven't heard from her since."

"You've called her parents?"

"I did. She left them yesterday afternoon to come back here."

It was a statement that hit like a punch to the gut. My breath left in a wheeze, and fear surged. Something must have happened. Something *bad*.

I closed my eyes and rubbed my forehead. "I take it you've tried to track her phone?"

"I have. It's either switched off or dead."

"Do you know the location of the last cell tower it communicated with before it powered down?"

"Castle Walk, which isn't that far away from where we are in Southport."

I took a deep, steadying breath. "Have you driven around the area, just in case?"

"Yes, and we didn't find anything. Not her car, not her phone, not her."

Fuck. Fuck, fuck, fuck.

Darkside had her. I had no doubt of that. None at all.

"Tell Ginny to stay at Southport and make sure Barney does as well," Mo said. "The spells I wove around the mansion will protect them in the short term. We'll head to Mia's and grab the stuff we need to do a tracking spell."

"Heard that, and will do," Ginny said. "Where are you now?"

"Just outside Launceston."

"What the hell are you doing all the way down there?"

"Long story, and one that can wait."

She grunted. "Be careful, won't you? This may be but the first step of them taking us down one by one."

Undoubtedly, and it was one of the major reasons I

really hadn't wanted the two of them so deeply involved. But that horse had well and truly bolted.

"Let us know if you hear anything or if she suddenly reappears."

"And if she does suddenly appear," Mo said, "be a little cautious. It might not truly be her."

"I take it there's a story behind that comment too?" Ginny said, frustration and worry very evident.

"Yeah. Keep her in light, don't go into a darkened room with her, and knock her unconscious if she does even the slightest weird thing."

"God, now I'm even more worried."

She had every right to be. "I'll see you soon."

I hung up but before I could say anything, the phone rang again. This time, it was a private number.

My heart rate leapt several more notches. It was them. I knew it was them. I glanced at Mo, my fear so fierce I couldn't even speak. I simply showed her the screen.

"Answer it," she said. "You have no other choice. Not if you want to save her."

I pressed the button and then said, "Who's this?"

"That's none of your fucking business" came the harsh reply. A woman's voice, not a man's. Not Max's. "If you want to see your friend alive again, you'll meet us on King Island at six. Don't bring the knives, your grandmother, or the Blackbird. We see any of them, and your friend is meat for our evening meal."

And with that, she hung up.

CHAPTER FIVE

I threw the phone onto my lap then scrubbed my hands through my hair. "If they've hurt her, I'm going to burn their asses to hell and back."

"It wouldn't be to their benefit to hurt her—not at this point. They'll know you'll want to see her alive before you meet any of their other demands."

"Which they haven't yet made." Not that they really needed to. They'd been trying to either capture or kill me for weeks now. "It's odd that they've given us so much time to get there, though. Do you think they know where we are?"

And, more importantly, what we were doing?

Mo wrinkled her nose. "I've had no sense of Darkside's minions—"

"Would you though? It's not like you've been given that sort of info in the past."

"True, but in a place as unpopulated as Bodmin—and in weather as foul as we had today—I'd have felt the weight of a watcher, both on the earth and in the air. Besides, the fact they've chosen King Island as a meeting point suggests they think we're still near there."

"And the time?"

"That's easy when you're actually thinking rather than panicking." She cast a wry look my way. "The sun will have set, and the demons can come out to play."

"And if they do, I'll burn their asses too."

Mo smiled, though it failed to reach her eyes. "Which is also why they no doubt told you not to bring the knives. I dare say they'll check before they bring Mia out into the open."

"It's just as well I no longer need to hold them to unleash their fury." But even if that hadn't been the case, I still would have walked into this trap. There was no way known I'd allow Mia to remain in Darkside hands a second longer than necessary.

I flexed my fingers in an effort to remain calm, but it was an action that had the opposite effect thanks to the sparks that flew at the movement. The inner lightning was very ready for action, and its ferocity scared the hell out of me. If I fully unleashed, I might not be able to control it. And while Mo might have said I couldn't be killed by the forces I raised as a mage, that didn't mean they couldn't affect me. Using the knives had knocked me out more than once, and if that happened *this* time, it would land me in Darkside hands.

"We both know they're not actually going to release Mia," I added, "no matter what else happens."

"Not unless you force the issue."

"How the hell am I going to force the issue when they're holding the only card that matters?"

"*You're* the only card that matters. So you walk onto the

island via the bridge rather than flying over, and you stop halfway and tell them to release Mia or you go no further."

"They'll just kill her." Or, even worse, start consuming her while I watched. Bile rose, and I swallowed heavily, trying to ignore the images crowding my mind. Unfortunately, they were derived from memory rather than imagination—from the mass of bloody destruction that lay within the hecatomb we'd discovered. Those deaths might have been the result of human lives being traded for information, but I had no doubt Mia's bones would be picked just as clean.

"Oh, I don't think they will," Mo said.

There was a note in her voice that had my eyebrows rising. "You have a plan to stop them?"

"I always have a plan, my dear. You should know that by now."

I smiled at her words, though in truth they did little to calm the inner fears. Nothing would. Not until Mia was out of Darkside's hands.

But we had a good five hours of driving before we got anywhere near Ainslyn, let alone King Island, and that meant there was plenty of time to learn exactly what she had in mind.

We pulled into the parking area just as the first wisps of pink stained the evening sky. There was only one other car there, and it sat at the far end of the lot, well hidden from anyone who might be watching from the island or the bridge.

As Mo drove toward it, the vehicle's doors opened, and two men and a woman got out. The men were both members of Ainslyn's witch council, and I knew one of them rather well, thanks to the fact I'd dated his son for most of my teenage and adult life. I had no idea yet if Jun and his wife—May—had been informed of Tris's death, but the lack of grief in his face suggested not. Perhaps the preternatural division didn't want to risk the news getting out while they were still attempting to trace all of Tris's Darkside contacts.

The woman wasn't anyone I'd seen before, but she was a sharpshooter Mo had apparently worked with in the past. Why she'd needed such a service was something she *hadn't* clarified.

We parked next to the other car and then climbed out. I was still wearing Mo's oversized sweater, but it was now teamed with the black leggings and singlet top we'd found in a thrift shop just off the A30 near Launceston. Neither of us had wanted to waste time heading into the city's heart to hunt for something more suitable. To be honest, I'd have pulled on my sodden clothes if it had come down to it.

Mo stopped beside the taller of the two men and thrust her hands on her hips, her expression contemplative as she studied the barely visible shore. "Everything set, Tim?"

He nodded. He was probably ten years older than me, and very much a Valeriun in looks—silvery hair that glinted with blue highlights in the evening light and eyes the color of the deepest, darkest seas. "I've placed the dingy on the island's shore and will reel it back once she's climbed aboard."

"And the three two-ways I requested?"

He handed her a box. "The one with the red dot is set to receive only, as you requested."

She opened the box then handed me the red-dotted radio and an earpiece. The second one she gave to the woman, and the third she kept. She glanced across to Tris's dad. "Jun?"

"There're currently seven on the island. Six tread on the earth lightly, which suggests they're human rather than demon."

"And the demon?"

"Waits on the outside of the stone circle."

"Anyone near the bridge at this point?"

"One squats behind the rocks to the right of it on the island side, while two more wait under it on this side."

And no doubt *their* purpose was to block any prospect of a retreat.

"Jess?" Mo said.

The small, sharp-faced woman smiled, a distinct look of anticipation in her eyes. "It'll take me five minutes to get into position. And I hope you don't mind me saying this, but I'd really love it if some winged demons came out to play. Haven't shot any of those bastards for a while now."

Mo snorted. "Just make sure you keep undercover. I don't need to be rescuing your ass tonight."

"The scars I got from our last little jaunt are all the reminder I'll ever want about the need for caution." She dragged a long case from the car, slung it over her shoulder, and then saluted lightly. "See you all on the other side of this."

She disappeared into the trees. Mo glanced at her watch. "Right, we'd better get in place. Tim, Jun, no matter what happens—no matter what you hear or see—your absolute priority is to get Mia out of here. Clear?"

The two men nodded and headed down to the shore. Mo's gaze swept me and came up concerned. "You okay?"

"Luc hasn't confirmed he's here yet, I'm about to walk into a trap, and I'm doing so without the two weapons I've come to rely on so heavily over the past few weeks." I waved a hand. "I'm perfectly okay."

A smile tugged at her lips. "We both know which of those three items worries you the most."

"I can't help but think they'll be waiting for him."

"Even dark elves can't see a Blackbird in full cover."

They didn't have to see him; they just had to hear him. Blackbirds might be able to manipulate light and shadow to disappear from sight, but they couldn't similarly manipulate sound ... I shoved the thought away. Luc was a soldier—the modern-day version of the knights of old. Aside from Mo, he was the most capable person I knew.

And that *included* me.

I squinted up at the sky and felt the wash of its vibrancy deep inside. Which was an utterly weird sensation and yet one that oddly filled me with hope. Darkness might lie on the horizon, but it wasn't holding court here just yet.

We could do this.

I could do this.

I just had to keep trusting the people around me, even though trust had already betrayed me twice. I also had to believe in my own abilities, even though they were still so new and raw.

But I also knew that while it might eventually come down to a confrontation between Max and me, there was a whole lot of ugly to traverse before that happened. This was but the starting battle—and one we had to win. And not just for Mia's sake.

It was time to send Darkside the message that we were done fooling around. Done with reacting rather than acting. If they wanted a fight, then they were damn well going to get it—and with Elysian in my hands rather than Max's, we had every chance of winning.

I lowered my gaze to Mo's. "Are you sure the conceal-ment spell will stop anyone spotting the sword and the crown?"

She nodded. "Even if someone decided to steal the SUV, they won't find either item. Not without the corona-tion ring."

I lightly touched the ring that now hung on a chain around my neck. Though the contact wasn't direct—the ring was tucked safely under my singlet, between my breasts—heat nevertheless pulsed through the stone. In the trunk of the SUV, the crown responded, sending a small but jagged bite of light through the air—something I felt rather than saw.

The spell—though only a temporary one—was working exactly as Mo had said it would. I drew in a breath and released it slowly. It didn't do a whole lot to calm the gath-ering nerves. "Please be careful up there. They'll be watching for you."

"They can watch all they want, darling girl. Blackbirds aren't the only ones who can disappear in plain sight, though my method somewhat differs to theirs." She leaned forward and kissed my cheek. "Keep alert, keep aware, and listen to the whispers of the air and the earth. They'll guide you when I can't."

With that, she shifted shape and disappeared into the treetops. A few seconds later, I felt the surge of her magic, but I wasn't close enough to see the telltale wisps the spell would have left behind to understand its intent.

After another deep breath that did little to calm the churning in my gut, I resolutely took off my shoes and socks. Plotting and planning hadn't been the only thing we'd done on the long drive to get here. Mo had used the time to give me a few quick lessons on mage-craft. It'd been extremely bare-bones stuff, and had basically centered on the need for a newbie like me to be grounded. In feeling the dirt between my toes and the pulse of the earth under my heels, I'd form a connection that would not only give me easier access to that power, but also create a full circuit that would hopefully stop the energy from frying my mind. The caress of the air against bare skin would offer the same sort of protection, but there wasn't a chance in hell I'd take off the sweater before it was absolutely necessary. The storm might have blown itself out, but the night's chill had well and truly settled in.

Once I'd tossed my shoes into the car and locked it, I shoved the keys into the leggings' phone pocket and walked across to the well-worn path that meandered down to the old suspension bridge. It was the only way those without wings or a boat could get onto the island, though using the latter had always been a risky proposition. Not only were the seas surrounding the island treacherous at the best of times, there were only a couple of truly suitable locations on which to land a boat. The shore, like the island itself, was covered in rock, though a wide variety of trees and shrubs now thrived there, providing shelter for the array of wildlife that called it home.

The path swept around a corner, and the suspension bridge came into sight. It was simply constructed, with four parallel load-bearing cables stretching across the narrow causeway between the island and the mainland. Two of those cables supported the wooden walkway while the other two provided walkers with something to grip. Crisscrossed metal mesh filled the gap between the two, preventing anyone who slipped on the old boards from falling into the water.

There was no official record of how old the bridge was,

or even who was responsible for its construction, though most believed it was Uhtric's doing, given his shield was the centerpiece of the archway that marked the far end of the bridge. There was likely to have been some form of bridge here well before then, however. The island was home to the King's Stone, which had held Elysian—or at least her copy— since Aldred's time. While we De Montforts could fly across to perform the yearly blessing that had always protected the sword from both would-be thieves and destruction attempts, the Aquitaines could not.

Though I guessed that as kings, they could simply command a Valeriun witch to calm the seas.

I scanned the rocks on the other side of the island, but couldn't spot the man who hid behind them. There was no indication that a couple waited in the growing shadows under the bridge on this side, either, but I didn't need to see either when the earth felt their weight so clearly.

Did this sort of understanding come so easily for all mage apprentices? Or was it just a combination of luck, good genes, and the fact that I'd at least learned a little about elemental energies through Nex and Vita? I suspected the latter to be true, though Mo hadn't exactly confirmed it when I asked her.

Though she hadn't discounted it, either.

I took a step onto the bridge. The churning in my gut immediately worsened, though I did my best to ignore it. It was far harder to ignore the fierce pounding of my heart, especially when it felt like it was about to tear out of my chest.

Other than the crash of waves on the rocky shoreline and the creak of the bridge as it swayed slightly in the breeze, there was little other sound or movement—a sign of trouble if ever there was one. It was dusk, and the multitude of birds that called the island home should have been flying here en masse to claim their nighttime roosts. That they weren't had to mean there was something happening on the other side of the island.

Something like winged demons, perhaps?

I hoped not, but Darkside was well aware I could take winged form, so their presence would make sense. Which meant that even if our plan *had* included me changing shape to escape, that option was now out of reach. My alternate form simply wasn't equipped to fight demons on the wing—neither my beak nor my claws were capable of tearing through their leathery hides. Just one of those bastards could take me down easily enough; any more than that, and it would be a massacre.

My massacre.

I pushed on, breaking my connection with the earth in the process. The evening instantly felt a lot colder and definitely more dangerous. I shivered and tightened my grip on the top cable—to counter the bounce, I told myself fiercely, not the fear.

When I reached the halfway point, I stopped and shouted, "I go no further until I see Mia."

For several—very tense—minutes, there was no response. Then the man from behind the rocks up ahead rose, his outline almost indistinguishable from the shadows that gathered around him. "Go no further, and she dies."

"Kill her, and you lose your ace." Despite the turmoil deep inside, my voice remained even. "You want me; I want her free. One hostage for another is a pretty fair exchange—and it's one we both know your dark masters would agree to. But feel free to check—they should be coming out to play any minute now."

There were a few more seconds of silence, then he said,

"Take off that sweater. We want to be sure you didn't bring your knives."

Which was exactly what we'd hoped they'd say. I needed a good percentage of bare skin to hear the wind's whispers, but given how damn cold it was, if I hadn't come appropriately dressed, they would have been suspicious. Although I wasn't wearing shoes, so suspicion would no doubt be stirring anyway.

I stripped off the sweater and dropped it onto the boards near my feet. The air immediately swirled around me, its cold, crisp touch raising goose bumps even as whispers filled my mind. As I'd suspected, winged demons were patrolling the shoreline. Four of them, to be exact.

The wind's whispers only vaguely mentioned the demon waiting just outside the stone circle; maybe she couldn't see past whatever magic he was using to conceal himself. But she was oddly specific about the other concealed man who stood inside the stone circle.

Luc.

My heart lifted, even if the inner tension didn't. He was here, just as he'd promised. And while it was ridiculous to think one man could make any real difference if things went sour, his presence nevertheless made me feel safer. Aside from the fact I was no longer alone on the island, between his battle skill and my own unrefined powers, there was now a good chance I'd survive this trap.

But first, I had to get Mia out of harm's way.

I raised my arms so that the watcher ahead could see the full silhouette of my body. "No knives, as ordered."

"Turn around."

I did so. "Show me Mia."

Another pause, then a scrape of sound and a soft gasp had my gaze jumping back up to the ridge. Three figures appeared, their forms silhouetted against the fading glory of the sky. Mia was one of them—I knew that even without the wind telling me. And in even better news, there was no immediate sign of major injury, even if the wind spoke of a multitude of minor cuts and bruises.

Whether she'd escaped without mental trauma—or god help us, being inhabited by a wraith—was another matter entirely.

Rising above the three of them, their outspread wings glowing like fresh blood, were the red demons. They were big bastards, too, bigger even than the one I'd confronted here on the day of the blessing. They really were taking no chance of me escaping this time.

I clenched my hands and fought the urge to unleash. I had no choice but to play their game until Mia was well and truly safe.

"There's a boat waiting on the shore below," I said. "I want her in it—alone—before I go any further."

"Oh, I think your time of making demands has come to an abrupt end" came a guttural comment from behind me.

I turned. The couple who'd been hiding under the bridge now stood at its end, both holding guns that were pointed at my body. I smiled benignly, though my heart hammered and my mouth felt drier than a desert. "On that we'll have to disagree. But feel free to shoot, because we both know your masters want me alive and won't be pleased if the opposite happens."

"Alive, yes," she said, cold amusement evident. "That doesn't mean we can't shoot a limb or two."

As if to demonstrate, she lowered her gun a fraction and pulled the trigger. The bullet tore into the wooden plank inches from my bare toes and sent splinters flying.

A heartbeat later, another shot carved a chunk out of

the plank closest to *their* feet. They jumped back, the man cursing loudly.

"You might have banned any sort of magical backup," I said evenly, "but you certainly didn't say I couldn't bring in a sharpshooter. Oh, and send one of those red bastards after her, and he's dead. She has special bullets for the likes of him."

The woman bared her teeth, a low sound rumbling from her throat. It reminded me of the growls I'd heard in Mryddin's cave and left me wondering if she was perhaps a halfling—one crossed with some sort of dark hound. It was a hell of a leap, but the more I stared at her, the more her features leaned toward canine rather than human.

"Fine," she barked. "We'll release her."

Her companion made the call while she kept her gun trained on the lower part of my body. I didn't so much as twitch—I had a vague feeling she was itching to follow through with her threat.

The wind picked up, tugging lightly at my hair as she continued her trickle of information. I glanced sideways; Mia and her two guards had disappeared from the hilltop. Tension surged, as did the inner energy. I crossed my arms to hide my clenched hands. The last thing I needed was visible sparks dancing across my fingertips; they'd give the game away far too soon.

Minutes ticked by. I kept my gaze on the boat below, well aware of what was happening with Mia thanks to the wind. Every other sense was trained on the two people in front of me and the one behind. *He* might not have moved, but he was definitely armed, and his weapon was aimed at my spine. Not a killing shot, perhaps, but certainly a disabling one.

Mia finally appeared below. One of the men roughly

shoved her forward, and she stumbled more than climbed into the boat. As she regained her balance, the seas surged, tugging the boat away from the shore, then whisking it across the turbulent waters back to the mainland.

The red demons swooped toward her, but a sharp bark from the woman had them retreating. She was obviously the leader of this little lot, which in itself was rather unusual. The winged demons were generally a higher rank than halflings—who were mostly considered disposable—and they'd always been the ones in charge the few times I'd come across them. The only other halfling I knew who'd had any sort of control over Darkside ranks had been Winter, and I'd presumed *that* had come about simply because he'd been Max's lover.

This woman suggested there might have been more to it than that.

"Right," she said. "Get a move on."

"Not until she's on the mainland and safe."

The woman made another of those low sounds but didn't push the matter.

The boat skimmed swiftly across the sea and hit the shoreline with enough speed to push it high up the stony embankment. Mia immediately scrambled out and quickly disappeared into the trees. A few minutes later, an engine roared to life. As it left the parking lot, two of the red demons broke away from their brethren and followed.

Though there was no sound of a shot, one of them jerked sideways and then fell as his wing collapsed. A heart-beat later, his face exploded. He dropped like a stone into the sea and was quickly dragged down.

The wind stirred urgently, but even as my gaze darted back to the woman, something hit my arm with enough force to spin me around. Pain bloomed, and I swore, dropping to one knee as I sucked in air and fought the wave of anger and agony that burned through me. She'd shot me. The bitch had *shot* me.

But as much as I wanted to cinder her ass right here and now, I couldn't. Not until I'd gotten the all clear from Mo. Jess might have taken out one red demon, but the other one still chased after Mia, and two more still circled the island.

I just needed to be patient, even if it went against every instinct I had right now.

"Try something like that again," the woman shouted, anger contorting her features and making her look even more hound-like, "and she's fucking dead. Clear?"

There was no response from Jess—it would have given them her location.

"As for you," the woman continued, "get up. *Now*. It's only a fucking flesh wound, so stop the carry-on. Or I'll shoot out your legs and we'll carry you across to the island."

I slowly pushed to my feet. Breath hissed through clenched teeth and, for an instant, everything spun. It might only be a flesh wound, but the bullet had plowed a fairly decent channel through the fleshy part of my upper arm, and it fucking *hurt*.

I breathed deep, fighting the pain and pushing back the inner fire. Both retreated, and I couldn't help but wish it were possible to stem the blood that easily. It pulsed down my arm, a warm wet rush that was cooled by the wind by the time it hit my fingers.

My gaze met the halfling's. I wasn't entirely sure what she saw there, but hers narrowed, and uncertainty briefly touched her expression.

She raised her gun. "Move, or else."

I obeyed. I really had no other choice. But this was the

most dangerous section of our plan, simply because we really had no idea what Darkside intended.

The bridge's bounce was more pronounced with three of us on it, which made me walk like I was drunk. I didn't dare risk gripping the guide cable just in case the inner lightning made a showing.

Thankfully, the bounce eased as we neared the end of the bridge and the archway onto the island. Though the bridge was basic in construction, the arch was the opposite. Time and weather might have taken their toll on the decorative metalwork that adorned its two stone pillars, but it nevertheless remained an ornate and beautiful piece of work. The shield itself was an oddity—aside from being too small to be at all useful in battle, it was completely untouched by the rust that was prevalent everywhere else. In fact, it could have been placed there yesterday.

In the fading evening light, the decorative cross adorning the center of the shield gleamed bloodred, while the white rose that lay across its heart held the luminosity of the moon. The same two symbols adorned the hilt of the fake sword, but not the real one. Did that confirm my earlier suspicion the shield had little to do with Uhtric and was simply another piece of subtle misdirection by Mryddin?

Maybe—but to what purpose? It wasn't like shields had ever played a major part in the stories of witch kings. At least, not in any of the stories I'd ever been told.

But then, it was becoming increasingly clear that none of us—not even Mo—knew the whole truth when it came to the Witch King's line.

A bright glimmer caught my attention, and my gaze narrowed. After a moment, I saw it again—a sliver of red light that pulsed around the edge of the cross.

Once. Twice. Thrice. In time with the beat of my steps, I realized.

That was something it had never done before, and there could only be one reason for it doing so now—Elysian. Or rather, the fact that I'd drawn her today.

But if the shield now recognized me—and it definitely seemed to—did that mean it was connected to the first Witch King rather than the last? And if *that* were true, why had no one ever mentioned it? How had it come to be stuck on this arch rather than in a museum like many other important artifacts?

All good questions I'd only get answers to if I survived the current situation.

I strode through the arch and headed up the long path that led up to the monument. My connection to the earth renewed, and its warming pulse offered enough strength to chase away the pain that came with walking on gritty ground with bare feet. My arm still hurt like blazes, but the blood flow had at least eased. Whether that was due to the energies that moved through and around me or was just a result of my own natural healing ability kicking in, I couldn't say.

Trees loomed, their branches entwined over the path ahead, their trunks twisted and surreal-looking in the quickly fading light. Mia's two guards had scrambled back up to the top of the ridge and were now waiting beside the demon whose presence weighed heavily on the ground. The wind remained mute about him; her concentration lay on the remaining winged demons. I wished there was a way to direct and refine the information she was giving me, but that was likely a future lesson.

We came out from under the trees onto the open ground atop the ridge. My gaze darted to the right. Ainslyn lay before us, a twinkling array of lights and life that seemed so far removed from the gloom that currently infused this island it could have been another world entirely.

Damn it, what was taking Mo so long? Surely she would have taken care of the demon tailing the car by now?

I did my best to ignore the churning in my stomach and studied the stone that dominated the skyline. It was a sharp projection of rock that jutted out at an angle on the highest point of the island—therefore earning it the moniker "king's knob"—and it held the stone in which the king's sword had been sheathed for hundreds of years.

Of course, neither the knob nor the King's Stone currently visible were the real ones. Mo had buried them deep in the earth a few days ago in order to prevent any possible attempt Darkside might make to destroy them. *This* one had been fashioned out of the nearby earth and stone, and only the keenest eye would be able to see the difference —and only then because this version didn't quite have the same depth of erosion.

The Darksiders here were unlikely to notice. It was doubtful if even Max would, given his attention the few times he'd come here would have been on the sword he coveted, rather than the stone that held it.

The stony path gave way to grass, making things a little easier on my feet. While those grasses covered the majority of the peak, the area within the stone circle was barren—not even weeds survived there. No one really knew why, although, according to Mo, it had happened when Aldred had thrust the blade into the stone—apparently, the last vestiges of the sword's power had bled into the ground and forever sterilized it. I'd always thought it to be little more than one of her tall tales, but now that I'd actually gained the same connection with the earth, I knew it was no lie.

The ground immediately under the stone had been totally and utterly sterilized of life. Even the earth's pulse was muted there. Which was odd, considering Elysian was merely the means through which all the elements were channeled. I wouldn't have thought she could kill the life within the soil, given a good percentage of her power came from it.

But maybe it wasn't the fault of Elysian, given it was possible she'd never been sheathed here.

Movement caught my eye, drawing my attention to the left of the circle. Mia's two guards stood there, but it was the shimmer between them that caught my attention. It spoke of magic—dark magic, if the tells were anything to go by. It hid the demon who stood so heavily on the earth.

My gaze flicked to the circle of stone monolith beyond him. Though I couldn't see Luc, I nevertheless knew exactly where he stood. His presence sang through me, a joyous note of heat and desire that warmed my insides and chased away at least some of the trepidation.

His readiness to move—to fight—was a more dangerous undertone that accompanied the joyousness. One filled with a deep, deep anger aimed solely at the three people behind me. They'd dared to shoot me, and he wanted them dead.

The man really *did* care.

"Stop," said the woman behind me.

I obeyed. The two winged demons swooped low, causing a maelstrom of air that had my hair flying everywhere. There was a barked order, and one of them immediately banked away, flying toward the other end of the island rather than the mainland. I sent the wind chasing after it, and it very quickly became evident it was taking an indirect route off the island and to the mainland to go after Mia. I wished there was a way to warn Mo, but that had never been part of the plan.

"So," I said, my voice still amazingly calm despite the continuing inner churning, "I'm here, as you demanded. What do you want?"

The two men didn't reply, but the dark spell fell away and the demon stepped free.

A gasp tore from my throat.

Winter.

It was fucking *Winter*.

CHAPTER SIX

But that was impossible. I'd killed the bastard in the dark altar's cavern—I'd thrust Nex so deeply into his eye that she'd sliced his brain in half.

This *couldn't* be him.

And yet he was identical—the same delicate build, gray skin, and pointed ears. Same long white hair pinned back from sharp cheekbones by a dangerous-looking, trident-shaped hairpin. Same effeminate features and sky-blue eyes.

What the hell was going on? Was he a twin? Or maybe a clone of some kind?

I fought to remain calm and raised my eyebrows. "I had no idea Darkside was capable of reanimating the dead."

Amusement touched his thin lips. "We aren't."

The lightning that burned through me was now so sharp, the hair on my arms stood on end and a faint, sulfur-like scent filled my nostrils. I dug my nails deeper into my palms in an effort to hold the force back, but it was a battle I was beginning to lose. If Mo didn't contact me soon with the all clear, all hell *would* break loose.

"Then who are you?" The roiling inner power was causing my vocal cords to vibrate and the words came out ... odd. I swallowed heavily and hoped the man ahead didn't notice. "Because you can't be Winter. I killed that bastard and watched him die."

Something flashed through his eyes. Something dark and very scary. "And his death was one we all felt. For that, you will suffer greatly."

We all? That not only suggested there were more than two versions of Winter but also that they were linked by some kind of collective consciousness—one that shared thoughts, emotions, and experiences even if they could act independently.

I scanned him again, but I really hadn't seen the original version often enough to spot whatever minor differences there might be.

"Does my brother know there's more than one of you?"

He raised a pale eyebrow, his expression mocking. "What benefit would there be to that?"

For Darkside? None. For my brother? To be honest, he might well welcome multiple versions of a man he was extremely attracted to. He'd never been a huge believer in one partner for life, and even during his so-called serious relationships he'd indulged his sexual needs elsewhere.

But he didn't like to be played, either, and I suspected that's what they were doing here. Hell, it was even possible that one of the Winters led one of the factions. Just because we believed half-breeds couldn't take up positions of authority didn't mean we were right.

"So how many of you are there?"

"Enough."

Meaning that even when I destroyed this one, there were plenty of other clones or whatever the hell he was waiting in the wings to take his place. Not that *that* would stop me. Besides, they'd surely have to run out of replacements eventually.

"So," I said, the vibration getting stronger. "Back to the reason I'm here—what do you want?"

Another smile, but this one had chills racing down my spine. "You are your brother's blood price. What do you think we want?"

"If you wanted me dead, the bitch behind me could have done it easily enough when we were on the bridge. We both know you weren't overly worried about the presence of a sharpshooter—you've plenty of minions to replace those we kill."

And we certainly both knew that Darkside didn't actually care if it lost hundreds of said minions, as long as the end result was what they wanted.

"Oh, blood price doesn't always mean death." His gaze fell on my arm, and lasciviousness gleamed briefly. "Though the sweet smell of your blood does make me hunger for its taste."

"It'll be a cold day in hell before *you* ever get to taste it."

That gleam got stronger. "Fighting only makes the taste that much sweeter."

"And you really think Max is going to allow anything like that to happen to me? Even if you *are* his true love?"

"He may have done all he possibly can to protect you thus far, but in the end there is no escaping a deal done, and he is well aware of that."

"I wouldn't place any bets on that. This blood—the blood we share—just might be thicker than his desire for a throne."

He laughed, the sound cracking harshly across the

night. "You're his twin—surely even *you* cannot believe that."

Perhaps not, but god, I wanted to. Badly.

Winter—or whatever the hell this one's name actually was—glanced at the man on his right. "Order the boat in."

As the man obeyed, Winter added, "As much as I would have preferred Gurra to fly you off the island, it is impractical given the nearest open gate is some distance from here. It would give the bitch you call grandmother too much time to rescue you."

I raised an eyebrow. "And you think she won't attempt a rescue if I'm in a boat? Really? Even you can't be that stupid."

"If she attacks, we sink the boat. Given you'll be chained within it, it'd have a cataclysmic result for any hope of a future you might hold."

"You sink the boat, and you'll also die. Demons can't swim."

He shrugged. "Death for the greater good is an honor, not a problem. And while the dark elf who has claimed reproduction rights with you will be displeased at your loss, it would be but a minor blip in their plans."

So I'd been right all along—the bastards *did* want me as a goddamn brood mare. I smiled, and I really hoped it looked as fierce as it felt. "Oh, I plan to be much more than a minor blip, trust me on that."

The earpiece finally crackled.

"Mia's safe" came Jun's voice rather than Mo's "but a second winged demon has appeared, and Mo's in the process of taking care of it. She said she probably won't get back in time to join in on the fun, so feel free to unleash any time you want."

Relief stirred even as tension ramped up. While Luc

had Hecate and I had my lightning, it was still six against two, and at least three of them had guns at the ready. When I moved, I'd have to be fast.

"Really?" Winter was saying. "Because last we heard, your grandmother can't control large bodies of water, and therefore would not be able to save your life. And we all know you've never had the capability to control ... well, anything really."

It was interesting they knew about Mo's inability to control large bits of water, given I'd only discovered it today. Had Max told them? Or had someone been researching just what her capabilities were as a mage? Maybe the answer was even more simple than that—there were demon equivalents of mages, after all, so it was possible the knowledge came from one or more of them having crossed swords with her in the past.

"Perhaps that's true on the mainland, but we're not there, are we?" I replied. "We're standing on King Island, the place my ancestors have protected for countless centuries."

He waved a hand in a dismissive manner. "It is but a worthless piece of rock now that the sword has been claimed."

"You think it was just the sword we were protecting?" I smiled benignly. "My, my, what lies has Max been telling you?"

His gaze narrowed and, from behind me, came a snick of sound—the safeties being unlocked on three guns. My nails were now so deeply pressed into my palms that I was drawing blood. "I suggest you all leave now, while you still can."

He laughed again. "You're alone and without your knives. Both the numbers *and* the outcome are in our favor."

"Who said I'm alone?"

With that, I dropped flat and unleashed the pent-up inner power at the three people behind me. Multiple forks of fierce white light burned from my fingertips and shot across the darkness, hitting all three weapons at the same time and turning them into nothing more than liquid metal. In the process, it cindered the hands of those who held them. Their screams of agony and disbelief filled the night air.

A different type of scream rose from behind me, but it was one I recognized—it was Hecate's battle cry. Luc had joined the fray. A man bellowed, the sound followed by the sharp retort of a gun.

My heart leapt into my mouth. I twisted around, but all I could see was Winter coming straight at me.

I slapped a hand onto the ground and called on the earth to entrap him. She responded fiercely, her power burning into my fingers then on through my body before erupting from my feet. She swept up the dirt and stone, forming it into a liquid wave that rolled toward Winter with ever increasing speed and ferocity. A brief flash of horror crossed his face then he turned and fled. *This* Winter was not as brave as the first.

"Gurra!" he shouted. "Stop her!"

The winged demon screeched in response and dove at me, his talons gleaming like fresh blood in the shadows of the night. I flicked lightning upward, and he banked sharply, his wings a blur as he fought to outfly the bolt.

More footsteps on earth, their weight clean rather than foul. I twisted around. The two men were coming at me, pain and madness etched into their faces.

I recalled the lightning and lashed it toward them, punching a hole the size of my fist through the chest of one before wrapping the lash around the neck of the second. His eyes went wide in a brief moment of lucid horror, then the energy severed his neck, killing thought as it separated body from brain. His head hit the ground and rolled back down the path. The dog-faced woman took one look, then ran. She got five steps before a bullet tore through her head and sent blood, brains, and gore flying.

Jess, putting her sharpshooter skills to good use.

I pushed upright; weariness hit like a hammer, and I swayed briefly, battling to remain standing against the specter of exhaustion and pain that threatened to sweep me away.

Up ahead, Winter's two companions lay on the ground, their bodies cleaved in two. Luc was now visible, but he was surrounded by half a dozen demons who'd come from god knew where ... Another screech had my gaze jumping up. All I saw was demon claws.

I threw myself sideways, hitting the ground hard on my injured arm. Agony bloomed, and a bellow tore up my throat, but I somehow managed to clamp down on it. The last thing I wanted was to distract Luc, however momentarily. Tears blurred my vision, but I didn't need to see to know where the demon was. I could feel him on the wind. I flicked up a hand, and the air responded, swirling toward the diving demon. He abruptly switched direction, but the maelstrom caught him and sent him tumbling toward Ainslyn's shore and Jess.

I twisted around to watch; multiple wounds appeared across his body, and black blood flowed. He was dead long before the wind smashed him onto the rocks.

I sucked in a breath, then once again wearily pushed to my feet. Everything ached, and my vision continued to go in and out of focus. At least the wind's whispers were clear of immediate threat, even if the sound of fighting still echoed. But the demons surrounding Luc now numbered three, and Hecate's thirst was far from quenched. Two of the remaining demons were dispatched as I walked over to Winter.

Though he was stuck neck-deep in my wave of earth and stone, his expression was furious rather than fearful. That probably wouldn't change now, even if this version *had* run when confronted by an example of my power.

"Before you die, I wanted you to know that I will stop you. *All* of you." My voice was flat, devoid of fury and anger. It had all burned out of me; the only thing that remained was bitter determination. "Neither Max nor anyone else in Darkside knows as much about the De Montfort line and the king's sword as they think."

Winter sneered. "The sword—and the only man who can wield it—is ours. He *will* open the main gate, and there is nothing you can do to stop him or us."

"A pleasant fantasy, but a fantasy nonetheless. Or did you think there was only ever one sword made?"

He snorted, though a touch of uncertainty flicked through his eyes. "You think we'd believe such a patently obvious lie?"

"I'm many things, Winter, but a liar isn't one of them. Ask Max. Or rather, have one of your counterparts ask him, because you'll certainly never have the chance to deceive him again."

And with that, I asked the earth to complete the cage. She responded so swiftly—so eagerly—that the ground vibrated underneath my feet, forcing me to fling out my arms in an effort to maintain balance. The ground swept up his face, filling his mouth and nose, and cutting off his air.

Then stone encased him, until all that remained was a small monolith that vaguely resembled humanity.

As deaths went, it was far too damn swift, given the pain and hurt he'd inflicted on someone I cared about, but I doubted *that* would have stopped him passing on the information about the sword—not if all the versions of him truly *did* share a consciousness.

I was okay with that. I *wanted* them to know we were coming after them. Wanted them to fear that the sword they owned—via the man who'd raised it—was not the only sword of power.

If nothing else, it might just delay any planned attack against the gate.

Of course, it would undoubtedly cause them to ramp up the attacks on Mo and me, but that was infinitely better than Mia, Ginny, or even Barney, getting caught in the crossfire.

I drew in a deep breath, then glanced up as Luc approached. There was a small backpack slung around one shoulder, and his clothes were splattered with demon blood, but other than the cut across his cheek—one that looked to have been made with a knife rather than a bullet—he appeared unhurt.

I smiled wearily. "Glad you managed to join the party."

"I wouldn't have missed it for the world. That was quite a show you put on." The lightness in his voice failed to reach his eyes. "Why aren't you wearing any shoes?"

"They're wet." They weren't, of course, but I really didn't want to get into explanations right now.

"And this is problematic why?"

A smile tugged at my lips. "I hate wet shoes."

"That is a ridiculous statement, and one that could have come out of your grandmother's mouth. How's the arm?"

"Painful, but there's not much we can do about that right now. We need to get off the island before that damn boat they called arrives. You might have the strength to fight hordes more, but I'm just about out of it."

He nodded, sheathed Hecate, then—before I could protest, though in truth it would only have been a token effort—swept me up into his arms and strode down the ridge toward the path and the bridge. I smiled and leaned against his chest. Every breath was filled with the musk of man and sweat, and it had an oddly calming effect. Or maybe that was a result of the tenderness with which he held me and the steady beating of his heart under my ear. He was strength and caring and harmony, and just for a moment, I absolutely believed that Vivienne's dream of unity for our long-tortured souls would finally come true.

Which was utterly stupid given the shit storm of darkness that still lay ahead. Then there was the whole problem of the sword concealed in the SUV and what it actually meant for the two of us.

As the deeper darkness caused by the overhanging trees closed around us, I said, "What do you know about the shield on the arch?"

"Probably nothing more than you do." He glanced down at me, features shadowed, but jade eyes glowing with awareness. "Why?"

"Because when I crossed the bridge earlier, it reacted to me."

He frowned, something I felt more than saw. "Are you sure it wasn't a trick of the light?"

"Positive."

"But—" He paused. "That would mean it's connected to one of the witch kings, and as far as I'm aware, it's a replica, not the real thing. It's too small to be of any use in a battle, for a start."

"That's what I thought, but maybe that's another of Mryddin's tricks."

"It's possible." His voice held a mix of doubt and concern. "But why is it reacting to you now when it's never done so before?"

I hesitated, internally bracing for his disbelief. "Remember Mo's theory about me being the true Witch King's heir?"

His amusement sang through me. "I could hardly forget, given the tongue lashing she gave me for not believing it possible a woman could draw the sword."

I smiled, but the inner tension remained. "Well, she wasn't wrong. We found Elysian today and I drew her."

"What?" He stopped abruptly. "Where is she?"

"In the car, with the crown." I cupped his bristly face. "I'm sorry, Luc."

"Why on earth are you *sorry*?"

"Because it's not a fate you wanted—for me or for you."

"What has my fate got to do with—"

"The role of the Blackbirds is to protect and guard the Witch King," I cut in gently. "My drawing Elysian locks your fate into mine, whether you want it or not."

And it also meant that what lay between us—the desire and the promises—might never be fulfilled, simply because Blackbirds traditionally didn't mix business with pleasure. Not since Aldred had banished the Blackbird who'd dared to steal the heart of his queen, at any rate. The consequences of *that* event had rebounded endlessly through the centuries until we'd reached the current point—the two of us now facing the same damn decision even if I was now the "king" rather than his queen.

Which was no doubt exactly what Vivienne had planned all along.

He drew in a deep breath, inner turmoil briefly evident in the arms that held me so gently. I knew why—the woman in the red dress who I so often saw in his thoughts. He'd been assigned to guard her when he was much younger and had fallen in love in the process. She'd been snatched by demons on his watch and had died in a hecatomb despite his best efforts to save her. He'd sworn that day never again to mix duty and pleasure, and yet, here I was, another woman he was battling to resist.

He wouldn't bend before it. Not this time. Not when his memories of that woman dying at his feet now bore my face and name.

His Adam's apple bobbed as he swallowed heavily. "You drawing the sword doesn't matter one way or another. My duty is with you regardless."

"Because of Max?"

"Initially, perhaps. Things are not so clear now." His mouth twisted, though it was as far from a smile as you could ever get. "Fate and an old goddess are very intent on controlling the narrative, aren't they?"

"Old women—goddess or not—do tend to like getting their own way."

"Mo being the perfect example of that." He shook his head and continued on. "Where did you find Elysian?"

I filled him in on everything except for the discovery that I'd inherited Mo's mage genes, and then added, "Will you be able to hide Elysian in much the same manner as you hide Hecate? Mo believes it best if I keep her with me at all times, but Darkside can't know that."

"Then why tell them she existed at all? It might buy us some time while they attempt to uncover the truth of that, but in the end it will only intensify the attacks on you."

"Yes, but I can defend myself."

"The lightning takes a severe toll on your body and your strength and, if they swamp you, you will eventually be overrun. Besides, they can't actually touch Elysian."

Which was something we knew thanks to the fact that after Uhtric's horse had been cut from beneath him and the sword had slipped from his grasp, the dark elf who'd tried to claim it had been instantly incinerated. "And that's the whole point—the only person who possibly *can* is Max."

"So you made yourself bait? And Mo agreed to this madness?"

"It's the safest way of drawing Max out of the shadows."

"The safest way would be to use his hair or something similar to make a tracker."

"Something we may yet be forced to try, but the thing is —he's well aware of Mo's capability in that regard. He'll have arranged some way to counter it."

"And if he does take the bait?"

"I'll have a decision to make."

Did I try for reason and hope, or did I simply accept, once and for all, that the brother I'd grown up with only existed as an outer shell? That the real Max—the one I loved and who had loved me—had died long ago, replaced by greed, madness, and the need to conquer and rule.

"He'll hardly come alone," Luc said. "Not now."

"I know. But I have Elysian, Nex, and Vita. I can counter anything he throws at me."

"Anything except a bullet—and don't think he won't resort to that."

"Others might. He won't. He's done what he can to

protect me thus far, Luc. He'll keep doing that until the bitter end."

"I think you're leaning too heavily on your memories of your brother, rather than the reality."

"Possibly, but he's my brother and I owe it to him." I poked him in the chest. "And you know damn well you'd do exactly the same thing if it was one of your siblings."

Sadness briefly washed through the connection between us, and I silently cursed. The last thing I'd intended was to remind him about his sister.

"She'll be okay," I added softly. "It's not the first time the displacement team has encountered a wraith infestation, and Mo was pretty damn sure they could get it out of her."

"I hope so." It was bleakly said, suggesting he wasn't so certain. "Back to the shield—do we leave it where it is, or try to detach it?"

I turned my gaze to the arch up ahead, though it was little more than a vague shadow in the darkness. "I don't think we can risk leaving it—not if it is somehow connected to one of the witch kings and the sword."

"You'd think *we'd* fucking know," he grumbled. "If Mryddin ever does emerge from his cave, we Blackbirds are going to have some serious words with him."

I smiled, as he'd no doubt intended. "According to Mo, Mryddin takes about as much notice of other people's opinions as a duck does rain."

"I'll just note here that he's not the only mage with *that* particular gift."

I laughed. He walked under the arch, then turned around. The flicker of red once again ran around the edge of the shield's cross, its rhythm matching the beat of my heart rather than my steps.

But this time, magic stirred through that pulse; it was very different in feel to the force I felt through Elysian and my knives.

"Whether or not this shield was ever used by a Witch King," Luc said, "it's definitely magically active."

Surprise flickered. "You can *feel* it? Not just see it?"

"Yes, but I rather suspect it's simply a result of the not-quite-telepathic connection that seems to occur whenever we're touching."

I couldn't help grinning. "And I for one cannot wait to discover how much more fun sex will be with said connection."

"Concentrate, dear Gwen." His voice was dry. "Sex is still a very long way off in our future."

"Yes, but that won't stop me anticipating. Set me down."

He did. I rose onto my toes and reached for the shield. While my fingers barely brushed the base, its response was immediate and fierce. Light burst from the rose in several quick pulses and shot across the water. I swung around to see what the moon-colored beams would highlight. At first, there was nothing. Then, from deep in the heart of old Ainslyn, came a responding flash.

"Any idea where that's coming from?" Luc asked.

I hesitated, eyes narrowing. "Hard to be sure at night, but if it's not the King's Tower, then it's close to."

The King's Tower was the only intact remnant of Uhtric's castle and, to most, was little more than a tourist attraction and museum. It did, however, hold a whole lot of witch history—and weapons, apparently, though I hadn't yet seen them—in secret vaults well protected from the museum staff and accidental discovery, by multiple layers of spells.

"There's nothing left in the castle that *could* be responding," he said. "Very few true artifacts remain there these days."

Not even Uhtric's throne. The Blackbirds had taken it for safekeeping after a dark elf had tried to destroy it. There were still a number of other personal and furniture items from the reigns of the other witch kings, however. "Mo might know a bit more."

"To point out the obvious, she's not here."

"No, but she'll probably be on her way back by now." *If* Mia had proven to be wraith free, that was.

I crossed mental fingers that she was and returned my attention to the shield. After a moment, I shifted my grip and then lightly tugged. The thing dropped so suddenly, I squeaked in surprise and jumped straight back into Luc. He steadied me with one hand and grabbed the shield with the other.

"It's surprisingly light," he said, studying it through narrowed eyes.

I ran my fingers along the top edge. No new moonbeams appeared, though the pulse of red light continued to run around the cross. "It feels like ice."

He nodded, his expression thoughtful. "There's a Norse myth involving a shield called *Svalinn* that's icy to the touch. It was supposedly used by the gods to stand between the chariot of the sun and the earth to prevent the latter from being set on fire."

"Viking shields were made of wood, not metal."

"Yes, but if an old goddess can make a sword for a king, why can't an old god make a shield? Or are you being sexist?"

I smiled. "If this shield *is* even older than Elysian, why on earth is it responding to me?"

109

"I think you'll find the key is the aforementioned 'old gods.' Maybe they decided to repurpose the thing." He handed me the shield and then scooped me up again. "I know this is a stupid question, but do you want to head home or investigate the light?"

I smiled in answer and he shook his head. "You're as insane as she is."

She being Mo, obviously. "I'll take that as a compliment."

"Not surprising, given she probably would."

I laughed. "Actually, we can't head directly over, as much as I want to. Mo said she'd meet us at The Red Lion if she wasn't able to make it back in time for the fight. I think we should wait for her before we do anything—especially given she's familiar with all the spells in that place and neither of us are."

"That's actually a good idea, as I think we could both do with a shower and something to eat."

The only thing I really wanted to eat right now was *him*, and that was currently out of the question. Nevertheless, enticing images rose.

He cleared his throat. "Um, can you stop that? I don't need to be distracted when we're on this stupid bridge."

I laughed, banished the imagery, and once again rested my head against his chest. Though the shield's handgrip was warm to the touch, cold magic continued to emanate from the steel. It had a very different feel to either Elysian or my knives, which in many respects confirmed that someone other than Vivienne had been involved in its forging. I doubted it was the Norse god Luc had mentioned, if only because the magic rolling off it didn't feel "godly" in the same sort of way that Elysian did.

Did that mean the shield really was another of Mryddin's subterfuges? If so, why? I guess there was only one way to answer either of those questions, given it was currently impossible to ask the man himself, and that was to find whatever had briefly responded to the shield's pulses.

Luc picked up Mo's sweater on the way over the bridge, then headed up the path to the parking area. Jess appeared out of the trees as we neared the SUV, the rifle case slung over her shoulder and a large grin on her face.

"Now *that* is my definition of a damn fine night."

"Anytime there're no major casualties on our side is a damn fine night," Luc said, voice dry.

"It is indeed always a bonus," she agreed. "You able to give me a ride back into town?"

"Sure." I glanced up at Luc. "You'd better drive though, I think."

"There's no 'think' about it—I want to get back to my motorbike in one piece, thanks."

"How did you get here if not on the motorbike?"

"Cab earlier this afternoon. They're too aware of the motorbike now, so she's parked in a secure lot, out of the way."

He placed me down next to the passenger door, then took the keys from my hand and opened the SUV up. As Jess climbed into the rear, he placed me into the passenger seat, dug a first aid kit out of the small backpack he was carrying, and quickly but efficiently tended to my gunshot wound. Then he ran around to the driver's side and started up the vehicle.

We wound our way out of the peninsula park then headed onto the main highway that ran around Ainslyn's more modern city center and on to the old walled town. By the time we neared the Petergate Gatehouse, my left arm was aching and I was barely keeping my eyes open.

"You can drop me off here somewhere," Jess said. "I'll walk the rest of the way."

Luc immediately pulled over. Jess jumped out, then leaned back in and added, "Tell Mo to give me a call if she needs any more of them red bastards shot. Hell, more than happy to shoot any of the other kind, too."

"I will," I said, amused.

"Catch you later then." She slammed the door shut and disappeared into the shadows of a covered laneway between two old houses.

Luc drove off. "Where on earth does Mo find these characters?"

"She likes oddbods. Always has."

His smile reached his eyes, crinkling the corners. "Another thing that runs in the family."

"I'm definitely her child more than I ever was Mom's." A statement that provided an ideal lead-in to the whole mage thing, but reluctance remained stronger than the need for honesty. He'd have to know, and sooner rather than later, but I really wanted to give him the time and space to accept me being the heir to the Witch King's crown before I hit him with another monumental piece of information that would affect our life together. Mages had very, *very* long lifespans. Humans had a relatively set time span. If we *did* ever marry, we'd both have to accept the fact that I would watch him grow old and die.

Not something I was ready to even think about right now. Especially when we hadn't even gotten around to doing anything serious.

I glanced out the window and watched the world go by as we wound our way through old Ainslyn and then across the river to The Red Lion. It was an L-shaped old coaching inn that had been considerably altered over the years.

What had once been a large manure heap now contained a lovely beer garden that ran down to the riverbank, and the old stables had been converted into rather quaint en-suite accommodation. Ginny's sixteenth birthday party—a bigger milestone in her family than the eighteenth—had been held in the beautiful medieval dining hall upstairs, rather than her family's large home, simply because between the inn and the nearby hotels, there'd been enough accommodation to house her extended family in the one vicinity. But it wasn't a pub we visited often, which was exactly why Mo had booked a room here. That, and the fact it was owned by a friend of a friend who'd agreed not to ask questions and who'd accept both cash and a false name.

The parking area only contained one other car, which wasn't really surprising given it was the middle of the off-season, tourist wise. I shivered into Mo's sweater and shoved on my shoes. "I'll go check in, then we can both have a shower before we get something to eat."

He nodded. I grabbed my purse out of the glove compartment, then climbed out of the SUV and headed across to the office. The proprietor—a good-looking man in his mid-fifties—was obviously disappointed I wasn't Mo, but cheered up considerably when I said she'd be here later. A past lover, perhaps? She certainly had plenty of them, and he did fit the type.

After collecting the key, I headed down to our room. Luc met me at the door, his pack over one shoulder and my wet clothes in the other hand. "I take it Elysian and the crown are in the trunk?"

"Yes, but they're spelled invisible and should be safe enough there for the moment."

He nodded. "Would you like first shower?"

I hesitated, then shook my head. "I need a cup of tea, and I also need to call Mo."

"If she's in the midst of flying here, she won't be able to answer."

"No, but she'll feel the phone vibrating."

He blinked. "Seriously?"

"The magic that takes care of whatever possessions and clothing we're carrying doesn't actually alter their form. It just ... miniaturizes and conceals, I guess." To be honest, I'd never really questioned the physics of it. It just was.

"Huh." He continued on to the bathroom, my wet clothes in hand.

I found the kettle and followed him into the bathroom to fill it up while he hung my clothes on the heated towel railing. "You're going to make a fabulous husband one day."

"Hmmm" was all he said, though anticipation and desire burned briefly through our link despite the fact we weren't touching.

And that suggested it was expanding. Which was both good and bad, given any possibility of deepening our relationship lay in a distant and very uncertain future.

Once I'd flicked on the kettle and found a cup and the tea bags, I grabbed my phone and made the call. It rang on and on, and I was just about to give up when she said, a little breathlessly, "Sorry, had a minor glitch with the second red demon. The bastard just wouldn't die."

"You okay?"

"A few scratches, but nothing serious." She paused, and in the background, I heard a familiar voice. Mia. She not only sounded okay, but also rather annoyed.

"Mia wants you to know," Mo added, voice droll, "that if she's ever captured again and in need of rescuing, she's not to be treated as a useless bit of baggage that has to be secreted away. She wants in on the payback."

"Tell said bit of baggage that if she *does* get captured again, I'll make sure she's securely locked up until all the fighting is over."

Mo relayed the message and then added, "Hang on while I put you on speaker to make things easier."

"Ha!" Mia said in response. "That's been tried before, and we all know how it went."

I grinned. Said triers had been her parents when she'd fallen in lust with a boy they considered unsuitable. "There's plenty of time to get in on the action, Mia. Trust me on that."

"Good, because the bastards destroyed my best set of bo staffs." She paused. "Though I guess that isn't really surprising, given I cracked open the heads of two of them and broke the leg of a third before they took me down."

I frowned. "Why didn't you use magic?"

She was, after all, a Lancaster. Personal magic of all kinds was their gift, and that included all manner of protection *and* repelling spells.

"I didn't have the time. They were on me before I knew what was happening. It was just lucky I was carrying the staffs."

"Maybe you need to start carrying them all the time."

"I intend to from now on."

"Good. Mo, are you still flying back tonight?"

"Yes—why?"

"Remember the shield on the arch?"

"Yes."

"Well, it came to life tonight."

"But it's a fake—"

"And it has magic. It pointed toward Uhtric's castle. I think we need to investigate it rather urgently."

"I agree. Be there in an hour or so."

"See you then."

I kicked off my shoes then made myself a cup of tea. Luc came out just when I was halfway through, still toweling his hair but fully dressed and smelling delightfully fresh.

"You want me to head over to the restaurant and order us some food while you shower? The kitchen will be closing in the next twenty minutes or so."

"Sounds like a plan." I took a sip of tea. "It also sounds like you don't want to be around my fabulously naked self in case temptation hits."

"And it usually does. Quite hard."

My gaze skimmed down his body. "Not quite there yet."

He tossed his towel at me. "You're incorrigible."

I batted it away with a laugh. "No, just horny. Expect it to get worse if you refuse to help ease the problem."

He rolled his eyes. "I'll see you in the bar. Please appear appropriately dressed."

I grinned. "I'll certainly consider it."

He rolled his eyes again and headed out. I finished my cup of tea, then made my way into the bathroom. He'd washed his shirt and pants and hung them on the railing besides my clothes. It was an oddly domestic moment in a world that had gone quite mad around me, and it had determination flaring anew that there would be plenty more such moments in my life with him.

I fashioned the shower cap into a protective wrap to cover the bandage on my arm, then took a quick but very hot shower. As I grabbed a towel to dry myself, I noticed the neat stack of clothes sitting on the closed lid of the toilet.

Jeans, a warm flannelette shirt, and fresh underwear. He hadn't only packed for himself, but also for me.

With a delighted grin, I dressed, then pulled Mo's sweater over the top and headed out to put on my socks and shoes. After grabbing my purse and the room key, I headed out.

The dining room was narrow and stretched the full length of the street-side section of the building. The bar dominated the space and was lined with old wood and leather stools. On the street side of the room there was a run of lovely old sash windows; a foot-wide table ran under the bottom of all these, its height perfect for leaning on. Luc sat at the far end of the bar, close to the open fire. I walked over, dropped a kiss on his cheek, and perched on the stool beside him.

"That's for the clothes."

He smiled. "I've ordered our drinks and our meals. Decided on the roast beef with roast potatoes, peas, and Yorkshire pud."

"A man who anticipates his woman's needs is a man to treasure indeed."

"Or a man who fears the wrath of his woman's grand-mother if he doesn't look after her well enough."

His voice was dry, and I laughed. "Yeah, right."

A bartender appeared with his beer and my whiskey, cheerfully said our meals wouldn't be long, and then disappeared again.

I picked up my glass and took a drink. The whiskey's fiery goodness burned all the way down and chased at least some of the tiredness away. Whether it would last long enough to get me through what we still had to do tonight was another matter entirely.

"If Mo doesn't arrive by the time we've eaten, can we go back to the room and properly conceal Elysian?"

He nodded. "It will take some time, though. It's not an easy spell to cast, and I've never actually tried it on a weapon other than Hecate."

"So it might not even be possible?"

"Oh, it is. We've had plenty of reasons over the centuries to conceal weapons other than our swords."

"How does the spell actually work? I mean, you were wearing Hecate when you were driving here, but she didn't seem to be restricting your movements or get in the way."

"Because she's not." He picked up his pint. "It's more than just a concealment spell. In some ways, it works along the same lines as Elysian, but instead of providing the wielder a means of stepping into the gray space, it pushes whatever weapon we want concealed into the outer edges of the gray. I can reach through the spell to grab her hilt, but for all intents and purposes, she's not physically present."

I frowned. "That would suggest if and when I have to step into the gray space, I'd also disappear."

"There are whispers of the witch kings fading in and out of focus during battle," he said. "But eyewitness accounts are understandably rare."

"I didn't disappear when I partially stepped into the gray space to call Nex to me."

He raised an eyebrow. "How can you be sure, given you were fighting for your life? It's not like you were standing outside your body observing what was going on, and Mo was busy with the dark altar."

"The bastard had his hands around my neck. I was very definitely on this plane, not the other."

"Meaning he might well have been anchoring at least a portion of you on this plane." He took a sip of his beer. "The fact is, you did reach for your knives via the gray and—from the little that's written on the king's use of it—that means there was at least partial immersion."

"If we survive the shit that's coming, you and I are going to sit down and detail every goddamn thing we know about the sword and the gray so that no future witch king *or* queen ever has to muddle through like we are."

He clicked his glass against mine. "Here's to survival and future detailing."

Our meal arrived, and our conversation moved on to less weighty subjects, like movies and books. I was pleased to discover he agreed with my declaration that *The Princess Bride* was one of the best fantasy movies ever, even if we did disagree on which of the *Lord of the Rings* movies was better.

Mo walked in just as our coffee arrived. Scratches covered her face, and she was favoring her right leg, but her grin was wide and her eyes sparkled. I wasn't entirely sure whether that was due to the sharp flight back to Ainslyn or besting two flighted demons.

"Looks like you let the demons get a little too close this time." Luc's voice was dry. "Reflexes slowing in your ancientness?"

Mo claimed the vacant stool on the other side of him, then lightly slapped his arm. "I'm late middle-aged in mage terms, and that's certainly not ancient, thank you very much. The bastard flew up from a culvert, catching me unawares."

I raised an eyebrow. "The wind didn't warn you?"

"It can't when I'm in blackbird form. The use of one ability mutes the use of the other."

Which was a useful snippet to tuck away and remember. "Is Mia as good as she sounded on the phone?"

"She is now," Mo said. "She did have a ton of bruising—and one of her kidneys was bleeding—but I've healed all that. She'll have to rest for the next twenty-four hours, but otherwise she'll be fine."

"So, she's not returning to the safe house tonight?"

"No. The last place anyone will think to look for her is Jun's."

No doubt because of Tris's involvement with Darkside. "She can't stay there forever."

"She won't—she'll head back tomorrow night via an Uber. It's too risky for her to use her car at the moment."

"Too risky for *any* of us," I commented.

She nodded. "Which is why I've extended the hire time on the SUV."

"And why I'll not be using the motorbike in the short term." Luc took a long drink of his beer. "Have you any idea why the shield pointed us toward the King's Tower?"

"None at all," Mo replied. "There are plenty of old weapons in the vaults, of course, but even if one of them had responded, it shouldn't have been visible. Where's the shield?"

"In the SUV," I replied.

She nodded and motioned to our drinks. "Once you finish those, we'll head off."

I picked up my coffee but didn't gulp it down. "Did Barney ever send you the enhanced images of the writing on the King's Stone?"

"Actually, yes. I just haven't had the chance to look at them."

She dug into her pocket and dragged out her phone. I slipped off the stool and stood behind her as she opened the first of the three images. The writing remained somewhat fuzzy, but you could at least pick out that it was text now, albeit a language that was ancient and probably long forgotten by most.

"Okay, this one says ..." She paused for several seconds. "That which is ... beautiful? is not always powerful."

"Obviously not a fan of De Montfort women," Luc murmured.

I laughed and nudged him lightly. "Smooth, Blackbird, smooth."

Mo flicked over to the next image. It was a little more legible and her translation was faster. "That which is plain often hides a mighty heart."

"This is where you make some comment about me," Luc said.

"There is nothing plain about you, I'm afraid," I replied obligingly.

He grinned but didn't comment as Mo moved on to the final image. After a few minutes she said, "The hand that claims one will never be worthy of the other."

I blinked. "Does that mean ...?"

"I believe it does," she said. "And thank the fuck for that."

"That's presuming the prophecy is true," Luc said. "There's nothing in the archives that suggests whoever draws the sword out of the King's Stone is incapable of drawing Elysian. And, in times past, she *was* the sword in the stone."

"Yes, but not for many, many centuries." Mo put her phone away. "We'll have to run on the presumption that he might be able to raise Elysian, but I have no reason to doubt what was written. Ready to go?"

I gulped down the rest of my coffee and then followed her out. The night was icy in comparison to the bar, and I crossed my arms in an effort to repress the shivers and contain some warmth. Luc immediately wrapped an arm around my shoulders and tugged me closer to his big body. I smiled and tucked an arm around his waist, determined to enjoy this moment of intimate normality before it all went south again.

He released me once we neared the SUV, and my body mourned the loss of heat and closeness. Once he unlocked the SUV, Mo opened the rear hatch door, then undid her coat and pulled out a rather plain leather scabbard.

"Where on earth did you get that?" I queried. "Or is it better not to ask?"

She dropped the scabbard into the trunk, retrieved the shield, and then slammed the hatch door closed. "I didn't steal it, if that's what you're inferring."

"Which doesn't answer the actual question." I opened the rear passenger door for her, then climbed into the front.

"The council has a number of artifacts on display in their chamber," she said. "None of the swords were as old as Elysian, of course, and the one I stripped the scabbard from is in fact eighteenth century, but it should fit quite nicely."

"And it certainly saves me having to make a temporary scabbard tonight," Luc said.

He reversed out of the parking spot and then headed out into the street. "Did you recognize the magic the shield's emitting?"

"Yes—it's Mryddin's."

"He made a fake shield as well as a fake sword?" I asked. "Why?"

"To annoy the hell out of me, no doubt," she muttered. "As I've said before, he always did like his games."

"Meaning the shield might not be connected to the witch kings?"

"Oh, it'll be connected. Whether it's relevant to our current quest is another matter entirely."

It took twenty minutes to get across to the King's Tower, thanks to many of the streets in the old town being inaccessible to a SUV. It probably would have been faster to walk, but we had no idea if Darkside had watchers out overhead. It was better not to take a chance, especially after the mess we'd made of them on King Island.

Luc didn't stop in the parking area behind the tower, but rather one of the nearby side streets. I climbed out and scanned the sky; aside from the faint glow of distant stars, there wasn't much to see. There was no whisper of darkness stirring on the wind and little in the way of life or sound coming from the surrounding neighborhood. This part of Ainslyn held a number of museums and had nothing in the way of after-hours nightlife.

The old tower dominated the area from its position on top of the mound. It was quadrilobate in shape, rather than the usual circular design, with each "lobe" holding different functions. The ground floor area contained a souvenir shop, a display room, toilet facilities, and the circular stairs down to the vaults. The upper floor—which was the most intact and original portion of the tower—contained the bedchambers. Though it couldn't be seen from this angle, a small chapel had been built between the east and south lobes, spoiling the symmetry of the building on that side.

Mo handed me the shield, and I pointed its face toward the tower. Once again the rose came to life, shooting a beam of light toward the tower that exploded over its old wooden roof. If anyone had been in the area, all they would have seen was a firework-like display.

Hopefully, any Darkside demons or halflings who might

be out and about nearby would think exactly the same thing.

As the display faded, two brief pulses of white shot skyward and then faded.

"They came from the other side of the tower rather than the tower itself," Luc said.

I glanced at Mo. "Would the chapel have anything Witch King related? I thought the place was empty?"

"It is—anything of worth was stripped from it centuries ago," she said. "Its only real point of interest these days is its medieval architecture. It was a private chapel built for the king alone, and far too small to be a useable display area."

"There has to be something in there—there's nothing else on that side of the building that could be responding."

"Remember who set this all up."

The more I learned about Mryddin, the more annoying he became. "How are we going to get into the tower without raising the alarms?"

"We won't," she replied. "We'll have to go in via the tunnel. But first, why don't you two take a concealed walk around the tower just to confirm where the response came from?"

Luc held out a hand. Once I'd twined mine through his, we headed toward the street that circled the tower. The surge of his power flowed across my senses, and the air began to glimmer gold. He was manipulating the darkness to conceal us and, as before, it felt as if a thousand tiny gnats were biting me. My skin twitched, but it was more uncomfortable than truly painful.

The glimmer formed a veil that not only covered us both but provided a visible boundary. To anyone beyond it, we were now completely invisible.

We crossed the road and walked around the base of the

mound to the parking lot side of the tower. As we neared the small chapel—a squared-off portion built between the two lobes—I raised the shield again. This time, the response from within the chapel was barely more than a sullen glow being emitted from a slit close to the chapel's stone foundations. Maybe proximity lessened its force.

I frowned. "Is there a room or vault under the chapel?"

"I daresay Mo would know better than me."

We continued around the rest of the tower, then headed back to the SUV. Mo leaned back against the rear hatch, her arms crossed and her gaze narrowed. Communicating with either the wind or the earth, I guessed.

"Anything?" she asked, though I daresay she already knew, given she'd basically been watching us.

It was a thought that suddenly had me wondering just how often she'd kept an eye on us like that when we were younger. There'd certainly been a number of times that she'd suddenly appeared to "save the day" when things had gone wrong for either Max or me.

And it might also explain the guilt she still felt over our parents' death—maybe she *hadn't* been watching that day. Although in truth, why on earth would she have been, given they were both adults?

Luc released his cloak of darkness. "The response came from an area close to the foundations of the chapel."

Mo frowned. "That's odd—the location would suggest a vault, but there's none in that area."

"This entire area was once a part of a wider castle complex," I said. "I know there's nothing much left of it above ground, but what about below? Have you ever asked the earth?"

She smiled. "Her power doesn't quite work that way. It hasn't a voice and can't answer direct questions, as such.

She is a force of energy that can provide impressions but nothing more."

"Surely the presence of a vault or some kind of underground structure would leave an impression on the earth though?"

She raised an eyebrow. "Can you feel the weight of the tower on the ground?"

"No, but that isn't surprising given—"

"Why would Gwen feel its weight?" Luc cut in, his brows furrowing. "That's not a skill that comes with the sword."

"No, it's not." Mo patted his arm lightly. "And that, dear boy, is definitely a conversation you and Gwen can undertake at a later point. Are you able to get the three of us unseen into the tower?"

Luc didn't look happy with her avoidance, but he'd been around Mo long enough by now to understand it was pointless arguing. "I can get us in, no problem, but I can only shield one other person. After the last break-in, they're monitoring the external cameras."

"Then we'll just go in through the abbey tunnels."

He nodded and, once we were all back in the SUV, drove across to the Museum Gardens, where the ruins of St. Mary's Abbey were. It had once been one of the richest in England, but it, like so many others, had been destroyed in King Henry's dissolution of the monasteries. Little enough remained these days—just a long sidewall and a solitary corner edge that was disconnected from the rest.

Though it was dark, there were spotlights on the abbey's walls, and they provided just enough light to see by. The entrance into the vault had been hidden in the smaller chunk of wall, and the thick veil of spells protecting it was probably the only reason it still stood.

Mo stopped in front of it and ran her fingers across the curve of a column. Golden sparks followed her touch, a comet tail of energy I now suspected was caused by her connection to the earth, rather than all the old protection spells that crisscrossed the entrance.

There was a soft click, followed by a soft rumble. The air shimmered, and the layers of protecting spells parted to reveal a slowly opening and very narrow stone door. Steep stairs descended into a deeper darkness, and they were just as wet and slimy-looking as they'd been the first time we'd come here.

I glanced up and down Luc's tall frame. "Are you going to fit in there?"

Devilment momentarily danced in his eyes. "I've been in tighter places."

"Oh, I just bet you have," Mo murmured.

I gave her the look—the one that said behave—but she merely grinned and motioned me into the lead. I dug out my phone and flicked on the flashlight, holding it in front of me as I squeezed sideways through the door then carefully moved down the steps until I reached the bottom. The air was rank and smelled of disuse, while the tunnel walls were wet with moisture and decorated with long strands of slimy green moss. The tunnel floor was little better than the walls, making any sort of speed impossible.

It was, to put it bluntly, a fucking horrible place to be in.

Our footsteps echoed hollowly in the otherwise dank silence, but this time, at least, there was no tightening in the air or any other indication of trouble waiting up ahead.

The tunnel did a long curve around to the left and ended in a solid wall of stone. It was an illusion—a very good illusion—rather than real.

I pressed on; the spell's energy tingled across my skin,

briefly resisting my presence, and then I was through into the main vault area. It was a large space that was these days used for storing whatever artifacts weren't currently on show upstairs. The human members of staff who worked here took the space at face value and had no idea that there were, in fact, multiple magically protected areas leading off it. I knew of two—one held an extensive library that included the full birth records of all seven houses dating back since before the time of the Witch Kings. The other was another—decidedly more decrepit—tunnel that had not only led down to the old sea wall and port, but also an open gateway into Darkside. Luc had sealed that thing pretty damn fast, but that didn't mean there weren't other gates out there we didn't know about.

I stopped and looked around. "Are there any other storerooms here we can't see?"

"Two," Mo said. "But neither of them lie underneath the chapel."

"The response came from inside the chapel at ground level," Luc said, "so unless there's a hole in the floor maintenance is ignoring, it can't be from a vault."

Mo grunted, though whether that meant she agreed or not, I couldn't say. She motioned me on.

I headed for the heavy wooden door that led into the unadorned stone corridor and ancient stairs that spiraled up to the ground floor. We climbed cautiously, making little sound even though the air gave no indication there was anyone else about.

I stepped over the rope barrier that stretched across the exit arch and padded across the foyer to the small, plain doorway that led into the chapel. It really wasn't anything to write home about. Medievalists might admire the oak beams that supported the ceiling or the decorative arcading that still lined the walls—and which had probably at one point held vibrant images—but as Mo had already said, everything else had been stripped away.

I stopped to one side of the doorway and studied the walls. After a moment, I spotted what looked to be an air vent near the base of the external wall. I knelt in front of it, the shield clanging loudly as it hit the stone with a little more force than I'd intended, and shone the phone's flashlight in. There was no mesh covering either end of the vent, which—considering the hole was big enough for squirrels or other very large rodents to crawl through—was rather odd. "There's nothing magical here."

Nothing other than old cobwebs and dead grass that had probably accumulated over the years of mowers going past, anyway.

"I doubt the beam would have emanated from within the vent itself." Mo stopped several feet away, her hands on her hips as she studied the floor. "Raise the shield and see what happens."

I obeyed. Nothing did. "Why would Mryddin lead us here if there's nothing to find? That makes no sense."

"Mryddin did a lot of things that make no sense to those with reasonable minds, but I suspect that's not the case here. The reason may be obscure, of course, but we won't know one way or another until we find whatever it is he wants us to find."

"Someone should have smacked some sense into that man ages ago," I muttered.

"Some tried, and more than once." Mo's voice was dry. "I think it's safe to say enjoyment rather than chastisement was the end result."

"Too much info, I'm thinking." My gaze went to Luc. He was studying the wall junction to the right of the vent, his brows furrowed and expression intent. "You found something?"

"This corner doesn't look right." He paused. "In fact, the whole wall is off."

I frowned at it, but it basically looked no different to the walls in any other part of this room. "In what way?"

He waved a hand toward the external wall and the vent. "It's not long enough. When we were outside, the vent was located roughly twenty feet away from the junction between the chapel and the south lobe. But inside, it's only ten feet."

I looked down at the floor. He was right. "Meaning there's a false wall."

"And it's not a magical one." He glanced at Mo. "Can you feel or see anything?"

She stepped up to the wall and pressed her fingers against it. After several seconds, she said, "There's a door close to the junction of the internal wall and this one. More than that, the earth cannot see."

"Because it's protected?" I asked.

"Because it's been sterilized in the same manner that the monolith's circle on King Island is sterilized."

My heart began to beat a whole lot faster. "That was supposedly done when Aldred thrust the sword into the stone."

"And would suggest whatever lies beyond this wall originates from that time, not Uhtric's," Luc commented.

Mo nodded somewhat absently as she trailed her fingers along the stone. Sparks chased after her, indicating she was still in contact with the force of the earth. A foot away from the end of the wall, she stopped. "It's here somewhere."

We walked over. The old arch in this section of the wall looked no different to any of the others. There certainly wasn't any indication that a door was set within it, be it physical or magical.

"If Aldred is responsible for the false wall, then perhaps it's not for you or me to find." Luc glanced at me. "Perhaps it will only respond to his heir."

"Possibly." Mo moved back and motioned me forward.

I hesitated, then stepped up and pressed a hand against the stone. It was warm and filled with a distant sort of power—the earth's energy still echoed through it despite the fact its connection had been severed long ago. Perhaps that echo was how Mo had refashioned the stone over on King Island.

After a few more seconds, a deep pulse began within the stone. It was intermittent at first but rapidly grew stronger, until its beat matched that of my heart. Light appeared, first encircling my hand, then spreading out across the stone, until the entire arch shone like moonlight.

Then, with a harsh grating sound, the stone retreated from my touch, revealing a staircase that plunged into deeper darkness.

CHAPTER SEVEN

I cautiously shone the flashlight's beam downward. The stone steps were narrow, but the air rising up the stairwell smelled a whole lot fresher than the abbey tunnel had, which suggested not only that whatever lay below was free from the runoff afflicting the other tunnel, but that it also had some form of ventilation.

I handed the shield to Luc, then cautiously went down, one hand on the wall for balance and the other holding the light. The steps might not be slimy, but they'd been designed for feet far smaller than mine.

The air got colder the deeper we went and, under my fingertips, the wall felt like ice. Unlike the wall and door above, this stone held no echo of the earth's energy—and hadn't for a very long time, I suspected. Had it been sterilized as a means of protecting whatever lay below? There might now be only three mages in existence, but the Chen line were earth manipulators and were often used to uncover artifacts on historic sites. Their services generally meant archeologists avoided spending years on hands and knees slowly scraping away dirt, though there were still many digs that did things the old-fashioned way—mostly because funding was limited and didn't always stretch to employing Chens.

But dead earth couldn't be read or manipulated, and I would have thought that alone would have been a major giveaway that something odd was going on under the chapel. Unless, of course, no one had ever bothered doing an exploratory dig this close to the tower.

The stairs continued to wind down, and the world above faded away until nothing was left except thick silence and expectation.

Some of the latter was mine.

Most of it wasn't.

Whatever we were about to uncover, it had been waiting for a very long time for our arrival.

For *my* arrival.

We eventually reached the bottom of the stairs, and I paused, shining the light down the narrow corridor. It spotlighted a highly decorated metal door riddled with protection spells. *Nothing* was getting through that thing without invitation—not fire, not flood, not a whole battalion of demons.

"Well, that's certainly unexpected," Mo said.

I glanced up at her. "What is?"

"The crest in the middle of that door—it's Ludvik's."

I raised an eyebrow. "Who the hell is Ludvik?"

"A king who reigned before Aldred's time. He was one of the few before Elysian came onto the scene who'd had any success beating the demon scourge."

"Is the magic protecting the door his?"

"No, although there was mage blood in his line, and he was rather hard to kill." She cocked her head sideways, eyes narrowed. "The spells are mostly Mryddin's, entwined within a few older ones that are Lancastrian in feel. Ludvik did have a number of them in his council, and from what I've been told, they were renowned not only as adepts but also fierce warriors."

"You didn't know Ludvik personally?" I asked.

"No, he was before my time, but I remember Mryddin mentioning him a few times." She waved a hand toward the door. "Perhaps this is why."

"You know, the current situation would have been a whole lot easier if Mryddin had just passed on shit like this," I grumbled.

"His tendency for secrecy is extremely annoying," she agreed. "But perhaps the very reason this place still exists is because he *didn't* pass the knowledge on."

I grunted and carefully approached the door. The spells protecting it became agitated as we drew closer, but nothing struck out at us. The door itself had no handle, but then, neither had the upper stairwell door. Unlike that one though, this door was highly carved and featured multiple images of battle. There were depictions of a king astride a horse, his sword raised as he plowed through demon hordes, multiple villages being overrun, and what looked to be Darkside gateways out of which all manner of evil poured. Ludvik's crest was set in the middle of the door, a crowned and rampant lion with a double-forked tail.

"I've not seen that crest in any of the heraldic references," Luc said.

He stood close enough that his breath caressed the back of my neck and an odd sense of security washed through me even as I crossed mental fingers that he would *always* have my back.

"It's possible Ludvik's line died out long before Aldred

came on the scene," Mo said. "It's also possible that Ludvik is in fact Aldred's ancestor."

"Surely something like that would have shown up in the genealogy records," Luc said.

"They might not go back that far. Gwen, press your hand against the crest—that's where the bulk of the spells lie."

I did so. Once again magic swarmed around my fingers, its touch warm and without threat. After a few seconds, it faded away and the door quietly unlocked. I hesitantly pushed it all the way open and swept the flashlight's bright beam around. The room was square in shape and the walls were covered with brightly colored images. A round oak table, on which sat a number of rolled-up scrolls, dominated the center of the room; evenly spaced around it were twelve chairs.

I glanced around at Luc. "Obviously the Blackbirds were *not* the first to use a round table."

"No." He walked across, placed the shield on the table, and then carefully picked up the top scroll. "These hides are in mint condition."

"The whole place is." Mo moved across to the nearest wall. "Look at these images—they're so damn vibrant they could have been done yesterday."

I stopped beside her and slowly swept the light left to right, revealing a crudely drawn map filled with locations and names I didn't recognize. There were creatures on it too —demons mainly, but also figures I presumed were dark elves, given the elongated point to their ears. In a couple of places, the images glowed faintly.

"Have you ever seen something like this before?" I asked.

"No." Mo's expression was thoughtful as she moved

further down. "There's magic woven into the mural though."

My gaze shot to her. "Where?"

She waved a hand to encompass the room. "It's embedded into the whole thing. It's not any sort of spell I've encountered before."

"It's not Mryddin's work then?"

"No, but he obviously knew about this place."

"You really need to have a stern word with that man if he ever bothers to make an appearance."

She nodded, though it was a somewhat absent gesture; her attention was mostly on the mural.

I glanced across to Luc. "Anything in those scrolls?"

"A whole lot of old script I can't read." He glanced at me. "Demon script."

"*All* of them?"

"The five I've checked so far, yes."

"Why on earth would a human king have demon scrolls stored here?"

"Perhaps they are the reason these maps exist," Mo said. "After all, the ancients appeared able to translate demon script, a skill we've long lost."

"There's far too many things that have been lost to the mists of time," I grumbled, "and we seem to be paying the price for it now."

"That is the way of the world, I'm afraid, and something you'll learn to accept over time." She moved on to the wall. "I do believe the mural on each wall depicts a different portion of the UK."

"What?" I returned my gaze to the images and studied them for several seconds. "None of those place names exist today."

She lightly touched the map. "Aquae Sulis is now known as Bath."

I frowned and stepped closer. "What are the two symbols underneath it?"

"They're rune symbols—if I remember right, a triangle half-mast on a stick means gateway."

My stomach did a weird sort of twist even as excitement stirred. "*Are* there two gateways in Bath?"

"There used to be. One fractured a hundred or so years ago, and that might just explain why the runes are pointed in different directions."

Meaning this thing could well be a map of the position and current state of all known demon gates at the time this was developed—something we didn't currently have, despite the fact we knew the locations of most of them.

"If that gate only closed a hundred years ago, then the magic in this thing has to be still active, despite appearing otherwise."

She nodded and moved farther along the wall, scanning each of the old place names, her expression intent. Once we'd done a circuit around the room, she grabbed my phone and brought the light closer to the nearest rune. "It's faint, but there's very definitely another name written under the current one. That would suggest this map has been updated at least once—perhaps even in Aldred's time."

"So why would something as useful as this have been forgotten by the other witch kings?"

"That I can't say. But Mryddin's magical fingerprints are all over the external layers of this place, so there's obviously some reason it was locked up and abandoned."

"I can't say why it was abandoned," Luc said, "but I think I found the reason why it ended up deep underground."

We swung round. He'd placed Hecate along one edge of a scroll and the shield on the other and was studying it intently. "This is written in Old English, which I'm somewhat rusty on, but it seems to be an account of an attack on this structure and what was done to preserve it for future generations."

Mo moved around the table to stand beside him. For several minutes, neither of them said anything, their attention wholly on the text.

I shifted from one foot to the other and tried not to be impatient. I failed. "Care to share before I die of curiosity?"

"This map room," Mo said, without looking up, "was part of a much earlier fort constructed on the site and was designed to not only indicate the viability of a gate but also whether demons were active near it."

My gaze shot to the faintly glowing figures. Some were brighter than others, which might be an indication of how many demons exited—the greater the number, the brighter the glow.

"After most of the fort was destroyed in a demon attack," she continued, "the decision was made to make this room disappear. Mryddin and loyalist Chens were called in to push the entire building deep underground. Mryddin then constructed a tunnel none but the king or his heirs could find or open."

"Was the shield a part of all that?"

"It would certainly explain why it is so much smaller than the shields in use at that time," Luc commented.

I looked around the room again. "There's no indication of a tunnel entrance now."

"No," Mo said. "But it would explain why Mryddin insisted Aldred build a castle on this spot."

"His original castle wasn't here?"

"It was in Winchester," Luc said.

Which was why it was also the ancient seat of the Blackbirds—as the witch king's guardians, they basically had to be where the king was.

"Do you know if Aldred used this map at all?" I asked.

"He could have, but Mryddin was his advisor, not me." A smile twisted Mo's lips. "I was relatively young in mage terms at the time, and neither man liked taking direction or advice from any woman, let alone a young one."

"More fool them," Luc commented. "But if Aldred *did* make use of this map, it's all the more unfathomable it was then locked away and forgotten."

"All magic has its costs," Mo said. "Perhaps it was decided the cost of this room was too great."

"Then why keep the *map* active?" I asked. "That makes no sense."

"As I have said many times, Mryddin's actions often made little sense to us mere mortals."

I gave her the look. "You're hardly a mere mortal."

"Well, no, but I am certainly closer to it than he ever was. I mean, he *is* half incubus."

"I daresay the answers to all our questions will be in these scrolls somewhere," Luc said. "They seem to have kept a studious record of things."

"Perhaps if we all took a pile ..." I stopped as an odd sort of awareness vibrated across my skin and made the hairs on the back of my neck stand on end.

Something stirred ...

I swallowed heavily and looked around. "Did you feel that?"

Mo's gaze sharpened. "Feel what?"

"That vibration ..."

"Define vibration," Mo said. "Magical or physical?"

I didn't answer. Instead, I swept my gaze across the walls. Nothing appeared to have changed, but the vibration caressing my skin was strong enough now that my whole body tingled. Then a flicker of movement caught my attention.

I walked across to the southern end of the room. "Mo, where's Lindum?"

"That's Lincoln—why?"

"Because the rune there is now flashing." Though the nearby demon or dark elf drawings weren't glowing in any way.

She hurried across. "I'm not liking the look of *that,* and I certainly don't like the fact that you felt the magic activate."

"It really isn't that surprising, given both the shield and the two damn doors reacted to me." I pointed at the flashing rune. "Do you think it's worth flying over there to uncover what, exactly, is happening?"

"I think we'll have to." She eyed me critically. "You up to that? Or do you want a boost?"

I held up a hand. "I'm fine. Tired, but fine."

"Which definitely should *not* be the case, given the forces you tapped up there."

I frowned. "You sensed that?"

"I'm a mage. I sense many things."

"If I were you, I'd be saying something along the lines of 'and yet you have so very little sense' right about now."

She laughed and lightly pushed me toward the door. "Let's go."

"I'll stay here and keep going through the scrolls," Luc said. "It's not like I can come with you anyway."

I frowned at him. "We can't leave the chapel door open, and I'd rather not lock you in here just in case something happens to me."

"I'll follow you up and conceal the open door," he said. "No one will be able to tell the difference between the real wall and the fake. But I *would* nevertheless appreciate you coming back in one piece. We still need—"

"To have sex?" I cut in hopefully.

"Eventually, yes, but that's not where I was going."

"That makes me sad."

"It makes *me* even sadder," Mo said, her expression sorrowful. "Have I not mentioned my need for grand-children?"

"Multiple times," he said dryly. "And you already have two, dear woman, so there is no rush. But I was referring to the need to shadow Elysian in the gray."

Mo patted my arm. "Better luck another day, my dear. Come along."

I rolled my eyes and followed her back up the circular stairs. Once we were through the top door and back in the old chapel, I grabbed Luc's shirt, hauled him close, and then kissed him. Because I wanted to. Because I needed to.

He slipped his arm around my waist, then pulled me hard into the steel of his body. Our kiss was fire and passion, need and desire, an affirmation and a promise. It made me hunger not just for him, but for time itself.

Time to get to know him better.

Time to explore all that could lie between us.

That time, however, was not now.

I sighed regretfully and stepped back. He cupped my cheek with one hand and brushed a thumb across my lips. It felt like he was branding me. "Come back in one piece."

"Oh, after a kiss like that, you can bet I will. The sad fact is, you're stuck with me now."

Warmth and caring spun through his eyes. "I can think of worse fates."

"Such a romantic thing to say," Mo said, voice dry. "Can we move on now?"

I grinned and motioned her on. She shifted shape but didn't head out the door, instead arrowing through the vent.

I shifted and followed, tucking my wings in close as I went through the vent. I nevertheless felt the scrape of stone along my body before I was free and climbing skyward again. The night sky had cleared while we'd been underground, and the breeze chased our tails, making flying faster and easier. It nevertheless took us too long to get to our destination and, as we arrowed down, I couldn't help but wonder if there'd be anything left to discover.

As it turned out, there was.

Bodies.

Seven of them, in fact.

We rode the wind for several minutes, circling the area and looking for demon activity or traps. A series of lakes stretched out below us, with heavily treed land bridges linking the six larger islands together. The bodies lay on one of the unlinked islands. Its shoreline was ringed with thick stands of trees, and a small clearing lay in the middle. In the center of *that* was a rock-topped mound I presumed was the gate. There was no sign of magic or movement anywhere on the island.

If this wasn't a trap, why were the bodies there?

Granted, demons considered human flesh a delicacy, but major hunts were rare these days. If these bodies *were* the result of such a hunt, why not immediately take them through the gate? Discovery might be unlikely thanks to the fact the island was only reachable by boat, but it was nevertheless odd behavior for them.

After circling for another few minutes, Mo flew on to a nearby island and shifted shape as she neared the ground.

I landed beside her. "Why are we here?"

"Just wanted to give you a heads-up—that island is shielded, and I've not seen a spell like it before."

I hadn't even *seen* the damn shield. "Is it dangerous?"

"It doesn't look like it, but I think I should—"

"No," I cut in. "Definitely not."

She gave me a long look. "Do not be daft, darling girl. If this *is* a trap, I'll need you free to rescue me."

I hesitated. It was a logical step, even if I hated the risk she was taking. "Squawk if it's clear. Squawk louder if it's not."

Her answering smile suggested she'd be doing neither. We reclaimed our blackbird forms and flew back to the other island. While she arrowed down, I remained aloft, the wind under my wings, allowing me to circle without effort. She swooped across the treetops and then through the clearing. Nothing happened. After a few more passes, she landed at the base of a tree, regained human form, and motioned me down.

I followed her entry line and landed beside her. She knelt and pressed one hand into the soil. While she communed with the earth, I crossed my arms and studied the mound. It was an actual cave rather than something the demons had built to cover the existence of the gate. The entrance was low to the ground and little more than an open slash that was at best two feet high. Obviously, the demons who used this particular gate were on the small side.

The seven bodies were randomly placed in front of the entrance and, at least from this distance, there was no immediate indication of how they'd all died.

Mo rose and brushed dirt from her hand. "There's definitely no life on the island, human or otherwise."

"And is there a gate inside that cave?"

"Most likely, but it's not something I can feel through the earth. Not unless Darksiders are coming out of it."

I frowned. "But the gates exist in our world, so why can't you feel them?"

"Because *technically* the gate sits in the gray, even if it is visible from both sides."

"That makes no sense, given the Blackbirds and the witch councils are always spelling closed minor gates. They couldn't do that if they were sitting in the gray."

"You're coming at the gates from a position of logic—"

"That," I cut in, "is the first time anyone has ever implied logic is a bad thing."

She half smiled. "Logic cannot be applied to the gates because their presence actually defies logic and the laws of existence as we know it."

"Then how are we supposed to think of them?"

"As a protected tunnel *through* the gray. The structures we see are basically a boundary echo—one that prevents the unwary unwittingly getting sucked in."

"Considerate of whatever causes these things to do that," I said. "Is that why we can't seem to permanently lock down the gates with magic?"

She nodded. "Elysian is our only means of locking down the gates, and even she does not provide a permanent closure. Time and whatever cosmic forces cause these things work against her."

"Did any of the kings use Elysian in an attempt to shut the minor gates down?"

"The gates do not close easily or willingly, and the longer you remain in the gray, the greater the toll it takes on your body. It's not possible to shut down the minor gates in bulk, and it's not survivable to do them one at a time." She rose and brushed the dirt off her fingers. "Let's go check those bodies. But keep an eye out."

I followed her across. The wind stirred around me but held no power and whispered no secrets. "Is the ability to hear the wind intermittent? Because I'm not getting anything from her at the moment."

"We can switch it on and off," she said. "It'd be pretty damn annoying if we couldn't. But you're untrained, so you pretty much have to be naked to make the connection."

"That's inconvenient."

"And something of a safety measure. Hearing the wind and feeling the pulse and pain of the earth twenty-four-seven can easily drive you mad if you don't have the means to switch it off."

"Why would the earth be in pain?"

"Why would it not, given all that modern civilization does to it?"

"I guess I never thought about that."

"Few do, even those whose element it is. That's the problem."

The first body we came to was that of a woman lying facedown. Her arms were underneath her, and her legs were splayed at odd angles from her body. She hadn't fallen like that—someone had thrown her onto the ground like so much rubbish. But, broken limbs aside, there was no obvious indication of what had killed her.

Mo knelt and pressed her fingers to either side of the dead woman's head. After a few seconds, she said, "Death occurred about two hours ago."

"How was she killed?"

"Her throat was sliced open."

"Not here, obviously." If it had been, there would be

evidence of blood spurts on the ground, either in front or to the side of her body. There was nothing.

Mo shifted her grip and gently turned the woman's head. A soft gasp followed. "My god, it's Elaine."

I touched Mo's shoulder lightly. "A friend?"

"A colleague of Barney's. She's a member of the Lincoln Witch Council."

My gaze shot to the remaining six bodies. "You don't think ...?"

"God, I hope not."

She thrust upright, stepped over Elaine's body, then walked over to the next body and gently rolled him over. He had dark hair, cherub cheeks, and a look of horror forever etched onto his face. His throat had also been cut and, once again, there was an absence of blood on the ground around him.

"Joel Okoro, another council member." She moved on, checking the remaining five bodies. "Damn it, they've killed them *all*."

"How the hell did demons manage to catch seven council witches utterly unprepared?"

"They couldn't. Not if they were all together, at least. But separately? Very possible, especially if they were hunted beyond the protections of their homes."

"But we're talking about council witches here—they're elected into the position because of their knowledge and proficiency in their particular element or skill set."

"Being the best doesn't mean you can't be caught unawares." She grimaced. "We can both certainly attest to that."

I raised my eyebrows. "I would hardly class me as being knowledgeable in anything right—"

I stopped abruptly and stared at the cave, unease prickling over my skin. There was no whisper of movement, no evidence of the magic that had led us here, and yet ... something stirred deep within the darkness of that cave. Something foul.

"Mo," I whispered.

She held up a finger and motioned me to the left edge of the cavern's entrance. I flexed my fingers and wished I had Nex and Vita with me. I might not need them to use the inner lightning, but there was something very comforting about their weight in my hands.

I pressed back against the rock and stared down at the entrance. Nothing came out of it. Not for several unbelievably long minutes.

Then Mo raised a hand and reached for the wind. As she did, a screaming black mass swept out of the cavern's entrance, split into two, and attacked.

They were bats.

Or rather, Darkside's version of them.

A cloud of leathery wings, sharp claws, and even longer teeth flew at me. They tore at my clothes, my hair, and my face, their red eyes gleaming with malevolence and hunger. A scream that was part fear, part rage tore from my throat, and I raised my hands to protect my face even as I called to the lightning. It erupted from my fingers and lashed at the striking swarm, burning one after another after another. Embers swirled around me, and the air became thick with the smell of burned leather and flesh. The bats didn't seem to care. They just kept on coming, kept on attacking, their number seemingly endless.

Then, abruptly, they were gone, wrenched away by a whirlwind of air that took them god knew where.

I blinked but didn't immediately release the lightning pressing at my fingertips.

"Sorry," Mo said into the silence. "That took far longer than I expected."

My gaze jumped across to her. She leaned back against the rock, her face pale and covered by numerous scratches. She plucked the broken body of one of the wretched things from her coat, dropped it to the ground, and then stomped on it. "But at least I discovered what the shielding on the island does—it prevents the use of magic in the area, including mage."

"You did get past it, though, so that's something."

"Yes, but it took a lot of effort, and had it been humanoid demons rather than bats, we might well both be dead."

I sucked in a deep breath and released it slowly. My head was aching, and a faint trickle of moisture leaked from one eye—which was definitely an improvement over both of them bleeding—but overall, I felt surprisingly okay.

Which didn't mean I wouldn't fall in a gigantic heap once we got back to the hotel room.

"So where did the wind take them?"

"I shoved them deep in the water and drowned the bastards."

"Good." I dragged out my phone, then squatted in front of the cave's entrance and shone the flashlight into it. It plunged so steeply down into utter darkness that even if the gateway had been close, it wouldn't have been visible. "Do you think they deliberately drew us here to test their shield?"

"Given the range of magics included, no. It's simply a means of protecting the gate against all of our witches."

"Why here, then? Why this one? It's not particularly large or well positioned."

"I think it safe to say this would not be the only gate that's now protected."

I pushed upright. "That surely means they're getting ready for a big push."

"Lincoln's council won't be the only ones on their hit list."

"Then we need to get a warning out." I glanced down at the gate again. "Darkside has to have a means of tracking the viability of the gates if this one has only just opened."

"That wouldn't be surprising, given they rely on Earth for much of their sustenance."

Something I didn't want to think about, especially given how close we'd come to being that sustenance. I thrust a hand through my hair, shaking loose bits of ash and leather. "What are we going to do now?"

"I'll ring Barney—he can put out an urgent alert to all the local councils. The High Council will also have to be informed."

While she made the phone call, I took off my shoes and socks and then pressed my toes into the ground. The earth's pulse was a distant echo—something I could hear, but not reach. I frowned and glanced around. Darkside magic might be darker in both tone and design than ours, but from what I'd seen of it, it followed the same basic principles. Which meant the shield would have a base—something onto which the spell was anchored. With a shield this large, there'd have to be at least three of them. If I could find those anchors, I might be able to destroy it. But even if that wasn't possible, finding them would help us understand the spell's construction. Knowing that would allow us to create a counter.

I walked across to the other side of the clearing. The earth's pulse remained distant, suggesting the barrier I couldn't see extended well into the trees. I cautiously continued on, trying to avoid anything prickly or sharp even though it was extremely difficult to see, given the darkness and the thickness of the leaf litter on the ground.

The gentle lapping of water against the shoreline soon filled the silence. I paused, placed one hand on a nearby tree trunk for balance, and then dug my toes into the leaf litter and dirt. The earth's pulse was stronger; I had to be getting near the end of the barrier. I pushed on. The forest thinned out, and from directly ahead came the shimmer of moonlight on dark water. Surely they wouldn't bother extending the protection out into the lake—

The earth's pulse jumped into focus so abruptly, a squeak of surprise escaped my lips. I swallowed heavily and took one step back. The earth muted again. I'd found the shield's edge.

I turned and followed its line, one foot on either side as a guide. About twenty feet further along, an odd sort of awareness crept across my senses, making the hairs at the back of my neck stand on end. There was no change in the pulse of the earth, but up ahead something was definitely off. I paused and scanned the shore, but it was nigh on impossible to see anything beyond trees and the large cluster of boulders that blocked my path.

I walked to the pile of boulders, then gripped the top of the nearest stone and climbed. The stone was cold under my feet, which was odd given that—up until now—the rocks had run with the earth's warm pulse. Did it have something to do with the anchor? Was its presence somehow altering the earth's voice? Or perhaps even my perceptions of her as I drew closer?

Mo would undoubtedly be able to tell me, but she was still talking on the phone—I could hear snatches of her conversation drifting on the breeze.

I slid down the other side of the rock and walked on. The earth's pulse resumed, and the creeping sense of oddness began to fade. I stopped and turned around.

The boulders were the anchor point.

I walked back. The creeping oddness returned. I scrambled up to the top again and then looked around. It was unlikely they'd use the whole rock pile as an anchor, if only because it'd be far too obvious to any witch who might be out on the lake boating or fishing. Making them small made them easier to conceal and harder to find. I might not be able to spell myself, but I'd certainly learned all about the intricacies after years of watching Mo, and even Mia, create them.

There were numerous fissures between the various boulders that would provide the perfect hiding spot, and there was no way known I was going to stick my hand down any of them. Not without first peering into each one with a light to ensure the demons hadn't left any additional nasty surprises.

What I *could* do was pin down a location by using the ebb and flow of that weird awareness.

I carefully scrambled around the boulders and, after five minutes or so, had narrowed the possibilities to two—the first was in what appeared to be a hairline fissure in the largest of the top boulders, and the other a gap between it and the next.

I sat down on a nearby rock to wait for Mo. She appeared after a few minutes, shifting from blackbird to human form as she neared the base of the mound.

"You comfortable up there?"

"No, because this rock is as cold as ice and my ass is freezing."

"Ah." Her gaze narrowed. "You've found one of the anchor points. Well done."

"Thanks. Did you contact Barney?"

"Yeah. And then I rang the High Council. They're going to send people ASAP to investigate the four Greater London gates."

"I take it they'll also send an official priority warning out to all witch councils?"

She nodded. "Barney did ring back after I'd finished that call and said the rest of Ainslyn's councilors are okay."

"That doesn't surprise me, to be honest. Darkside—through Max—would be well aware of your relationship with Barney. Attacking him or anyone else would basically advertise their intentions. I don't think they're quite ready for that just yet."

I leaned down and offered her a hand up. "The anchor is in either that crack or the fissure beside it."

Mo squatted in front of the fissure and shone the flashlight into it. After a moment, she grunted. "I can see it. It's a piece of darkstone lodged about three feet down."

"Just out of our reach then."

"Yes, but I wouldn't ever advise touching darkstone with bare hands. It'd give you frostbite in seconds."

I raised my eyebrows. "I take it that's why these boulders feel so cold and weird?"

She nodded. "It's a reaction against a substance generally not found here on Earth."

"Aside from the freezing thing, is it actually dangerous?"

"No. Nor will the foul freezing radiate out more than ten feet or so from its location."

"That will at least make them easier to find."

"Yes."

She pushed upright and wavered a little. I caught her elbow to steady her. She might be the strongest, smartest woman I'd ever known, but even she had her limits. Not that she'd ever willingly admit that.

I couldn't help smiling. I guess that was something *else* I'd inherited from her.

"Are you going to deactivate the shield?"

She shook her head. "It'll only warn them we've discovered what they're doing, and, for the moment, I'd rather not do that."

My gaze went to the clearing I couldn't see. "And the bodies of Lincoln's councilors?"

"Will be retrieved tomorrow."

If there was anything *left* to retrieve. She didn't say that, of course, but it nevertheless remained fact. I took a deep breath that did little to ease the frustration of not doing enough for the dead and then said, "So, back to Ainslyn?"

"You should, as you still need to conceal Elysian."

I frowned. "Where are you going?"

"To London. I need to bring the High Council fully up to date, but I don't trust the phone. Besides, I wanted to run a physical check on them, just to ensure we've no wraiths on board."

"Wouldn't they have already checked that, given you contacted them about getting a team in to disinfect Noelle?"

"That would be a logical step. Unfortunately, there are some on the council very set in their ways and very convinced no mere wraith would ever get the better of them."

"Then I'm glad you're heading there to smack some sense into them."

She half smiled. "I only resort to violence if it's absolutely necessary."

And it very much sounded as if it was. "How long will you be?"

"About a day. But I want you to keep an eye on the maps and tell me if anything happens."

"And if something does?"

"Then pray we can counter it," she said. "Because if I'm right, they're about to test our defenses. If we don't counter it, all hell will break loose."

CHAPTER EIGHT

"**A**nd on that cheery note," I muttered, "we'd both better get moving."

She smiled and dropped a kiss on my cheek. "Be careful, but don't behave—at least when it comes to that luscious man of yours."

I rolled my eyes. "He has this whole honor and duty before pleasure thing going on, so nothing *will* go on until Darkside is defeated."

"That man is not made of stone, despite appearances to the contrary."

"Want to bet on that?"

She laughed. "I've never been one to wager on the whims of a man. They can be fickle creatures. Fun, but fickle."

"They say that about us."

"Of course they do. Men have a long history of projecting their own failures onto us." She glanced at the sky, her nostrils flaring as she drew in a deep breath. "At least it's a good night for flying. Be careful, darling girl, and don't be seen. I'll be back as soon as I can."

I nodded and waited until she'd shifted shape and flown off before I did the same. It took longer to get back to Ainslyn, thanks to the fact the wind was against me, and I was shaking with weariness by the time I flew into the chapel via the old vent.

Luc glanced up from the stack of scrolls as I walked into the room. His gaze swept me, then came up concerned. "What's happened?"

"Everyone in the Lincoln council has been murdered. Mo thinks it's a precursor to a major attack, and is off to London to coordinate with the High Council."

"Have the Blackbirds been informed? They certainly should be involved with any retaliatory action."

I frowned. "Aren't your people guarding the queen and her family?"

"Six are, but they will need to be updated. If there *is* a major attack planned, then in all likelihood it'll involve the royal family. Remember, it's your brother's goal to regain witch rule of this land, and he can only do that if the entire royal line is erased."

I could hardly forget something like that. "You'd better ring them, then, because it's unlikely they'll be the High Council's first priority given what has happened in Lincoln."

While he made the call, I walked across to the wall that mapped out the Yorkshire area and found the main gate. Its rune was larger and a dark red rather than the gold of the other gates. Its color reminded me of dried blood, which was somewhat apt given if that gate ever opened, *our* blood would be flowing across all of England.

I raised a finger and lightly touched the rune. It was inert. I skimmed the rest of the map until I found an open gate and then touched that, just to compare. It felt like I was touching lightning.

Did that mean I could tell which gates were close to opening even just by touching them? I guess there was only one way to find out.

I slowly traversed the room and checked each of the runes. None of the closed gates sparked. Not until I reached the map detailing the southeast portion of the country and Greater London.

Three of the four gates there sparked even though their runes were still backward, indicating their closed state. The fourth was a known active gate.

I swore and thrust a hand through my tangled hair. At least none of the runes were currently blinking, and that meant we still had time. How *much* was the damn problem. Why on earth would Mryddin and the kings bury this place to protect it and then forget to leave a whole bunch of instructions on how to use it? My gaze went to the scrolls on the table. It was possible the instructions were somewhere amongst that lot, of course, but did we have the time to uncover and then transcribe them?

Maybe. Maybe not.

I sighed—a sound that was pure frustration—then sent a quick text to Mo to let her know what I'd discovered. She wouldn't be near London as yet, but she'd at least have the information at hand when she met with the High Council.

"Problem?" Luc said, as he got off the phone.

"The inactive gates in Greater London are fizzing under my touch. I think it might mean they're about to open. If I'm right, it means the demons are about to hit London en masse."

His gaze went to that portion of the map. "The demon images near the Horn's Green gate aren't glowing."

"That's not unexpected if they are planning a mass attack. They wouldn't do anything that would give us a warning. Were you able to get through to anyone?"

He nodded. "Jerold said he'd warn the palace team, then contact the council. If the Greater London gates *are* on the verge of opening, and they do attack the palace en masse, we'll need help to counter them."

"Why not just move the royal family to a more secure location?"

"They probably will if it's deemed absolutely necessary, but it's doubtful there'd be many places as secure as the palace."

Because Layton—the very last witch king—had handed his human descendants the means of curtailing any magical attacks. "Darkside won't attack it magically—they'll try to overwhelm it with sheer bloody numbers."

"Yes, but there are enough witches on staff to keep the barrier spells viable. And both the palace guards and the Blackbirds on duty there should be able to handle any who do break through."

"What if her staff or guards have been infected by wraiths? Hell, what if the Blackbirds on protection detail there are infected?"

"The Blackbirds within the palace have already been checked—no infection. The council has given them ultraviolet lights to check anyone wishing contact with either the queen or the royal family."

Which didn't solve the wider problem of possible infection within the guard ranks. "What about the remaining six Blackbirds?"

"Jerold and Kai are in the clear. The other three will be checked when they report in."

"And your cousin?"

"Ricker was shifted across to palace detail a day ago and was one of the first cleared."

"Thank goodness for that."

"Yeah, though it wouldn't have surprised me if he *had* come up as infected." Luc's expression was grim. "Not given the hate your brother has for us in general and me in particular."

I couldn't help smiling. "That's because you had the audacity to fall in lust with his sister."

"Guilty as charged." The heat that flared in the jade depths of his eyes burned all the way down to my toes. "I take it we're now making this place our war room?"

I nodded even as I half wished he'd give in to what continued to flare between us. Which was a stupid wish given what might be coming at us in the next few hours.

"One of us will have go out and grab some supplies—"

"One of us being me, no doubt."

His voice was dry. I grinned and didn't deny it. "I need Elysian, the crown, my knives, and food. And not necessarily in that order."

"Chocolate and tea the priority. Got it."

"You really are going to make me a fabulous husband one day."

"Let's not get ahead of ourselves. Besides, there's more to being a good husband than the ability to fetch tea and chocolate."

"Yes, but if you make love like you kiss, I think we're set."

He shook his head, his expression an odd mix of amusement and desire. "You really could be a clone of your grandmother."

"That's truer than you know."

He raised an eyebrow, but I once again sidestepped the

unspoken question. "You'd better go before I fade away from lack of sustenance."

Annoyance replaced the amusement, but all he said was, "I take it Elysian and the crown will still be concealed?"

"Yes, so take this." I pulled the chain holding the coronation ring from my neck. "It'll point you in the right direction."

He nodded and headed out. I took a deep breath that did little to curb the ache of weariness, then walked across to the section of the map that held Ainslyn. There were three gates in our vicinity—one to the north past the new business precinct, one situated near Chester, and the one we'd found near the tunnel close to the sewer outlet near the old port. My gaze fell on the latter. Unlike the other two, it was simply a stick—the flag pointing to the left or the right to signify its state was missing. Which was interesting, given Luc had recently used his magic to shore up that gate. I pressed my finger against the rune. It was fizzing. Did that mean Darkside was working to break down his magic and reopen it?

More than likely.

I did another walk around the room, this time looking for runes that were sticks, and found seven. None of them were fizzing, which seemed to indicate my instincts might be right. I sent another text to Mo and then walked back to the table. Until Luc got back, I might as well make myself useful and check some more of the old scrolls. It was a tedious task, especially when I couldn't understand either Old English or Latin. But I did discover a couple that were colorfully illustrated, and some of *those* appeared to be a glossary of the non-rune characters used on the wall map. None of the characters listed on either scroll reacted to my touch—I checked—but that didn't mean they weren't in some way connected to the gates. If they were drawn on the maps, they obviously had *some* function.

A couple of hours had slowly slipped past by the time the happy smell of pizza invaded the air. Luc appeared a few minutes later, a large pizza box in one hand and a green shopping bag in the other. Nex and Vita were tucked into his belt, and Elysian—now unconcealed and sitting in the scabbard Mo had nicked from the council's headquarters—was slung over one shoulder. The crown was hooked over Elysian's hilt.

"Sorry it took so long." He dumped the pizza and the shopping bag on the table, then unslung Elysian and hooked her and the crown over the nearby chair. The knives and the coronation ring he handed to me. "Got waylaid by a call from the team disinfecting Noelle."

I glanced up sharply. "Is she okay?"

"There's some residual memory and behavioral problems that suggest incomplete removal. They have to go in again."

How was it possible for removal to be incomplete—surely wraiths were either removed or not. Or did it mean that wraiths were able to reconstitute themselves if fragments of their bodies were left inside?

God, I hoped not, and not just for Noelle's sake. If they *had* infested a multitude of people in key positions within both the parliament and principal councils, the inability to successfully remove them would mean those positions could be left empty until replacements were found—and given how ponderous governmental processes often were, that could have disastrous results, especially if Darkside chose the right moment to attack.

I slipped the chain back over my neck, put the knives on

the chair holding Elysian, then sat on the next one and opened the pizza box. It was a meat feast—he was a man after my own heart.

I scooped up a slice and then said, "At least she's in the hands of people used to dealing with this sort of thing."

"Doesn't help ease the worry though."

It was doubtful anything would except seeing her whole and untouched by the darkness currently inhabiting her. And given what Mo had already said, that was highly unlikely. Not that I was about to tell him that.

He carefully removed a cardboard drinks tray and handed me a large cup. "What, no chocolate?" I asked, expression one of feigned horror.

He snorted. "As if I'd dare forget *that.*"

He pulled out a couple of assorted Cadbury blocks, as well as a big bag of jelly snakes. I raised my eyebrows. "Yours?"

"You don't like them?"

"I've yet to meet a lolly I *didn't* like. You just didn't seem the jelly snake type."

He raised an eyebrow, expression amused. "And what confectionary type did you think I was?"

I pursed my lips, pretending to seriously consider the matter. "Something traditional and retro, like humbugs or rock candy."

He shuddered. "Hate them both."

I laughed, and we got down to the serious business of pizza eating. Once that was consumed and the mess shoved back into the bag, he grabbed Elysian and offered me her hilt.

"I need you to grip but not draw her. The concealing spell will ensure only you can see and draw the blade when she's in the scabbard."

"So why is Hecate sometimes visible when she's sheathed, and invisible when she's not?"

"The spell surrounding her has multiple layers and exceptions woven into it. In your case, they're not needed. We simply need to hide her from anyone else's eyes but yours until she's needed."

"I won't be able to draw her in any hurry if she's strapped across my back."

"I doubt that'll be a problem, given you're unlikely to be physically using her as a weapon."

"True." I had Vita and Nex for *that*. "Why do the paintings of all the witch kings show them using Elysian in bloody battles?"

"Because they were warrior kings, trained in warfare and sword craft. You're not."

"And would probably endanger myself if I tried to use her that way," I finished for him.

He smiled. "Stick with the knives. They're easier to wield in battle."

"I'd rather avoid it altogether, thank you very much."

"Wouldn't we all."

He motioned to the hilt, and I immediately wrapped my hand around it. He took a deep breath, then began to spell. It was long and intricate, but also spoken in what sounded like Latin, meaning the spell was ancient and I had no hope of understanding its intricacies. I could, however, see each layer as it went down, could feel the build of power. Saw the shimmer of gray appear, weaving its way around the scabbard and then up to the hilt and my fingers. It felt … odd. Ethereal. Alien, almost. Which made some sense, given the gray was not of this place.

Luc spelled on. Sweat sheened his face, and his growing weariness washed through the link between us. I wished I could push some of my strength his way, but that was not my forte. And yet even as I thought that, Vita pulsed warmly against my thigh. I remembered the moment in Mryddin's cave when I'd leaned into Luc and strength had flowed from him to me. If, through Vita, I could siphon strength, why could I not send it?

I shifted in the seat, pressed my knee against his, and then imagined energy flowing from me to him. Vita's golden glow infused the shadows, and warmth coursed through my body and down into the connection of our knees. His face began to look less drained, even as weariness pulsed harder through me.

I broke the connection after a few minutes. I couldn't risk doing too much. Not when I was already pretty damn tired. But at least I now knew for sure that the De Montfort gift of healing hadn't skipped me; I'd simply needed a means of accessing it.

Luc's spell reached a peak, and the gray completely claimed the sword, drawing it from this world to the other. Though I could still see her, her shape was insubstantial, and she held no real weight.

Luc drew in a breath and then released the end of the scabbard and looked at me. "It's done. She's now in the gray."

"But not totally invisible."

"Only to you, and that's a necessity, as I've said. If you put her down, you want to be able to find her again."

"Makes sense." I certainly had no desire to lose her again after all the trouble we'd gone through to find her. "Will my shifting shape in any way affect the spell?"

"It shouldn't."

"Good." I shifted my grip on the sword, then slung her diagonally over my back. Though I could feel her presence, when I leaned against the back of the chair, there was no obstruction. I might not have been wearing her at all. "That's a pretty impressive spell. I'm surprised you don't use it for more than just swords."

He raised an eyebrow. "Who says we don't? But even in this day and age, an unseen sword in the hands of a similarly invisible Blackbird is a mightier weapon than a gun."

I wrinkled my nose. "But surely death by sword would instantly point the finger at Blackbirds."

"We haven't survived this long without learning how to hide our kills." He tore open the packet of jelly snakes and offered it to me.

I shook my head and grabbed the block of Darkmilk Salted Caramel instead. "So, there's no problem with me wearing Elysian full time?"

"Technically, no." He bit the head off a snake. "I wouldn't recommend wearing her to bed or even in the shower. She may be in the gray, but the constant interaction with the physicality of this world can put pressure on the spell and even unravel it."

"Good to know." I swung her off my back and hooked her over the chair again. "I don't suppose—when you've got your strength back—you could do the same to Nex and Vita?"

"Tomorrow." He hesitated. "Are we camping out here for the night or heading back to the hotel?"

"Mo wants me here to keep an eye on the maps."

"You can hardly do that when your eyes are just about hanging out of your head." A smile tugged at his lips. "Very unattractive it is too."

"So unattractive that your desire surges through our link?"

"That's because I'm a man and the body is always more important than the face to certain portions of *my* body."

My gaze swept down to his crotch. It was a rather impressive mound, even when seated. "Certain portions seem unimpressed at the moment."

"Will of steel." He grinned and popped another snake into his mouth. "Do you want me to head out and grab some camping beds and blankets?"

I shook my head. "I can kip on these chairs easily enough for one night."

He nodded. "Then do so. I'll keep watch."

I wasn't entirely sure I'd be able to sleep with him watching me, but was nevertheless disappointed when he rose, moved to the other side of the table, and picked up one of the many unchecked scrolls still in the pile.

I rearranged the chairs to form a basic bed shape, then stripped off my jacket to use as a pillow and lay down. Despite the ever-present awareness of Luc, sleep hit hard and fast.

The uncomfortable racing of my heart and a deep sense of wrongness woke me who knew how many hours later.

I thrust upright and looked around quickly. The room lay in darkness. Luc was asleep in a chair, his arms crossed on his chest and his feet up on another chair. I swallowed heavily and scanned the room, looking for changes or flashing runes. Nothing. And yet ... something was definitely off.

I stood up, and from the other side of the table came a scrape of movement.

"Everything okay?" Luc asked.

"I'm not sure yet."

But even as I said that, my gaze was drawn to the map

that held the image of the main gate. Whatever I was sensing, it was coming from there.

That surely couldn't be a good sign.

I walked across, flexing my fingers in an effort to ease the tension. Sparks flew in response, briefly resembling fairy lights that faded as quickly as they appeared.

The main gate wasn't flashing, but the wrongness was definitely emanating from it.

Luc moved up behind me, his heat pressing into my spine even though he wasn't touching me. "Is something happening at the main gate?"

"Yes, but I have no idea what."

I raised a finger and carefully pressed it against the rune. It remained inert, and yet the twisting sense of wrongness grew stronger.

"It's not opening, but whatever I'm sensing is coming from there."

"Could it be Mo's spell?"

"Oh fuck ... *yes*. Max is testing his sword against the gate." I grabbed my phone out of my pocket, even as the damn thing rang. It was Mo. Heart hammering, I hit answer and said, "Is your gate spell being tested?"

"It certainly is. How did you know?"

"Something felt off with its rune." I scrubbed a hand across my eyes. "Are you heading out there?"

"Yes."

"I'll meet you there."

"I'm not sure—"

"Don't fucking finish that sentence, Mo. Elysian is our one chance to put an end to Max's nonsense. I need to do this."

Had to do this. Had to ask him why.

She sighed. "Indeed, but be careful. Max is well aware I

alarmed the gate, and this might be nothing more than another of their traps."

"Meet you on the bridge?"

"Yes, if it's safe. Otherwise, remain aloft until I arrive."

"Will do." I hung up, shoved my phone into my pocket, and then met Luc's gaze. "I have to go."

"This is definitely one of those times I wish I had wings." Frustration and concern spun through our link, even though there was little evidence of it in his expression. "I'll follow you up in the SUV, just in case."

"Whatever is going on up there will probably be over by the time you arrive—"

"Then ring me and I'll turn around," he cut in. "Because I've got this bad feeling things will go very wrong if I'm not there."

I frowned. "I can take care of myself—"

"I'm well aware of that, and that's not what I meant."

"I'll be fine. I promise." And hoped, even as I said it, that I hadn't just tempted fate.

He gently touched my face, his thumb brushing my lips. "You'd better be. I have no desire to wait yet another lifetime to explore what might lie between us."

I grinned. "You already know what lies between us, because Mo's informed you often enough. It's kids. Lots of kids."

He laughed, though it failed to lift the worry in his eyes. "I think we'd better explore the sex thing for a few years first."

"On that, we agree."

I moved across to Elysian and slung her over my shoulder. But as I reached for Nex and Vita, I hesitated. If this *was* a trap and I did get caught, the knives would be taken from me and destroyed. Given I could use their power

168

without holding them—even if at a greater cost—it would be wiser to leave them here. Especially since I'd probably need Vita's healing help in the very near future.

It was an ominous thought. I undid the chain holding the coronation ring, hooked it onto the chair next to the crown, then turned and headed out. Once I'd reached the old chapel, I shifted shape and arrowed into the vent. The sword didn't hit the sides, and I didn't come to a crashing halt.

I flew toward Yorkshire as fast as I was physically capable. I had to get to the gate before Mo. If this *was* a trap, it was likely to be aimed at her more than me, given the number of attempts they'd already made on her life. Granted, they'd made just as many on me, but, as she'd already noted, Max knew she'd placed that block on the gate, so what better way to lure her back there than an attempt to smash it open?

Dawn was just beginning to creep golden fingers across the sky by the time I reached the gate, though the faint glimmers of light didn't mean the demons wouldn't be about. Until the sun actually crested the horizon, they were able to move around freely.

I circled the Gill, but couldn't see Mo—or anyone else, for that matter. No cars were parked on the side of the nearby road, which meant Max had flown here. I continued to circle, but couldn't see him. Either he was under the bridge or hiding elsewhere. After one more sweep, I dropped to the bridge spanning the small stream—or beck, as it was more commonly known around here—and shifted to human form.

The air was still, and cold enough for each breath to frost. I pulled out my phone, switched off the sound, and then sent a text to Mo, asking if she was here. There was no reply, which meant she was either still in the air or simply not in a position to answer.

I gnawed lightly on my bottom lip and fought the urge to fly into the Gill to see what was happening. But there wasn't a whole lot of fighting room down there, as I'd discovered the hard way last time we were here. Until I knew for sure where Mo was, it was far better to remain in the open.

But was the open any safer?

I scanned the fog-masked fields surrounding the Gill and the bridge, looking for the problems I suspected were here, but seeing nothing untoward. Yet unease continued to stir.

I walked to the bridge's rock wall and peered over. Hell's Gill was a narrow, five-hundred-meter-long slash in the ground that had been created over the centuries by the clear, cold waters that still ran at its base. Although the canyon was not particularly deep—at least in comparison to its US counterparts—it had become a favorite haunt of cavers and scramblers alike, all of whom had no idea that the presence of the main gate made this one of the most dangerous places on Earth.

Enough light had crept into the sky to see the dark pool of slow-moving water at the base of the Gill, but it was impossible to see the main gate from where I stood, nor could I sense any lessening in the old powers that protected this place. Even Mo's spell pulsed on, seemingly as strong as the day she'd cast it. Either Max's attempt at breaching it had spectacularly failed or this really was nothing more than a ...

The thought stuttered to a halt as Elysian began to pulse. A heartbeat later, energy punched through me, sending me stumbling backward. It burned through every cell and fiber of my body, a storm that spoke of fierce electricity and furious winds, of the cindering heat found deep within the earth, and of the rolling violence and power of the sea.

It wasn't the gate's energy. It was a combination of light energy and dark. Max's energy and that of the dark elves.

Nails scraped against stone. Alarm surged, and I spun. Eyes stared back at me. Red eyes. Demon eyes. I heard a similar sound behind me and spun again to see more of them crawling over the wall I'd been leaning on only seconds before. Then the wind started whispering, and I glanced up sharply; there were five winged demons in the air.

I'd been wrong in presuming this trap had been aimed at Mo. I was their target, just as Luc had feared.

I flexed my fingers but didn't unleash the lightning that flicked and buzzed across my fingertips. No matter how fast I was or how deadly my lightning, I wouldn't be able to kill them all. And that was no doubt the whole idea.

I backed into the middle of the bridge. None of them reacted; they simply watched, red eyes gleaming with anticipation and hunger. They wanted blood, wanted to rend and tear, but were being restrained by something.

Or some*one*.

My heart began to beat even harder.

Max. It had to be. He was the only one who could wield the fake sword. And *that* was no doubt the reason for the odd energy I'd sensed emanating from the gate's rune. Mryddin might have created the fake sword, but a man who'd crossed from light to dark now wielded it.

Elysian's pulsing grew stronger, and a gentle mist stirred around me, momentarily blurring my vision. There was an odd wrench sideways, though I didn't physically move, and suddenly I was neither in this world nor in the gray, but somewhere in between. There was no bridge, no demons, and no Gill. All I could see was a man-shaped sliver of darkness walking toward me. In his right hand was a sword; it was richly embellished with gold and emitted a twisting, writhing mass of blackish purple and golden energy that moved in time to Elysian's beat.

Were Elysian and the fake sword acknowledging each other? There were certainly some ancient artifacts that could recognize similar energies, but I really hadn't expected it in this situation.

I blinked, and normal vision returned. Max stopped at the beginning of the bridge; not only was he holding the sword, but a gun.

My heart stuttered to a brief halt. For several seconds, I could only stare at him, unable to believe that my brother—my *twin*—was willing to shoot me for his insane cause. I swallowed heavily and somehow said, "So it has come down to this? You'd kill your own sister to claim what will never be yours?"

Thankfully, my voice remained calm, untouched by the inner terror and heartbreak. I wanted to cry—to rant and rage at him—but it would do little good and leave me with nothing more than blurred vision. That could be fatal given the number of demons surrounding me. I needed to see if I wanted to survive, and while I might never be able to kill them all, I was more than willing to give it a damn good go.

Of course, it might simply be easier to kill my brother, even if he was the only reason they weren't currently attacking.

Could I do that, though? Could I stare into his eyes as I stabbed lightning through his heart?

I really didn't know.

Really wished I didn't have to find out.

A sad sort of smile touched his achingly familiar features. Unlike me, he'd inherited the full De Montfort coloring, which for the males of our line meant black skin and hair, and blue irises ringed by gold. He was the image of my father, while I'd taken after Mom.

What *was* new was the shimmer of darkness that surrounded him. It bore the same blue-black color that fought with the gold around the sword's blade, and I very much suspected it was a magical emanation of the darkness he had fallen into.

Had that descent started with Winter? Or had there been a tipping point well before he'd found his Darkside consort?

"I'm not going to kill you," he said softly. "I can't. But if you so much as twitch the wrong way, they *will* tear you to pieces. And we both know not even you can erase them all before they're on you."

Meaning he was well aware of my ability to use lightning. But I guess that wasn't surprising, given who his lover was.

"The only reason you can't kill me yourself is the fact I'm your blood price and they want me for their breeding program."

Something flickered in his eyes. Something that resembled sadness and regret. Or was that merely wishful thinking? The need to believe the boy I'd grown up with—the brother I'd shared everything with—was still in there somewhere? That he would in the end do the right thing, even if all evidence pointed to the exact opposite.

"They *will* look after you. You're my sister—the better half of my soul—"

"Your soul was lost the day you entered into a pact with Darkside, brother." My voice vibrated with an edge of violence, and I sucked in a breath to keep it contained. Calm. I *had* to remain calm. It was the only way I was going to escape this situation. "Just tell me why? Surely it's not just about the power."

"It isn't," he replied evenly. "It's about restoring what was stolen from us. We De Montforts are the rightful heirs to the throne, not the half-witch monstrosity who currently claims the palace as her own."

That sounded like something Winter had whispered deep in his ear late at night. Twisting my brother's soul, making him hunger for things that were neither right nor just.

Which really wasn't giving Max due credit. He'd always hungered for more, be it power, money, or recognition. No matter how much he had, it had never, ever been enough, even from a very young age.

"Witch king rule ended with Layton," I said. "Drawing that sword from the stone doesn't change anything, however much you might wish otherwise."

His sudden smile was so achingly familiar, it felt like a knife had sliced through my heart.

"You no more believe that than I do."

I didn't reply. Nothing I could say would alter his determination to take what he now saw as his due.

He raised the elaborate sword and pointed it at me. Elysian responded, her pulsing stronger. I had no idea what it meant or even if I could use her against Mryddin's sword or my brother, but I would try, if it came down to that.

But if I *did*, it would be the end of me, as it had been the end of Cedric. The only way to survive the forces she raised was to step fully into the gray. And that wasn't an instantaneous process—not if my experience with Nex and Vita was anything to go by. The minute I even tried to cross, he'd set his demons onto me.

"Tell me about this sword," he said.

I didn't immediately reply, my gaze caught by a glimmer of silver on his left hand. It was a ring, and very similar in design to the one I'd not only found in Tris's bag after he'd been murdered, but also on the demon who'd attacked Jackie but hadn't lived to tell the tale.

It was an oath ring—a ring that bound one or more demons to a dark practitioner.

This one was bigger—fancier—than the other two, and there could only be one reason for that. It was the control ring.

While it was no real surprise that Max was wearing it, it nevertheless was just another knife through my heart. Not just that he'd obviously approved the murder of a man we'd both grown up with, but also because it was yet another indicator of where his allegiances now lay.

I sucked in a breath and tried to remain calm. A hard task when all I wanted to do was unleash—verbally *and* physically—at him. "How about you tell me about Winter first?"

He raised his eyebrows, a casual movement that oddly spoke of anger. "I think you already know more than enough about him."

"I know he's been cloned and there's now multiple versions of him."

"You say that like you expect it to shock me, but I'm well aware of who and what he is."

"And you don't care that they're playing you?"

"Why should I? They are all of the one source, the one man, and it was that man I fell in love with. Having more of them simply means I can never lose him."

"And if one or more of them is in charge of the factions opposing you?"

"Treachery is always to be expected with Darksiders," he said with a shrug. "As long as you're aware, you can never be caught."

"Overconfidence will be your downfall, brother."

"I've played this game for a very long time now. I've earned the right to be confident."

He was also, I realized, perhaps a little too happy to talk. Nor did he seem in any particular hurry. Why? Was he waiting for something ... or some*one*? Winter, perhaps? God, I hoped not, and yet it would make sense given the one I'd killed on King Island had sworn his counterparts would make me pay.

I swallowed heavily and wished the sun would just get on and rise already. If nothing else, it would save me the effort of burning the bastards and allow me to concentrate solely on my brother. "When did you meet Winter?"

"Years ago."

"So was he the man in the car with you that day you were heading to the airport? The one you'd said was part of a deal that was going to change both our lives?"

"Yes."

"And I was part of that deal?"

"Yes, but you have to understand—"

"I don't have to understand anything more than the fact you betrayed me for personal gain, brother."

He sighed. "You were always so overly dramatic—"

"Being raped by dark elves in order to produce royal blood halflings is *not* being overly dramatic." My voice was rising, and I couldn't stop it. "I hate that you did this—"

"Enough." He slammed the point of the sword into the bridge so hard sparks rose. Though the blade remained intact, the force of the blow shook the bridge, and stone cracked. The demons screeched and shifted uneasily, their gazes darting between Max and me. He really was the one holding them in check, and that meant my guess about the ring had been right.

"Tell me what you know about this sword, Gwen." His voice was flat, holding little life or hope.

Something in me died. There was no coming back for him, however much I'd foolishly hoped otherwise. He was in this, heart and soul, and no one was going to get in his way. Not even the sister he still professed to love.

Tears stung my eyes, but I blinked them back furiously. I could mourn my loss later; right now, I had to keep alert. Had to keep looking for a way to escape even if the sheer weight of numbers was against me.

"That sword?" I said casually. "It's the one you drew from the stone."

"Yes, but is it the real one?"

"Ah, now that's the million-dollar question."

"Meaning what? Trust me, sweet sister, it'll be better if you tell me. Otherwise, Winter will be tasked with retrieving the information—and *that* is something I wouldn't wish on my greatest enemy, let alone someone I care about."

How I didn't laugh in the face of a statement like that, I'll never know. If he *truly* cared, he wouldn't happily hand me over to be tortured.

But the only things he now cared about were his own wishes and desires. And if I was being at all honest, it had always been that way.

"I know what the prophecy on the King's Stone says, if that's any help." I dug my fingers deeper into my palm in an effort to control the inner tension and the urge to lash out. The energy in his sword continued to build, as did Elysian's pulsing heat. I had a feeling one was the direct result of the other. I also suspected that his sword would protect him against anything I could throw at him. Anything except the multiple paths of energy that Elysian allowed me to call on, perhaps.

A choice loomed, but it was one I wasn't yet sure I was willing to make.

"How could you know that?" he said. "The writing is almost illegible and old script."

"It's not illegible if you know how to enhance it and can read old script. Which Mo can."

"Indeed?" His expression was one of tolerant amusement. "Then what does it say?"

"That which is beautiful is not always powerful. That which is plain often hides a mighty heart. The hand that claims one will never be worthy of the other."

He stared at me for several long seconds, his expression a mix of disbelief and consternation. "That inscription makes no sense. Anyone who thinks this sword isn't powerful doesn't know what they're talking about."

"The inscription was written by Mryddin, who also happened to make that sword. There's no doubting it holds power, brother, but it is not *the* sword of power. It's not Elysian."

"And you know this how?"

"I spoke to the woman who made Elysian."

He blinked. "Vivienne? You spoke to the *goddess* Vivienne?"

"Yes. Well, Mo did, but I was there. You might want to call off your Darkside dogs, because Mo's the only one alive who currently can summon her."

His fingers twitched on the gun. My heart rate zoomed yet again, and lightning pressed so fiercely against my fingertips, its heat burned my palm. The demons stirred, and several snarled. A warning, nothing more.

For the moment.

He raised the sword again. "Did Vivienne tell you where to find Elysian, if this *isn't* her?"

"No. She said something along the lines of 'you lost her, you find her.'"

"Huh." His gaze narrowed. "I believe you might be lying, dear sister. This sword is powerful enough to smash through Mo's protection spell. I have no doubt it will also open the gate for me."

"Then you haven't fully tested it?"

"There were a few things that needed to be taken care of first."

Like the Blackbirds? And the royal family?

Before I could ask, something darted across the edges of my vision. My gaze went left, but none of the demons there appeared to have moved. Yet there was a wave of expectation coming from them now. Their hunger for blood was growing, but, given what Max had said, whose blood had they been promised if not mine?

Mo's?

Was *that* why he was waiting? Why he was so casually standing there talking, rather than acting? Was he somehow tracking Mo's approach?

If that was the case, then I had no choice but to stop him before she ... The thought died as his phone beeped. He drew it from his pocket, took a quick glance, and smiled. "Finally—"

I unleashed the lightning before he could finish. He swore and raised the sword. The twisting threads of blue-black and gold reacted instantly, flaring out to form a shield, covering his body and repelling my attack.

He released his hold on the demons. They screamed and lunged at me, talons at the ready and wicked teeth bared. I unleashed the lightning and whipped the ragged forks around in a circle, ashing them all in an instant.

All except the ones above.

They screamed, and my gaze jumped up; the sky was filled with claws. I raised both fists and punched the lightning upward. As their soot rained around me, something hit my back, sending me staggering even as claws and teeth tore into flesh. Lightning erupted from my body, ashing not only the thing on my back but all those within close proximity.

But it came at a cost.

Crazy men with ultra-sharp daggers were now hacking away at my brain, and my heart raced so badly it felt as if it would tear out of my chest. I sucked in air and pushed more lightning at the demons that crawled over the wall and lunged at me. They died hard and fast, but blood now seeped over my eyelashes. I was pushing my limits; too much more and I'd—

The thought stalled as the air stirred behind me. I threw myself sideways but wasn't fast enough. Something hit the fleshy part of my arm, and an odd chill flared, spreading quickly to my shoulder and across my chest.

I pushed to my knees and looked down.

Saw a dart rather than a bullet hole in my arm.

Swore vehemently.

Heard footsteps and looked up, straight into my brother's gaze.

"I'm sorry" was all he said.

"You will be," I replied and raised a hand.

Nothing came out. The inner fires had flamed out. As had my strength.

I dropped my head and gave in to capture.

CHAPTER NINE

W aking was a slow and painful process. Every bit of me ached—even my damn hair pulsed in agony. My shoulders were on fire, and a river of energy surrounded me—one so foul it made my skin crawl even though it wasn't physically touching me.

That I was even awake was surprising—the last time I'd called on the lightning to the extent that blood blurred my vision, I'd been out for days.

Of course, I may well have been, but surely if I *had*, I wouldn't still feel this shitty.

As my other senses slowly came online, the first thing that hit was the stench in the air—it was a putrid mix of rotten meat and human waste. I had no idea what Darkside smelled like, but I didn't think this was it. It was more likely that I'd been dragged into a sewer of some kind.

If that was true, it really made no sense. Why not simply take me through the nearest dark gate and be done with it? There would have been no escaping and no possibility of rescue from Darkside, and they could have then taken their sweet time to torture the information about Elysian out of me.

Unless, of course, I was bait. Max might not believe the sword he held was fake, but he wouldn't chance that I was telling the truth. He also knew Mo would move mountains to rescue me, though it was doubtful he was aware that she could literally do that. He'd never really witnessed her using her mage gifts and had no idea just how powerful she truly was. Not even Winter had witnessed the full scope of her skills, though more than a few demons would have found their deaths via them over the centuries.

I tried to move my arms in an effort to ease the fire in my shoulders and discovered my hands had been bound tightly behind my back. It didn't feel like rope but rather tape of some kind. There was more around my waist—no doubt a means of keeping me upright against the thick pole or pillar or whatever the hell it was I'd been tied to.

My left foot was icy and shoeless. I was still wearing the sock, but it was wet and not helping the ice situation. Given the stench, I hated to think what it was actually wet with.

I tried to open my eyes, but they were caked shut, thanks no doubt to the blood that had dried on my lashes. I attempted to scrub them clean against an arm, but that was a pointless exercise given how tightly I was tied.

"Ah," a deep and familiar voice said. "You're finally awake."

I jumped; fear hit so hard that for several seconds I couldn't breathe.

Winter. Fuck.

I turned my face toward him and drew in a deeper breath, trying to pinpoint his exact location.

Big mistake.

The wretched foulness of the place burned into my lungs, leaving me gasping and coughing.

Winter chuckled. "Yes, it's best not to breathe too deep here. The fumes are somewhat toxic."

"Where are we?" It came out a croak. My throat felt raw and speaking hurt.

"Deep underground and well protected. Your witch of a grandmother won't be able to use her magic to find you here."

I wouldn't bet on that. Whether she could find me before Winter did whatever he planned to do was another matter entirely.

"If you fear her so much, why haven't you dragged me into the hellhole you call home?"

"Aside from the fact we couldn't, you mean?"

Of all the answers I'd been expecting, that certainly hadn't been one of them. "What do you mean, you couldn't?"

"Has the energy you unleashed at your beloved brother affected your hearing as well as your sight, dear sister-in-law?"

Another shock rolled through me. *Sister*-in-law? Surely Max wouldn't have ... I gave myself a mental kick. The time for being surprised by *anything* my brother did had long since passed. "No celebrant in their right mind would officiate a wedding between a human and a half-breed."

"Which is why we found one who wasn't in his right mind," Winter said with a laugh. "It's quite legal, I assure—"

"I hardly think so, given clones don't exist in our world let alone have any sort of legal status."

"Ah, but there are few in this world who would even realize we are more than one. Certainly the poor celebrant didn't."

A statement that suggested said celebrant hadn't survived long past the wedding.

"We will be consort to your brother's king," Winter continued, "and quite soon, if all goes according to schedule."

Not if I had any fucking say in it. Of course, I had to get out of the current situation before I wreaked havoc on their damn plans.

"To repeat, why couldn't you take me through the gate?"

"That is an extremely interesting question and one we have no answer to. Yet." Water splashed, suggesting he was moving closer. A vague sense of wrongness washed over me, then a hand forcefully grabbed my chin. I squeaked in surprise and instinctively kicked out—only to discover my legs were tied as well.

Winter didn't laugh, but he did enjoy my reaction. I felt the ooze of it crawl across my senses and knew then there was far more pain yet to come. "What are you hiding from us, Gwen?"

I spat in his face. I couldn't see the result, but his grip tightened so abruptly, I thought my jaw would crack.

"I'd personally kill you if the choice were mine. Fortunately for you, it is not. But such a restriction doesn't mean I cannot inflict a whole lot of pain, and my people have a long history of doing so without causing permanent harm. Perhaps you'll be more compliant after a little taste of what is to come if you do not give us what we want."

"What *I* want," I growled, even as my insides quailed, "is to see you suffer a long, slow, agonizing death. It will happen, Winter. I promise you that."

He laughed and released me. "We shall see how long that bravery lasts. Give her ten minutes, no more."

Meaning there was someone else in the room with us? Someone I hadn't sensed? I swallowed heavily, but it did nothing to ease the rising tide of tension and fear.

His footsteps retreated. For several long minutes, nothing happened. Deep in the distance water dripped, a soft and steady sound that gnawed at my nerves. Then the whispers began. I had no idea what they were saying, because they weren't speaking English. It didn't even sound like any of the Darkside languages I'd heard over the years.

They circled around me, moving the air but not the foul water, spiraling ever closer, filling my nostrils with their acidic scent.

Something hit my face. I jerked away, felt warmth trickle even as my skin began to move, to crawl, with life. Dear god, something was burrowing into my cheek ...

Horror erupted, and I snapped my face from side to side, trying to shake the thing loose. The whispers grew louder, more excited. Another sting, this time on my arm. I couldn't move, couldn't shake the thing from my skin as it dug into my flesh.

More stings, more life eating at my flesh. Then a dark heat began to crawl from the various entry points and flooded my veins with utter agony.

I screamed. Screamed long and loud. Screamed until my throat was raw and my voice broke. Screamed on in silence until the pain broke me and I collapsed into the welcome arms of unconsciousness.

Waking was another nightmare. My heart raced, my chest ached, and my body was slick with moisture. Whether it was sweat or blood, I couldn't say and honestly didn't want to know.

But deep in the pit of my stomach, a thick knot of determination had formed. I would survive this. I would get free.

And then I'd fucking make Winter, the whisperers, and most of all my brother, pay.

I was *done* playing nice.

But to do any of that, I first had to escape.

I drew in a careful breath and took stock. I remained tied to the post, though the tape around my waist didn't feel as tight. Maybe I'd thrown myself around so much when the bastards had been burrowing that I'd stretched it.

The burning ache in my shoulders had given way to numbness. I wasn't sure that was any better, given it was a sure sign the muscles—and maybe even the blood vessels—in my arm were under deep stress.

There was no sign or sound of the whisperers. Nothing to suggest I was anything but alone. There was no guarantee that was true, of course, especially since I hadn't sensed their presence initially. The rolling wave of dark energy remained, but otherwise, the place was silent. Even the faint dripping had muted.

I raised my head fractionally. Nothing stirred at the movement. I looked sideways to the spot where Winter had stood and saw the vague outline of a curved wall.

It took a moment to actually register the fact that I could now *see*. Not well, and not fully out of both eyes just yet, but joy nevertheless surged. Sight definitely improved my chances of escape.

I blinked a couple of times and felt the muck gumming my lashes move. The moisture that still ran down my face and slicked my skin must have softened it. I blinked like a crazy woman and eventually managed to pry my eyes fully open.

The barrier I'd felt was a constantly flowing river of dark, purplish energy that emitted just enough light for me to see. I was in some sort of sewer junction that was about ten feet wide. The ceiling was high and arched and made from slabs of stone rather than brick or concrete, suggesting this place was very old indeed. Or even, perhaps, that it was something *other* than a sewer, despite the stench.

Three tunnels led off it. Water trickled in from two of these, pooled around my ankles, and then trickled off into the third. My gaze returned to the barrier. I had no idea whether I'd be able to get through it, but that was something I could worry about once I'd gotten free from the restraints.

I started flexing my arms, trying to gauge how much give there was in the tape around my wrists. After a few minutes, the tape shifted. The moisture slicking my skin was obviously enough that it was affecting adhesion.

I continued twisting and pulling my hands apart, trying to force enough slack in the tape to get a hand through. The movement eased the numbness, and the pins and needles hit instead. I bit down on the instinctive curse and kept twisting and pulling at the tape. Eventually, it loosened enough that I managed to pull one hand free.

I sucked in a relieved breath, bit back the resulting cough as the air burned my throat again, then ran my fingers around the outside of the tape at my waist, looking for the end of it. Picking it free from the rest of the tape seemed to take forever, and frustration surged. I couldn't afford this delay. I had to get out of here before the bastards came back.

As if to emphasize this point, something heavy splashed deep inside the tunnel to my right.

I stilled, my heart in my mouth, barely daring to breathe as I waited to see if that splash was repeated. It wasn't, and there was no sense of anyone approaching, but urgency nevertheless pounded through my veins. If I was caught now, when I was so damn close to getting out of here, it would break me.

But maybe *that* was the whole idea.

I thrust the thought away and continued to unwind the tape, my shaking fingers making the task all that much more difficult. Once it was off, I tossed it onto the ground, then repeated the process with the tape around my ankles.

I was free. But as I stepped away, my legs went out from underneath me, forcing me to grab wildly at the pillar to keep my balance. It wasn't weakness as much as the slipperiness of the stone underfoot that was the problem. I kept one hand on the pillar and reached for my phone. Thankfully, it was there, but I couldn't ring out because there was absolutely no reception in this hellhole. I shoved it away and checked Elysian; she remained strapped to my back. It seemed the only thing I'd lost was one goddamn shoe.

But Elysian's presence did raise an interesting point—was *she* the reason they'd been unable to take me through the dark gate?

There'd never been any suggestion she was capable of such a feat but, in a way, it would make sense, given Darkside's beings couldn't physically touch her.

And if that *was* true, then I was damn well going to keep her strapped across my back, no matter what, until this whole goddamn mess was sorted.

I released her hilt and glanced around again. I had no idea where I was, other than deep underground somewhere, and no idea which of my three exit options would take me back to the surface. There was a way to find out, however. I tugged off my remaining shoe and both socks. It would no doubt be dangerous to run barefoot through these waterways, but it would be calamitous if I picked the wrong tunnel and ran into either Winter or those whispering things. I needed the connection to the stone and the earth if I was to have any hope of escape.

There was no immediate response, and it took me a few seconds to realize why. Not only were my feet numb with cold, the stone in this place was so old that any resonance had all but leached from it. But after a few more rather anxious minutes, the faint and very distant pulse of the earth began to beat against my toes.

I pressed them harder against the stone, though I doubted it'd make accessing that distant heartbeat any easier, and studied the three exits. The one the wastewater emptied into was the most logical escape route, but that fact alone probably meant it was the one I shouldn't follow. The distant pulse of the earth wasn't relaying the weight of anyone—or anything—down there, but that didn't mean there weren't physical or even magical traps waiting.

Which left me two others. I studied them silently for a few more minutes and eventually walked toward the smaller of the two, simply because the pulse of the earth seemed stronger down there. The stone underfoot was slimy, and the air drifting out of the tunnel reminded me somewhat of the stench that had come from a tanning factory we'd passed in Spain when Mia, Ginny, and I had holidayed there a few years ago.

I reached the dark barrier and stopped. It didn't react to my closeness, but given I had no idea what the spell was designed to do, that didn't mean anything. Its construction had some similarities to the entry-refusal spell Mia sometimes used when she didn't want her parents walking into her room uninvited, but there were lots of other lines of magic woven through this spell that bore absolutely no resemblance to anything I'd ever seen.

I lifted a hand and carefully reached out. Once again there was no reaction from the barrier, and that was odd. I mean, why have it here if it wasn't designed to stop anything?

Unless, of course, it was never intended to stop me leaving, but rather someone from entering. Someone like Mo, perhaps.

I hesitated and then finally touched the thing. The magic's energy caressed my skin, thick, foul, and oddly oily. But it didn't in any way stop me. I pushed my hand all the way through without harm or setting off an alarm.

Had it been designed to restrict entry, as I'd guessed? Or was it primed to react only when a certain percentage of flesh went through?

There was only one way to find out.

I sent a silent prayer for luck to any goddesses who might be listening and then stepped through.

The slick, foul magic moved around me and made my skin crawl, but little else happened. Of course, that didn't mean alarms weren't screaming somewhere else, but it was still weird given the power within ... The thought died and I felt like slapping myself.

It couldn't affect me because I was *immune* to magic. Whoever had created this spell was either unaware of that fact or had forgotten.

I stepped into the small tunnel, my nose wrinkling at the stench. The barrier's purplish light leached just far enough in to reveal wet walls ribboned with slime. I eyed the deeper darkness and thought about shifting shape, but quickly dismissed the idea. While my blackbird's night vision was similar to that of my human, there was no way known I could safely fly in utter darkness. At least in my human form I could use the slimy walls as a guide, however much the thought of running my fingers through the muck revolted me.

I forced my feet on. The water was thick and sludgy and certainly didn't feel like storm water. It made me glad I couldn't see exactly what was in it. I had a feeling it was better *not* to know.

After what seemed like hours later, a tiny flicker of light appeared in the darkness up ahead. It was too yellow to be daylight and too warm to be moonlight. I slowed fractionally and looked for a trap or an alarm but couldn't see anything either physical or magical.

The earth gave no indication that anyone waited up ahead, but I couldn't discount the possibility that the remoteness of the connection meant she simply wasn't able to sense the weight of anyone or anything.

The light became one, then two, and then more, their numbers and their light growing stronger the closer I got. The darkness peeled away, highlighting the ribbons of slime that hung from the tunnel's roof and the thick gray sludge that ran past my feet. There were chunks in that sludge, chunks that almost looked fleshy ... Bile rose, and I swallowed heavily.

Don't think, just concentrate on escaping ...

It was a mantra that grew harder as several fingers drifted past.

The lights, it turned out, were actually foot-long threads that rotated lazily around a bigger, darker shape. I had no idea what the latter was—it wasn't a light and it didn't appear to hold any weight. It was amorphous and surreal, and its presence sent a cold chill down my spine.

My pace slowed even further. Every instinct I had said stepping into the same space as those things was a very bad idea, and yet, what other choice did I have? It was too late to go back and try the other tunnel. I had to push on.

But as I *did*, the whispers started. Horror surged and I

froze. The whispers weren't coming from the tunnel behind me, but rather from up ahead.

From the threads.

Oh god, no ... I stepped back instinctively, only to catch my heel on something sharp. I flailed my arms in an effort to keep my balance but ended up on my butt in the foul water. A shockwave of pain reverberated up my spine, and I bit down on the gasp, hoping against hope the things ahead hadn't heard the noise.

But as the water splashed around me, soaking my clothes with its stench, one of the threads paused and looked at the tunnel.

It was then I saw it had eyes. And teeth. Razor-sharp, saw-like teeth within a small circular mouth ...

Lightning burned through my body, but it held little of its usual heat and threat. I swung the scabbard around and quickly drew Elysian. As her form solidified, a strange, blue-white light flickered down her fuller. She was ready for action.

I really wished I was.

As one, the threads turned and surged toward me. I raised Elysian high then thrust her, with all my might, into the stone.

The stone split and the earth responded. A fierce, bright wave of heat and power erupted from the blade, flooding the darkness as it rolled toward the threads. Their whispers turned into squeals, and they fled back toward that amor-phous shape, only to be caught by the wave and turned molten. As their remains dripped to the floor and ate into the stone, the wave swept over the shape and completely encompassed it.

The resulting explosion wrenched my grip from Elysian's hilt and sent me tumbling backward. I landed facedown half in, half out of the thick sludge, tasting death and god knew what else. My stomach rose, and this time there was no stopping it. I vomited until there was nothing left except dry heaves, then wiped my mouth and crawled back to my sword.

In the fading glow of the eruption, I spotted the cracks. They were spreading fast, finger-thick webs that motored along the tunnel's floor and up the walls. Walls that were now moving, shifting, sending bits of dust and stone raining down.

This whole area was about to collapse ...

I surged upright, pulled Elysian from the stone, and bolted into the area that had held the threads. It was another junction. I hesitated, my gaze darting between the two exit tunnels, not knowing which was the better option.

The decision was made for me when the roof of the tunnel to my right collapsed, sending a thick wave of dust and muck my way. I spun and went left, desperately trying to keep my balance on the wet and slimy stone. I gripped Elysian tightly with both hands, holding her in front of me, the light burning in her fuller washing away the darkness, allowing me to move faster than I otherwise would. Behind me, the trembling grew, the noise of the collapse a fast-approaching freight train. It would be the mother of all ironies to escape Winter's clutches only to be caught by my own inability to control the powers that were now mine to call.

I raced on, my pulse beating so damn fast it felt like one long scream of terror. I had no idea where I was going or what lay ahead, and I didn't care, as long as I escaped the collapse. The tunnel rose and curved away to the left, suggesting it was moving toward the surface. Rusting metal tracks appeared on the floor, and there were pockets of deeper darkness pressed into the walls. They weren't tunnels but rather some sort of wait spaces. Maybe this tunnel had been part of a mine at some point ... Out of the corner of my eye I caught the briefest glint of silver. I swore and twisted around, automatically raising Elysian to protect my body. Steel clashed against steel and sparks flew, reflecting brightly in the red eyes of a demon. I swore again and pushed Elysian down the demon's blade, severing his fingers and partially slicing his arm. As the sword clattered to the floor, he snarled and lunged forward. I jumped back, shifted Elysian, and allowed the demon to impale himself. He died between one breath and another.

But as I kicked his body free from the blade, I became aware of the weight of footsteps behind me.

Demons. *Lots* of demons.

I half leapt, half stumbled over the body and raced on. The trembling in the earth was so bad now, thick clouds of dust and stone were swirling around me, making it nigh on impossible to see. I had no idea how to stop it—not without physically pressing my hand against the ground, as I had on King Island, and with the speed of the demons behind me that could prove deadly.

I sucked in another breath and only then realized the air no longer burned my throat and lungs. Instead of thick foulness, it smelled and felt electric—the sort of sensation you got just before a major storm hit.

And that *had* to mean there was an opening to the world above somewhere ahead.

The knowledge sent a fresh spurt of energy into my aching legs. As I raced on through the muck, the darkness eased and the deeper chill in the air dissipated. But the demons were drawing closer, the walls around me were cracking, and big chunks of the ceiling were now falling. I raised Elysian above my head in the vague hope that she would protect me and ran on.

Another long, sweeping corner. The heavy steps of the demons echoed through the stone under my feet. They were so damn close that if I turned, I'd see the glow of their eyes. It didn't matter. The bastards were *not* going to catch me now. If I had to push every last ounce of strength into getting free from this place, I would.

I sucked in another useless breath, then gathered together the flickering remnants of my inner lightning and flung it behind me. The shadows lit up as the multiple forks shot back down the tunnel. A few seconds later, the footsteps stilled and the stench of burning flesh filled the air.

I had minutes, if that, to escape.

I slid to a halt in front of the crack. It was a long, thin channel that promised freedom and yet, at the same time, withheld it. Even my blackbird form wasn't going to get through it. I had to widen the damn thing.

I plunged Elysian into the crack and called on the earth to widen it. She responded fiercely, her power burning into the soles of my feet, through my body, down Elysian's blade, and into the stone. The channel's walls started to glow with a fierce yellow-white light that reminded me somewhat of lava, and then, ever so slowly, the gap began to widen.

Hurry, hurry, I wanted to scream, but there was little point.

My gaze darted back to the tunnel. They were coming.

Fuck.

The channel remained too narrow. I was out of time and out of choices. I swore, briefly closed my eyes against the sting of useless tears, then ripped Elysian free and shoved her through the stone and into the earth underneath. Awareness hit; the heavy weight of over a dozen feet pounding on stone, the ruins of the tunnels I'd destroyed, and the foul stain of blood surrounding a stone pillar driven like a knife into the earth. And, in the deeper distance, something that sat like a whisper on the earth, radiating an energy that was of this world and yet not. That was dark, and yet not.

A gateway?

Elysian pulsed, and something within me sharpened. An odd sort of mist blurred my vision, reminding me of the gray, though I was very definitely anchored to this world, not the other.

The whisper of the gate's weight on the earth drew me closer—mentally rather than physically—and suddenly I was there, in front of the gate, a ghostly figure watching as dark forms spewed from the portal. Their weight shuddered through the ground, through me, and their screams rent the air, a sound so loud it hurt my ears.

But not all those screams were distant. Some were way too close.

My attention snapped back to the here and now. The demons were so close now, I could smell them; if I didn't stop the bastards in the next few seconds, they'd be on me.

I reached for the earth's might and flung it at the tunnel. As the ground began to shake with the force of her response, I called on the lightning. I expected little more than a splutter, but instead got something entirely different. Something that wasn't just lightning but rather a storm of heat and fury that swept down Elysian's blade and chased the earth's wave of power through the ground. As huge cracks appeared in the ceiling, walls, and floor of the tunnel, multiple forks of lightning erupted through the gaps and targeted the demons. By the time the tunnel collapsed, there were none left.

I dropped to my knees and leaned heavily on Elysian, wishing I could move but physically unable to do anything more than breathe. And even *that* hurt.

I closed my eyes and rested my head against the sword's hilt. The gentle pulse of her power caressed my skin but gave me no strength or healing. I needed Vita for that, and she was simply too far away.

And yet, had Nex been here, I might not have needed Vita's help, because I would have been able to channel the power of the storms through her rather than my body.

How I'd been able to do that was certainly something I needed to talk to Mo about. But to have *any* hope of doing that, I had to get up, had to move. I couldn't stay here, no matter how much my body and brain hurt. I might have temporarily stopped the demons, but I had no doubt they'd find a way around the blockage. If they hit me again, it would be the end.

And yet, despite the pulsing need to get the hell out of here, I just couldn't force my legs to move.

I wasn't sure how much time had passed before I became aware that the earth was again shuddering. I frowned and opened my eyes. Elysian's light was muted and the earth under my toes still.

A squawk had my gaze jumping to the channel. A familiar black shape emerged. I blinked and wondered if utter exhaustion had made me delusional.

I wasn't. The shape was real.

My heart leapt. *Mo.*

Tears stung my eyes, and a sob escaped. She swept into the tunnel, did a quick circle, and then shifted shape in front of me. I dropped Elysian and fell into her embrace, shuddering and crying with relief.

"Hush." She wrapped her arms around me and held me close. "You're okay. You're safe."

"Mo, he betrayed me." It came out broken, full of hiccups and tears. "My own fucking brother willingly handed me over to Darkside."

"I know." She brushed a kiss on the top of my head. "I know."

"I hate him."

"No, you don't."

"I *am* going to kill him."

"Yes."

"I have no choice."

"No. Not now."

I didn't say anything else. There was no need to. She knew. She understood.

I wasn't sure how long we knelt there in the dusty gloom, but it must have been a while, because the daylight was fading fast by the time I pulled back.

She touched a hand to my cheek, her smile understanding. "I'm so sorry, darling girl. I'd truly hoped it would work out differently, that he would at least hold true to you if no one else, but I guess that was not to be."

Tears stung my eyes again, and I brushed them away resolutely. They were nothing more than the shattered remains of hope and love. My brother had proven himself unworthy of either up on that bridge.

"How long was I missing?" I asked.

"Just a day, but it was the longest day of my life." Her gaze scanned me. "Let's get you healed and out of here. You need a feed and a bath, and not necessarily in that order. You, my girl, stink."

She placed her hands on both my temples. The warm, golden heat of her healing energy flooded my body, fixing the myriad of wounds and chasing away the worst of the pain and tiredness. The deep ache remained in my head, but I suspected at least some of that was a result of severe dehydration.

She pulled back and studied me through narrowed eyes. "That'll have to do for now. I think we'd better get out of here before night hits and this entire area is crawling with demons."

I grabbed Elysian, then pushed to my feet. "Where are we?"

"Not that far out of Carlisle."

Meaning Max and his crew must have had cars nearby, even if I hadn't seen them. Hell's Gill was a good hour away from Carlisle, and it was doubtful he'd have risked using the flighted demons to get me here. Even if most people these days seemed to have their eyes glued to their phone screens rather than what was going on around them, a pack of flighted demons carrying a limp body was a rare enough sight that someone would have noticed.

I tugged the sword sheath over my shoulders, slid Elysian into it, and then slung her back on. "Are we flying back to the safe house?"

She shook her head. "It's too far a flight to risk with night coming on so fast. As I said, they'll be out in force looking for you."

"Then where are we going?"

"Windermere."

My stomach clenched "That may not be safe. I told Max Vivienne was the only person who might be able to find the sword. He's probably there right now trying to summon her."

"Except Windermere is not a lake traditionally linked to Vivienne. Aside from Dozmary Pool, there're six others."

"There are?" I asked, surprised.

She nodded. "Depending on which legend you read, she can be found at Llyn Llydaw, Llyn Ogwen, Loe Pool, Pomparles Bridge, Loch Arthur, or Berth Pool."

I blinked. "I've never heard of any of them."

"Hopefully, he won't have either."

"So *can* he summon her?"

"He can certainly try. He does hold the right blood, but he also has the wrong sword. The latter will likely cancel the former."

"Does that mean I can also summon her?"

"Yes, and not just because you drew Elysian. You are a mage in the making, and we remain her connection to this world. But this is a conversation we can continue later." She motioned to the channel. "We need to move. Ready?"

I nodded and motioned her to precede me. She shifted shape, then jumped into the air and flew into the channel. I followed, the very tips of my wings brushing either side of the channel but not hampering my flight. Relief hit hard as I flew out into a gloriously golden sunset.

I was free. Against all the odds, I was *free*.

If I'd been in human form, I might have started crying again. Which was daft, especially given I still had a whole lot of shit ahead of me to survive.

Despite Mo's healing, tiredness soon pulsed through me once again. I needed to eat, and I needed to sleep, but most of all, I needed to see Luc. Needed to have his arms wrapped around me and just lose myself in his warm strength and solidity for a few hours. Mo might be my rock —the one constant in my world, now that Max had betrayed us all—but Luc was both my past and my future. I might have only recently met the man in this incarnation of our souls' journey, but he was quickly becoming as important to me as life itself.

Dusk gave way to full night. Ribbons of light appeared below, the highways brighter than minor roads, all interspaced by pockets of brightness that were towns or hamlets. As the glimmer of water finally appeared, Mo arrowed down, heading toward a deeper patch of darkness that was at least several miles outside of Windermere's boundaries and nowhere near the shores of the lake. A house appeared out of the gloom, warm lights shining from several of its windows. She flew over its roof and headed toward several smaller shapes off to its right—barns that had been converted to guest accommodation, I guessed. She angled across to the larger of the them. Though there were no lights on, smoke drifted from the metal chimney at the barn's far end. Someone had lit the log burner, and I couldn't help but hope that person was Luc. As we dropped toward the ground, I saw the SUV we'd hired.

He was here.

I'd barely shifted shape and landed beside Mo when the door opened and his big form appeared. He didn't move, didn't say anything, but his relief washed over me, a wave so thick and fierce it snatched my breath and squeezed my heart.

The man cared. Really, really cared.

I was running toward him before I even realized it and then I was in his arms, wrapped in his strength and his warmth, feeling safe and secure and loved. My brother might have betrayed me, but this man never would. I was sure of that, if nothing else. The past had become my present and it *would* be my future. *He* would be my future.

There would be no repeat of mistakes made in the past.

"You okay?" he asked, his soft, warm tone cracking slightly with emotion.

He didn't mean physically, I knew. "I will be, once I've grabbed some sleep."

His arms tightened. I closed my eyes and listened to the rapid beating of his heart. It was a rhythm that matched my own and spoke of words neither of us were willing to say out loud yet. It was too soon, at least for him.

Mo cleared her throat. "Can we take this inside? The night is bitter, and these old bones need to get in front of the fire."

"And I," I said, "need to eat."

"No," Luc said, amusement in his voice. "You need to shower."

I laughed and pulled away. "It can't be too bad, given how tightly you were hugging me."

"Oh, it is, but relief momentarily overwhelmed my sense of smell. *That* is no longer the case."

"Then I shall go and shower while you, dear man, can prepare my dinner."

"As you wish." He bowed regally and stepped back. "You'll find fresh clothes and your knives waiting for you upstairs."

I glanced at him sharply. "You risked going back to our place for clothes?"

"No. I stole them."

My gaze widened. "Really?"

"Truly. A man my size buying women's clothing will always be memorable, and that's something we couldn't risk once you were freed." Amusement shone in his eyes. "A Blackbird's ability to become invisible to the eye isn't always used for good."

"That's a certainty." Mo closed the door and brushed an

alarm spell across its surface. "I've got a myriad of tales about the less-than-salubrious actions past Blackbirds have taken."

"We've never claimed to be saints." The gleam in his eyes was decidedly wicked. "And I'm betting some of those actions would involve women."

I raised an eyebrow. "Speaking from experience here, are we?"

"I refuse to answer that question on the grounds I may incriminate myself." He paused. "But no instances involved married women, just in case you were wondering. I've always steered clear of *that* sort of problem."

"Well, good, because a man who'd stray with a married woman is a man who would stray when he's married." I crossed my arms, my expression one of mock severity. "And I'll have you know here and now, there will be no such straying when we're married. Or nuts will be severed."

He laughed. "My nuts will never be in any sort of danger, of that I can assure you."

"Good," I said primly, and finally looked around.

The ground floor of the old barn was one long room, its stone walls and beams on full show and utterly gorgeous. The log fire blazed at one end, the kitchen and the stairs leading up to the next floor were at the other.

I walked around the large, comfortable-looking sofa and headed up. There were three rooms up here—two bedrooms and a bathroom. I walked into the latter, stripped off my stinking, putrid clothes, and switched on the taps, waiting until the water was hot before stepping under. I scrubbed at my skin with the flowery soap, needing to remove the stench and the grime from every part of my body. It was a task that took far too long and, even after I'd stepped out, I could still smell traces of the thick, foul sludge. But maybe that was simply memory playing tricks.

I headed out naked to look for my clothes and found them sitting on the bed in the largest room. Luc had not only gotten a couple of pairs of jeans and sweaters, but also bras, panties, and boots. All of them fit perfectly. Obviously, the brief time we'd shared a bed at the safe house Ginny had organized had not gone astray.

Once I'd pulled on the new clothes and boots and strapped on my knives, I headed back down the stairs. Luc's gaze swept me and came up pleased. "Glad they all fit."

I walked over, dropped a kiss on his cheek, then leaned past his arm to see what he was cooking. "Yum. Spaghetti."

"And it's just about ready. You want to grab some bowls? They're in the drawer to your left."

I got them out and, after he'd dished everything up, grabbed two of the bowls and walked over to the L-shaped sofa, handing Mo one before dropping down beside her.

"We need a plan of attack."

Luc sat beside me, his thigh brushing mine and sending all sorts of delicious heat tumbling through me. "We tried tracking Max when you were snatched. He's protected."

"Against any magical means of tracking, yes." I glanced at Mo. "But is it possible we can find him via his weight on the earth?"

She pursed her lips. "Possibly, but it'll take some time. The bigger problem is the fact it will likely require a constant connection, and I'm not sure either of us have the strength to waste on something like that."

"Meaning," Luc cut in, "that Gwen has inherited some of your mage abilities?"

I swore internally. I'd forgotten I hadn't gotten around to telling him that.

"It would appear so," Mo said gravely. "But it's not something we realized until she drew Elysian. There'd been no indication before then."

"Does this mean she's inherited your long life as well?" His gaze was on mine even though the question was aimed at Mo.

She hesitated. "At this point, that's an unknown. But I would say most likely."

I had no doubt he was thinking about sharing a life with someone who'd basically never age while he grew older and eventually died.

Would that fact kill our relationship before it truly got off the ground? Fate was all very well and good, but living with someone who'd barely age in any normal way would undoubtedly take an emotional toll, no matter how great love was.

"The males of my family are very long-lived," he said eventually. "I guess I'll just need to hope those genes were passed on to me."

"That," Mo said, voice a little wry, "sounds like an acceptance of fate to me."

A smile tugged at his lips. "As you delight in reminding me, my fate was a foregone conclusion. We just all need to survive the current situation to put acceptance into action."

Something *I* had every intention of doing. I scooped up more spaghetti and then said, "What about the wind? Would she be able to find Max for us?"

Mo smiled. "The wind—like all the other elements—is a force we can plug into and use, but she is not a dog. You cannot simply give her a 'find' command and expect her to obey."

"Well, that's damn well disappointing." I paused.

"What about Winter, then? If we could grab one of them, we could use him as bait to draw Max out."

"Max wouldn't fall for such a basic trap," Luc said. "He's many things, but he's not stupid. Besides, we have no idea how many clones are out there, so capturing just one isn't going to give us much leverage."

I growled in frustration. "There has to be *something* we can do. We need to take the attack up to them rather than simply reacting."

"I agree," Mo said. "But Darkside has always had one major advantage over us—a place of safety to retreat to."

"Have any witches ever tried crossing over to Darkside?" I asked. "Willingly, I mean, with the intent of attack."

"There were mages once who tried." Her face twisted. "It did not go well."

"They died?"

"Five of the six did. Darkside might be a dark echo of this world, but her energies are very different. We are not equipped to deal with them. It twists the soul and sends you mad."

"Is that what happened in the case of the one who made it back?"

She nodded. "He was ... different."

"In what way? Physically or mentally?" I asked.

"Both."

"But was that caused by the power they'd tried to use?" Luc asked. "Or by Darkside itself?"

I looked at him. "It can't have been the place. Max's twins have both been there, and Rione, at least, hasn't been affected."

"Perhaps she was never taken fully into Darkside, but rather into some midpoint between our two worlds," he said. "There have been multiple rumors of Darkside way stations over the centuries, though we've never found any evidence of them."

"How would that be possible when neither side has any control over the forces that create the gates?"

"Darkside may not be able to control those forces, but it's likely they've learned to manipulate them, at least to a certain extent," Mo said. "The gateways are a necessity to them, whereas for us, they're an evil that needs to be contained."

"If these way stations *do* exist, why have we never attacked them?"

"Because we have never been able to find them."

I finished the last bit of my dinner, then placed the bowl on the table. "Riona said Winter took her and Reign to Darkside to be schooled in demon script and magic. What if she meant a way station rather than Darkside itself?"

"I'm not sure either of them would be able to give firm directions," Luc said. "They're only young."

"Riona is an old woman in a young body," I said. "And I don't think there's much she'd ever miss. It'd be worth ringing Jackie and getting her to ask. We've really nothing to lose."

Mo nodded. "You have her new number?"

I got out my phone and scrolled through the contacts. I'd listed Jackie's new number as "hairdresser new number," simply because I couldn't risk Max getting hold of my phone and using the number to track her down. He'd know Mo wouldn't hand his children over to anyone she didn't utterly trust, and there were few enough people in her life that applied to.

I handed Mo the phone, but before she could ring, her own phone rang. A heartbeat later, so did Luc's.

Coincidence? Something within doubted it.

My pulse began beating a whole lot faster as the two of them rose to retrieve their phones, then glanced at the screens and answered. Luc walked to the far end of the room, speaking softly but urgently to the caller. Whatever had happened wasn't good, that much was clear.

I returned my gaze to Mo. She wasn't saying anything, but her expression grew ever darker. I clenched my fists against the urge to rip the phone out her hand and put it on loudspeaker. I could wait. I *could*.

The minute she hung up, I said, "What's happened?"

Her gaze rose to mine, her expression bleak. "The worst. London is on fire and the palace is under siege."

CHAPTER TEN

"Fuck," I said. "How bad is the damage? And is the royal family safe?"

"First reports say the palace's protections are holding, but things are chaotic in the surrounding streets, and demons are everywhere. Full details remain somewhat sketchy at this point."

"Are they going to move the royal family to a more secure location? There are tunnels under the palace built for that purpose."

Luc might have said they wouldn't unless it was absolutely necessary, but if things were already this bad ...

"They'll only evacuate if the palace is in danger of falling—and not just because Layton's magic protects it. There's been no time to screen all the staff at the other locations for wraith infections."

I swore again. "Was it just the palace and its surrounds that were hit?"

"The five main business districts are all under some degree of attack. The council's air witches are calling in storms to take care of the fires, but demons flood the streets, killing anyone and everyone they come across."

"Which plays into their game plan of causing utter chaos in order to prevent police, military, and witch coordination."

Mo nodded. "A level-three emergency has been declared by the government, which means COBRA, the Civil Contingencies Committee, and the High Witch Council are working together to coordinate engagement and response, so it won't remain chaotic for too long."

"What the hell is COBRA and the CCC?"

"The government departments whose duty it is to deal with the various levels of disasters and emergencies."

Obviously. And I guessed the "who" didn't really matter as long as there was a coordinated, real-time response to this disaster. I thrust a hand through my wet hair. "What are we going to do now? Go to London?"

"There's little point in doing so—there's nothing either of us can do right now."

"We can fucking fight—"

"Gwen," she cut in gently, "London is *not* our battlefield. We need to find your brother and stop him before what is currently happening in London is repeated across every city and town in the United Kingdom."

"And how in the *hell* are we going to do that, given he's apparently protected against any of your finder spells?"

"By starting with your suggestion—destroying their way stations and blocking their gates."

"Riona will only know the location of the station they were being taken to. She wouldn't be able to tell us about the rest."

"Perhaps not, but there has to be some means of differentiating a way station's gateway from a regular one. Your regular type of demon isn't the brightest spark, and they're not magic capable, so it would have to be something fairly obvious. Once we know the indicator, we can send an urgent request for all gateways to be checked."

"That's not going to get us any closer to finding Max, though."

"It depends entirely on what the way stations are used for. I doubt they were devised solely as a means to teach the twins the dark arts. It's also doubtful they'd go to such lengths to provide a safe resting place for weary demons."

"Not given how little their commanders value lives," I muttered. "I still think Winter is our best bet. We *do* have the body of one his clones—"

"We do?" Mo cut in sharply.

"I didn't mention it?"

"Obviously not."

"Ah, well, I buried the bastard in a wave of earth and stone over on King Island."

"Clever girl."

"It wasn't so much clever as desperate." My voice was dry. "It's amazing what you can achieve when you're staring the possibility of death in the eye."

"As motivators go, there's certainly little better." She pursed her lips. "I'll ring Jackie and see if they're able to question Riona tonight. We'll fly back to the island in the morning and use that bastard's DNA to spell find the rest of them."

I frowned. "Why not go now? The sooner we find him, the sooner we can drag Max out of hiding."

She lifted an eyebrow, her amusement evident. "Have you already forgotten you barely escaped a hellhole?"

"Hardly, but that doesn't alter—"

"They'll have all their forces out tonight looking for you.

Not only is it safer if we lie low until dawn, it has the bonus of giving you time to fully recover."

"But—" I stopped and waved a hand in frustration. "I need to be doing something."

Because I didn't want to think. Not about my brother, and not about the task that lay ahead of me. I might have accepted the need to kill him, but I had no doubt the decision would haunt my dreams. Not just now, but long into the future.

And the saddest thing of all was the fact that—had the situation been reversed—he would have killed me without a second thought and continued to sleep very soundly at night. He'd proven *that* on the bridge.

Mo leaned forward and wrapped a hand around mine, squeezing lightly. "I understand. Trust me, I do. But you can't risk running yourself into the ground. It's going to take all your strength and cunning to end your brother's madness."

"That sounds like you think I'm the only one who can deal with him."

"I do."

"But why? Because we're twins?"

"In part, but mostly because we're at the end of a very long game. Remember what Vivienne said—that destiny and blood has converged in this current timeline."

"Which doesn't explain anything at all when it comes to Max."

"Old gods and goddesses find nothing more enjoyable than a good old battle between light and dark—between good and evil. And if that battle is between fraternal twins on opposites sides? Practically orgasmic."

"I'm seriously beginning to hate the old gods and

goddesses," I muttered. "The world would have been much better off—"

"No," she cut in softly. "It wouldn't. Trust me on that."

Given her age and familiarity with the gods, I had no choice but to believe her. It still didn't make me like them any more.

I glanced around at the soft echo of footsteps. Luc's gaze met mine, his expression grim and unhappy. "We had a traitor in our midst. The royal family came under attack."

My heart clenched. "From another Blackbird?"

"Yes, but luckily for us all, Owain realized something was off and used the council's ultraviolet light on Daniel. The reaction was immediate and almost deadly."

"Shit."

"Yeah. Owain's currently in emergency being patched up, and Daniel is now under the care of the council specialist team."

"I take it the royal family is now being moved?"

"No, because this whole attack might be nothing more than a setup—a means of getting the royal family *out* of a location that hasn't been breached for hundreds of years."

"There will be more infections within the palace ranks," Mo said.

"Yes, which is why no one but the core team will be allowed to enter the secure apartments. There'll be no shift rotations or relief until this is over." He hesitated. "All other Blackbirds have been ordered back to London to deal with the invasion—including me."

My heart just about leapt into my throat and, for several seconds, I couldn't breathe. "And are you going?"

His gaze came to mine. "No. My duty is here. You are the Witch King's heir, and it's our goddess-given duty to protect you at all costs. That doesn't alter just because the king is now a queen, and one who no longer sits on England's throne."

Relief hit so hard, tears stung my eyes. I blinked rapidly and said, "And the response from your fellow Blackbirds?"

"Let's just say I may not have a job to go back to if this all goes to hell and we don't stop Max and Darkside."

"If we don't stop Max and Darkside," Mo said gravely, "none of us are going to care one jot about jobs or anything else. We'll all be either dead or enslaved."

"And on that cheery note," Luc said, "why don't you two go upstairs and get some rest. I'll stay on watch."

I frowned. "Why? We're perfectly safe—"

"I'm not going to risk losing you a second time," he cut in, voice steely. "You need to recover from your ordeal without any sort of distraction."

"You're hardly a mere distraction," I murmured.

He ignored me. "Besides, I don't for one instant think it's wise to be taking *any* sort of chances right now."

"On that, we agree," Mo said. "But in the morning, Gwen and I will be flying back to King Island."

"Why?"

She quickly updated him on all our plans, and then added, "There's a dark gate in Kendal—it might be worth you checking it while we're grabbing the DNA."

"Unless Riona can give us more information about the gate she was taken through, it could be a pointless exercise."

"We should have the information by the morning, but even if we don't, it's worth placing a light lock on it. It won't stop dark elves, but at this point, demons are our main worry."

He nodded. "And if it *is* one of the way station gates?"

"Then we open it and magically blast the shit out of the fucker."

Amusement creased his features. "While I highly approve of the strategy, if it was actually possible to destroy the connection between our worlds that way, wouldn't we have done it before now?"

"If we were talking about a regular gate, yes. But way stations, if they do exist, have somehow been altered via dark elf magic. What they create, we can destroy."

"Anything that inconveniences the bastards is a good thing at this point in time," I said. "Especially when we're still playing catch-up."

"Only to a point," Mo said. "We have Elysian, remember."

"And the hand that drew her is untrained in any sort of magic. The sword Max has is still very powerful, and he's been well trained in the use of elemental magic."

"A fact that may yet work to our advantage."

I raised an eyebrow. "And how did you reach this rather unbelievable conclusion?"

A smile tugged at her lips but didn't quite reach her eyes. "Because you've already used Nex and Vita in ways none of your ancestors ever have. Then there's the fact that Elysian responded to you so fiercely in the tunnel, it brought the whole thing down. Let's just say that I doubt any of the previous witch kings would be your equal when it comes to what you can achieve with her."

"Let's not forget that using Elysian cost one of those kings his life."

"Because he didn't step fully into the gray to call on her full power. You will not be that daft." She gave me a steely look. "Will you?"

"Of course not."

"That didn't sound convincing to me," Luc said.

I glanced up at him. "Trust me, I have no intention of dying until I ravish a certain Blackbird."

A heated mix of amusement, desire, and determination burned in his bright eyes and washed through our connection. It warmed in a way that was hard to describe and yet utterly delicious. "Thus with one statement ensuring you and I will *not* be having sex until this war is completely over."

"Something I've become resigned to anyway."

"Which doesn't mean you'll in any way stop testing my resolve."

"You'd be hugely disappointed if I did." I returned my gaze to Mo. "I take it we're leaving at dawn?"

"As soon as the sun hits the horizon, yes."

I pushed up from the sofa. "Then I'd better go to bed. I'll see you both in the morning."

Luc's gaze fell to my lips and, for an instant, I thought he was going to lean across and kiss me. "I'd offer to tuck you in, but that could be dangerous."

"You can tuck me in," Mo said, her eyes glinting wickedly. "I wouldn't object."

"I'm betting Barney would."

My voice was dry, and she waved a hand. "He's a dear but, seriously, not a patch on the magnificent specimen that stands before us."

"She window-shops," I said, glancing back to Luc. "You're perfectly safe."

"True enough," Mo said. "Had I been a few hundred years younger and you, my dear Blackbird, unattached, it might have been a very different matter."

"A compliment indeed," he said gravely.

"Which is a polite way of saying thanks, but no thanks,"

she said, with a laugh. "You Blackbirds are always so damn polite."

"Not always," he said, amused. "And certainly not when it comes to women—as was noted before."

She harrumphed and climbed to her feet. "I expect breakfast to be ready for us in the morning in compensation, then."

"That I can do."

I walked around the sofa, blew him a kiss, and then headed up the stairs. Mo followed and disappeared into the smaller bedroom. I stripped off, tucked my knives under my pillow, and then climbed into bed.

I kept Elysian on. Just in case.

———

It was close to seven when I went down the following morning. Luc was at the stove, frying up enough bacon and eggs to feed an army. There was also a stack of toast waiting on the bench, along with butter and various condiments sitting nearby.

"There are only three of us, you know." I dropped a kiss on his cheek, then snagged a slice of toast and slathered it with butter.

"And at least two of us have very healthy appetites."

"Make that three," Mo said as she appeared. "Especially if we're not talking about food."

"We are," I said dryly. "Mind out of the gutter and all that."

"Ha. When you get to my age, you've won the right to do and say what you want."

A point I couldn't argue with. "Has anyone had an update on the situation in London?"

Luc nodded. "The palace is holding, but London is burning."

"How badly?"

"Westminster is the worst hit."

No surprise, given Westminster was where both the House of Lords and the House of Commons were.

"Many casualties?"

"Hundreds, from what's been said on the news, but there's not that much getting out. Greater London has been entirely locked down in an effort to contain the bastards."

"I hope it works."

"It should," Mo said. "It has before."

"It still feels very wrong for us not to be there." I held up a hand, stopping the comment Mo was undoubtedly about to make. "And yes, I understand and agree with the reason, but that doesn't alter the fact I think we should be there."

Didn't alter the certainty that our path *would* lead us there, and sooner rather than later.

Mo patted my arm, then perched on one of the stools. I did the same, then leaned on my arms and distracted myself by watching Luc. There was something very sexy about a man who knew his way around a kitchen. "Did you manage to get any sleep last night?"

"Some."

There was a slight edge in his voice that had my eyebrows rising. "Was there a problem?"

"Something was sniffing around."

"A demon something?" I asked, alarmed.

"Hecate was flickering, so yes. But the presence was distant, and it might just have been a juvenile out on its nightly hunt."

"Did you go out and check?" Mo asked.

He shook his head. "Figured it might have been bait."

"They couldn't have known we were here."

"Unless they placed a tracker on Gwen," Luc said.

"There's nothing magical—I would have seen that."

"Which doesn't discount the possibility of a regular old tracker."

"They're generally distance limited, though," Mo said, nose wrinkling, "and it's highly unlikely they would have found us so quickly, given they have no idea which direction we fled in."

"Unlikely doesn't mean impossible." Luc motioned me to stand and then drew Hecate and walked around the kitchen counter. He ran the flat of her blade down my body, front and back, then grunted. "She's not reacting, which means there's nothing even remotely related to Darkside on you or embedded in your flesh."

"Surely I'd feel it if something had been shoved into my skin?"

But even as I said that, I remembered the burrowing whisperers and shuddered. Maybe pain wasn't all they'd intended or done.

"Depends on the size," Luc said. "Trackers are miniscule these days."

"Maybe we should check, then," I said. "It might be safer."

"After breakfast," Mo said. "The sun's risen, and we're leaving this morning anyway."

Luc immediately dished up the mountain of food and motioned us to help ourselves. "Did Jackie get anything out of Riona last night?"

Mo nodded. "She said there were no bad pictures on the gate they were taken to, just lots of thorns and angry faces."

I grabbed a plate and loaded it up. Luc was right—I did

indeed have a very healthy appetite, especially after last night's efforts. "I didn't think there were any gates that weren't decorated by the 'bad' images."

"There aren't, as far as I'm aware," Luc said.

"What about the Kendal gate? Is it decorated?" I asked.

"To be honest, I can't say," Mo said. "It's been centuries since I've been near it—as gates go, the Kendal one has always been fairly inactive. It might be worth Luc heading up to Carlisle first to check the two there."

He nodded. "Are we meeting back here?"

Mo shook her head. "Southport. We'll need Barney's help coordinating with the various councils—he's got the contacts, I haven't."

"For checking the various gates, or for hunting Winter's clones?" I asked.

"The clones need to be our task," Luc said. "It's dangerous enough outsourcing the gate check, given we have no idea how widespread wraith infections are. We can't risk word getting out about our hunt for Winter."

"Oh, no one else but us was *ever* going to go after those bastards," I growled. "I very much intend to make all variations of him pay for the part they played in Max's slide into darkness."

"Kill one, and the rest will be aware that we're after them," Luc commented. "There's no spell that can stop the sort of connection they have."

"So we shoot all but one, and use him to trap Max."

"Shooting them isn't much better—it'll create a dead connection that'll tell the rest something is wrong."

"Yes, but they won't know what, which gives us the chance to track them all down."

"As much as I hate to say anything good about your

brother," Luc said, "he's not stupid enough to fall for such a trap."

"Max *married* Winter," I said. "He wouldn't take that step unless he truly cared."

"Unless," Mo said, "marriage was another part of the bargain he made for Darkside's help."

I frowned. "Why would Darkside want that?"

"To claim the throne," she replied. "It wouldn't be the first time a consort has plotted to overthrow a king and rule in his stead."

"I seriously doubt ruling us is what they have in mind," Luc said.

"And what would be the point of it, anyway?" I wondered. "Winter's obviously half demon—no one is going to accept him."

She raised an eyebrow. "If it ever *did* get to that point, do you think any of us would actually have the choice of disapproval or resistance?"

I sighed. "Of course not."

And it wasn't as if our world didn't have a history of people doing whatever was necessary to survive tyrants and dictators. Dark elves might be far worse than any home-grown evil our world had ever experienced, but there would always be some who'd willingly work with Darkside against the rest of humanity in order to ingratiate themselves and survive.

"Let's worry about the details after we get the DNA," Mo said. "We won't know if hunting the various Winter incarnations is even possible until then."

"If you have one annoying fault, that's it. You're just too sensible." I paused and narrowed my eyes. "Well, that and your habit of working on a 'as needed' mode when it comes to information."

She laughed and patted my shoulder. "After a few hundred years, you too will learn both are requisites for a happy life."

"Oh, trust me, the latter is a lesson she's already learned *very* well," Luc said, laughter crinkling the corners of his eyes.

I chucked a bit of crust at him. He laughed and ducked. "It's nothing but the truth, and you know it."

I smiled and didn't deny it. Once I'd finished the rest of my breakfast, I went upstairs to clean my teeth and wash my face, then headed into Mo's room and stripped off.

She carefully examined me for anything to suggest I had a bug aboard, but thankfully didn't find anything. I got dressed and then plonked down on her bed. "I have a question."

"About what?"

"The gray space—did any of the other witch kings step into it to do anything more than draw on its energies to lock down the gates?"

"Not that I know of—why?"

I half shrugged. "It's never going to come down to a battle between only Max and me. He'll always have the demons at hand—he might not believe I could ever best him, but he won't take the chance of it happening, either. Not now that he knows I can draw down lightning. But if I can draw him into the gray—"

"The gray is nothing more than the emptiness between our world and Darkside," she cut in. "No one has ever successfully managed to enter it beyond the witch kings, and only then because of Elysian."

"But it's not exactly empty, and we can exist there."

"The claimant of the sword can. It doesn't mean Max will."

"Doesn't mean he won't, either."

She eyed me, her expression a touch uneasy. "I wouldn't suggest leaving him there, if that's your plan. Even if it *were* possible, his presence may well stain the gray and make it unusable for future generations."

"I wasn't intending to leave him. I was just trying to think of a way to detach him from Darkside." I shrugged. "It was an idea, nothing more."

She hesitated, and then said, "Fully transferring into the gray is dangerous. You merely brushed its outer veil when you called Nex to you in the dark altar's cavern. You survived it because Vita also responded."

"But why is it so dangerous? Is it because it's a 'between' place, neither of this world or Darkside? Or is there some other reason?"

"It's because the energies that exist within the gray are more cosmic in nature, despite the earthlike appearance—"

"How do you know it's earthlike if you've never been there?"

"By comments made by the two kings who survived."

Ah, of course. "So does that mean what we see there doesn't actually exist?"

She nodded. "I think it's merely a brief reflection—a static image that's caught and held by the gray when Elysian tears through her shrouds."

"So if I release Elysian, I die?"

"Unknown." She patted my knee. "Please don't, just in case."

I half smiled. "I'll definitely try not to."

"Good." She hesitated. "I got a call from Mary this morning."

Dread stirred. "And?"

"She managed to get hold of Mryddin. The news isn't good."

"Let me guess—the bastard's decided to stay in his hole and not help us?"

She nodded. "I'm afraid he sensed the power you raised when you drew Elysian. He's decided that since another mage has risen, he doesn't have to."

"Did Mary explain the other mage knows jack shit?"

"Yes. He said I was more than capable of passing on the necessary skills, then impolitely told her to leave."

"If we survive all this, can we go down to the bastard's cave and shake the hell out of it until he's forced to come out? Just to piss him off?"

She laughed and slapped my knee. "Indeed, I think we should. Let's go."

I hastily gathered my knives and lashed them together as I ran after her.

Luc was just finishing cleaning up as we came down the stairs. "It could take me a couple of hours to get to Carlisle, depending on the traffic conditions. If I check Kendal as well, I'm not going to be at Southport until early evening."

Mo nodded. "That'll give us the chance to organize the hunt."

"Just be careful," he said. "I'd hate anything to happen to my two favorite ladies."

"You really are going to make a most excellent grand-son-in-law."

He snorted and followed us across to the door. The morning was fresh and clear, the sky blue, and the wind light. A perfect day for flying.

Mo shifted and leapt skyward. I spun, claimed Luc's luscious lips, and kissed him with all the hunger and need that burned within. Then I shifted shape and followed Mo into the sky.

We didn't immediately land when we arrived at King Island, but instead circled for several minutes, looking for any indication that Darkside's human helpers lingered. There was no reason for them to, of course, but there was also no point in taking chances. But aside from the comings and goings of the various birds that called this place home, the island appeared deserted.

Mo arrowed down, regaining shape close to Winter's man-shaped coffin of earth and stone. I landed beside her.

"Considering this was the first time you properly called to the earth," she said, "you did a rather good job if it."

"It just about wrecked me, though."

"And yet you were able to fight on." She smiled. "Of course, that's no real surprise, given you've inherited my stubbornness as well as my gifts."

"Something else Luc would agree with."

She chuckled softly and knelt, pressing a hand to the rock and the earth that encased Winter. "No indication of life."

"Why would there be? He's half-human, and no human can survive being buried like that. I'd have thought a demon couldn't, either."

She wrinkled her nose. "There are a few who can survive for quite a long time on the air that filters in through the microscopic gaps between earth and rock."

"Meaning the next time I bury one of these fuckers, I'd better make sure there're no damn gaps."

"Always prudent, just to be safe." Energy stirred around her fingertips, then the rock and the earth slowly peeled away from Winter's body, revealing his neck and shoulders.

A look of horror and desperation was forever etched onto his pale features—not surprising given I'd buried him alive.

Mo rose and moved around to one side of the body. "Can I borrow Nex?"

I untied the knives and handed her Nex hilt first. Light flickered briefly down the blade; recognizing our shared bloodline, perhaps, even though it had never happened before now. Maybe it was just another sign that in drawing Elysian, I'd altered far more than I could ever have imagined.

Mo sliced off several large chunks of hair, then returned Nex to me. I didn't immediately sheath her; while we'd not seen anyone on the island, there were plenty of trees and rocks that could provide hiding spots. At least with Nex gripped tight, I'd be able to respond to any threat that much faster.

"Do we know how many versions of Winter there are?" Mo said.

I shook my head. "I did ask, but all he said was 'enough.'"

"Unhelpful bastard." She sighed and dragged a clean tissue out of her pocket. "I'll divide the hair into six. That should be enough."

"Are you going to activate them all now?"

"That would be risky."

I frowned. "Why? There's been no indication he's magic capable or even sensitive to its presence."

"There's been no indication that he's not, either. Always best to fall on the safe side when doing this sort of stuff." She plucked free a small amount of hair then carefully wrapped the rest in the tissue and tucked it back in her pocket.

"So we're not going after at least one of the bastards

right now? I think we should."

"That would be your need for revenge speaking," she said, amused. "However, I happen to be in agreement. Southport can wait."

"And Luc's theory that killing one Winter incarnation will warn the rest of them?"

A cold smile touched her lips. "Oh, if we do this right, he literally won't know what hit him. And neither will the rest of them."

I raised my eyebrows, but she didn't elaborate—no surprise there. While she weaved her spell around the hair, I pulled out my phone and sent a text to Luc.

His response was immediate. *Color me unsurprised.*

I could almost hear his dry tone and smiled. *How'd the gate check at Carlisle go?*

Neither fitted the description Riona gave us. I've just filled the SUV, so I'll head on down to Kendal.

And then back to Southport?

No. Seeing as you two are jaunting off elsewhere, I might as well check the Leeds gates while I'm down that way.

Surely the Leeds witch council can do that?

Have you met the Leeds council?

No, but they can't be incompetent—they wouldn't get elected if they were.

They're not. They're just sticklers for the rules and, with the mess in London at the moment, it's doubtful the high council would have had the chance to send out the full alert.

Yes, but Barney would have called them.

And they would not have moved unless they got clearance from the High Council.

But that makes no sense—all we're asking them to do is send someone out to check the damn gates. Why would they be hesitant to do that?

Because of a rash act years ago in which over a hundred people died. Council regulations now state they cannot act without prior approval unless they come under attack.

I would think that, after London, new orders will go out to all the councils not to wait for High Council approval on matters of national security.

Undoubtedly, though Leeds is probably the only one that will need it. And to repeat what I said earlier, be careful. Your brother and Winter will be watching for reprisals.

And so they fucking should. See you in Southport.

I shoved my phone away and then watched the developing spell. The orb Mo was weaving around the hair was far more complex than a mere tracking spell, and there were multiple layers within the spell that I'd never seen her use before.

Once she'd fully cast it, she glanced at me and said, "Ready to go?"

I hastily lashed my knives back together and then nodded. She immediately tossed the glowing orb into the air and spoke a command. The orb pulsed and shot off toward Ainslyn. Mo leapt after it, catching me a little flat-footed. I shifted, swept up my knives, and raced after her.

The orb rolled past Ainslyn and Chester and then swept inland. I had a bad feeling that—just as I'd predicted—we'd end up in London.

But I was utterly wrong, at least in this particular case. The orb spun through the middle of England, bypassing distant London and its plumes of smoke, and continuing on.

To Winchester.

The ancient seat of both the witch kings and the Blackbirds, and a location that still held many ancient documents and artifacts.

Winter had come here looking for information to clarify whether the statements I'd made to Max were true.

The orb shot across the cathedral's imposing spires and then descended. The still-impressive ruins of the Witch King's Winchester castle came into view, but the orb didn't stop there, instead swooping across the roof of the nearby great hall and residence before flying into the canopy of the nearby evergreen oak. Mo and I landed on a thicker branch close to the grand old tree's trunk but didn't immediately shift shape. Two birds in a tree weren't going to be noticed by many. Two women perched in said tree certainly would.

The orb hovered a few inches above the end of our branch, its pulse slow and steady. My gaze went to the building. While we were too far away to read the small information plaque situated where the path split into two—one going on to the residence, the other the ruins—I presumed either the residence or the hall was being used by the Blackbirds. Maybe even both.

The three-story residence beyond the fork was much newer than the great hall, and highly—almost outrageously—decorated. There were no protection spells evident, but I had no doubt they'd be present.

If Winter *was* inside searching for information, then the Blackbirds had at least one more traitor in their midst. He surely wouldn't have gotten inside otherwise—not when he was all too obviously a half-blood.

Time ticked by without Winter making an appearance. If not for the orb's gentle pulsing, I'd have wondered if he'd somehow eluded us.

After what felt like forever, the residence's rather grand rear door opened, and an all-too-familiar figure stepped out. Hatred and anger surged, and I shifted from one foot to the other, desperately fighting the urge to swoop down and kill the bastard. The whole idea of this expedition was to remain anonymous, and that would hardly be the case if I gave in to anger. Even if I swooped in from behind, he'd know I was there the moment I hit the ground in human form.

He didn't take the path toward our tree, but rather the fork that led to the old gates dividing the hall and residence from the castle ruins. There were several scrolls tucked under his arm, suggesting he'd found whatever information he'd come here for.

I wished I knew what that was. It surely couldn't be about Elysian—not after such a relatively short search, especially when the Blackbirds hadn't been able to uncover anything about either the sword in the stone or Elysian.

As he disappeared through the gate and started across a grassed inner court, Mo dropped to the ground, shifted shape, and then pressed her hand into the grass. My gaze shot back to Winter. He was now walking along to one of the remaining walls, obviously heading toward the gatehouse. His phone rang sharply, the sound loud in the peaceful stillness of this place. He shifted the scrolls, pulled out his phone, and kept walking.

As he did, Mo murmured a command. Fingers of energy shot from underneath her hand and silently rolled toward the castle's remains. They crawled up the wall and surrounded a massive stone at the top. Then, just as Winter stepped under that section, sent it crashing to the ground.

He wouldn't have known what had hit him. The force of the stone's fall was so great, half of it ended up buried deep into the ground. The orb flickered and then disintegrated, a sure sign that the life it had been designed to find had been extinguished.

Mo rose and brushed her hands together to clear them of dirt. "One down, two to go."

I dropped to the ground and became human. "I take it you felt the presence of the others when you set the tracker on this one?"

She nodded. "They're clones, so their echoes came through. One is in London, and I suspect the other disappeared through the Ainslyn Gateway, because the pulse cut off abruptly."

"Meaning he's probably up to no good." I glanced toward the old gates. "Is it worth checking if there's anything remaining of the scrolls this one was carrying?"

"I'd rather not disturb his remains. Besides, there's little point, given whatever information he found would have already been passed on to his counterparts."

"If that was true, he wouldn't have needed the scrolls."

"Unless he wanted proof for your brother."

I grunted and glanced at the residence. "And what about the traitor who let him in?"

"That's a problem for the Blackbirds." She glanced at her watch. "We need to get back to Southport. I'd rather not be flying after dark, and we're going to be cutting it rather close as it is."

"Let's just hope they have plenty of food in the pantry," I grumbled, "because I'll be absolutely starving by the time we get there."

"It's a mansion," she said, voice dry. "Their pantry is probably bigger than our whole damn apartment."

"No doubt, but I might send Mia a text, just to give her a heads-up of our approximate arrival time and the need to have dinner ready."

"Good idea. Meet you up high."

She circled the area while I sent the text, then we flew

231

north toward Southport. The wind picked up before we were even a third of the way there, chasing storm clouds toward us. The sky grew progressively darker, and the full fury of the storm hit just as we reached the halfway point. It ended up being a fucking miserable flight, and I'd never been so happy to see the modern mock-Tudor home that had become our safe house in my life. We swooped into the large covered porch and shifted shape. Though my black-bird form was basically waterproof, the cold had neverthe-less leached into my body, and my extremities felt like ice.

The front door opened, and a sharply dressed elderly gentleman with neat white hair and merry blue eyes appeared. It was Henry, the mansion's majordomo. "Wel-come back, ladies."

"It's a pleasure to be back, Henry," Mo replied. "Is there time to warm my old bones with a shower before dinner?"

"Of course." He stepped to one side and waved us in. "The other ladies and Mr. Lancaster have requested it be served in the small breakfast room."

Which was something of a misnomer, given it was large enough to seat at least twenty people.

"Could you let them know we'll be there in twenty minutes?" Mo glanced at me. "That long enough for you?"

"Depends how thick the internal ice is." My voice was dry. "But at the very least, defrosting should have occurred. A large whiskey can do the rest."

I followed her across the entrance hall. It was a double-height space dominated not only by a large and rather grand oak staircase that swept up to the galleried landing above, but also by the huge gold-and-crystal chandelier that sprayed rainbows of light across the white walls and ceiling.

The upstairs hall was wide enough to drive a car through, and parties could definitely be held in the bedrooms we'd each been allocated. I stripped off, dumped my clothes and Elysian on top of the blanket box that sat at the end of the super-king-sized bed, and then strode into the bathroom. Like everything else in this place, it was a vast and opulent space; gold-veined white marble on the floor and walls, with gold hand basins and taps. The huge shower had three ceiling-mounted showerheads and two flexible wall ones—also all gold.

I collected body soap, a sponge, and a towel the size of a tent from the inset storage shelves, placed them on the stand provided at one end of the shower, then turned on the water and stepped under. A long hot soak went some way to easing the weariness, but I'd be as sore as hell tomorrow. It had been a while since I'd flown that far in one day.

Once dressed, I slung Elysian on then headed down to the breakfast room. Barney wasn't about, but both Mia and Ginny were there. At five-ten, Mia was two inches taller than me, with blue-gray eyes, short brown hair, and a slender build. Ginny was typical Okoro in looks, with long plaited black hair and dark eyes. At barely five-foot-one, she was also something of a pocket rocket—and woe betide anyone who thought small equaled pushover.

Mia looked up from the papers they'd been examining when I walked in, her smile bright and somewhat relieved. I couldn't help but notice her bo staffs were on the table within easy reach and that Ginny was now wearing a gun. Detectives working in major crime units didn't typically carry unless they were working with the firearms unit, but Ginny had obviously gotten special dispensation, and that was something of a relief. Her skill set was the ability to track things via the trail of color and currents they left behind in the air, rather than the ability to control—or even weaponize—the weather that most of her siblings had.

"Did you find a suitably nasty way to deal with the bastards who snatched me?" Mia asked.

"I drowned the ringleader in a river of earth and stone, and Luc killed the rest."

She blinked. "Really? I mean, that certainly *is* a most excellent revenge, but I didn't think you could do that sort of stuff."

"It would appear Mo's bloodline is stronger in me than we all thought." I walked over and wrapped her in a fierce hug. "I'm so glad you're okay."

"So am I." She returned the hug, a smile in her voice. "But as I've already said, I want *in* on *all* the action. It can't be any more deadly than being snatched on the way home from my parents' party."

I wouldn't bet on that. But I kept the words inside. Even if neither she nor Ginny knew everything, they were well aware of the inherent dangers of dealing with Darksiders. They'd both lost family members over the years to the bastards.

Besides, it wasn't like I could keep them out of the action. Not now.

I pulled back. "So, what are you both doing?"

"We're transcribing the papers we found at that old church," Ginny said. "You know, one of the many tasks you gave us to keep us out of harm's way."

"That *wasn't* the intention." Though it was. "We needed to uncover what the demons had been trying to hide when they blew the place up, and it made sense for you two to help Barney out."

She harrumphed, clearly not believing me. "Well, it's a fucking slow and smelly process, let me tell you. I'm not sure what they used to preserve the translation scroll, but it reeks."

"It *is* centuries old, and skin to boot." My voice was dry. "Besides, weren't you and Barney supposed to be in Manchester, dealing with the mess there?"

"We were, but the High Council sent people in to take over." Ginny shrugged. "I know Mo made the dark altar safe, but they wanted to put additional protections around it so it couldn't be used again."

It was doubtful any of them would be able to raise the sort of protections Mo could, but I guessed it was better to be safe than sorry when it came to the rivers of power most knew as ley lines. I motioned to the papers they'd been transcribing. "Have you found anything interesting?"

"What appears to be several lists of names." She picked them up and offered them to me. "Barney recognized some of the people on the first list—they're mostly low-ranking government officials."

"Our theory is," Mia said, "that it's a list of people working with Darkside in some capacity."

"Be handy if it was, because it'll make it easier to weed them out." I scanned the first page, looking for familiar names but not finding any. "Why would a list like this be in the hands of mere foot soldiers, though? Darkside generally isn't that careless with information."

"Except not everyone killed in that church was a foot soldier," Ginny said. "The setup in the chancel area and the size of the desk where we found all these bits of paper suggests someone much higher in the ranks had been working there."

"So why didn't we find his body?"

"We can't be sure he wasn't there," she said, "especially given it's damnably hard to tell a menik from a controller when the explosion made an utter mess of them all."

A mess the preternatural team was still sorting out. I

flipped over the page. There were only a dozen names written on this, but one immediately jumped out at me.

Daniel Durant.

The name of the Blackbird who'd attempted to kill the queen.

This *wasn't* a list of people working with Darkside. It was a list of people who were *infected*.

My heart leapt into a whole other gear. "Well, I think we finally got a bit of fucking luck."

"How?" Mia asked.

I shook the second bit of paper at them. "We need to get this to the High Council ASAP."

"But why?" Ginny asked. "What is it?"

"I think it's a list of those who have been infected by wraiths."

"Wait—what?" Mia said.

I shot her a glance. "You weren't told?"

"About *what*?"

"That the reason you were first taken to a safe house rather than here was we needed to check you for infection," Mo said as she came into the room.

"But by *what*, though?" Mia's voice was filled with exasperation. "Just spit it out, ladies!"

"By a wraith," I said. "Which is a nasty sort of demon that infuses itself into human bodies and basically take over all thought and actions."

"Well, that's *fucked*."

Mo got her phone out and took a picture of the list I was holding. "You would have been, had you been infected."

"How long have these delights been in action?" Ginny asked. "And how come we've never heard of them?"

"Forever, I'm afraid, and very few know about them because it was deemed safer that way."

"Because giving people the opportunity to protect themselves against such an aggressor can never be a good thing."

Ginny's voice was dry, but there was little responding amusement in Mo's expression. "And neither is panic."

"I think you underestimate the witch population."

"Trust me, I don't."

Nex pulsed. It was only brief, little more than a couple of beats that warmed my thigh and then faded away, but it very much felt as if something had moved briefly into her sensing range.

Then I heard the scratch. Like Nex's pulse, it came and went, but unease nevertheless stirred. I cocked my head and listened intently.

"What's wrong?" Mo immediately asked.

"I'm not sure …" I stopped as the scratching repeated. "You didn't hear that?"

"Hear what?" Mia said, voice a little exasperated. "Seriously, can you not be a little more forthcoming with information?"

I held up a hand and cocked my head sideways. The noise wasn't coming from directly above us, but rather from the garage end of the house. Why I could hear it given the distance, I had no idea, but I wasn't about to ignore it.

It wasn't a squirrel, though. Aside from the fact they weren't active at night, I certainly wouldn't hear one running around on the roof from this far away.

Another pulse from Nex, though it once again faded as quickly as it appeared.

And *that* could mean only one thing.

There were people moving around out there.

People who meant us no good.

CHAPTER ELEVEN

I glanced out the French doors. The sun had dipped behind the horizon even if night had yet to fully fall, so in truth it *could* be demons out there, though there were no gates close enough for them to have gotten here so quickly. Besides, if it *had* been demons up on the roof, Nex would have done more than simply pulse for a beat or two. But that didn't make whoever the hell it was any less dangerous.

"Gwen?" Mo prompted, when I didn't immediately answer.

"I think we're about to be attacked."

"Demons?"

"On the roof? No. Elsewhere, I don't know. Maybe."

"Then we work on the principle that they *are* out there. Mia, Ginny, run down to the orangery at the other end of the house and check if anyone is trying to enter through there. Tell any staff you see to get down into the basement."

"And if we happen to find intruders? Or worse, demons?" Mia asked.

"Work on an attack first, ask questions later principle."

"A principle I highly approve of in this sort of situation."

Ginny drew her weapon and then glanced at Mia. "Let's go."

Mia's grin was one of anticipation. "Looks like I'm getting my wish to be involved in the action sooner rather than later."

As the two of them raced out, I glanced at Mo. "Do you want to grab Barney and check the other end of the house? I'll go after the thread of darkness Nex felt, just in case whoever or whatever is on the roof is a distraction."

She nodded. "It might be an idea to strip down to basics —that way, you can call on the earth and the air if it becomes necessary."

"Basics being bare feet, jeans, and my tank top. There's no way known I'm going naked, given how cold it probably is out there by now."

She tsked and shook her head. "It's a sad state of affairs when the younger generation is so much softer than the older."

"Says the woman who walks around in sheepskin slippers all winter bitching about the cold."

She laughed, squeezed my arm, and headed out.

I kicked off my shoes and socks, then tore off my sweater and tossed it onto the nearby chair. The floorboards were warm under my feet and the earth's pulse faint, but it nevertheless seemed free from the weight of anything that felt foul or wrong. I still doubted that meant our attackers were all on the roof, but there was only one way to find out.

I padded across to the French doors and quietly unsnibbed them. I didn't step out, instead studying the immediate surrounds, looking for anything or anyone that shouldn't be there.

The large patio area beyond the doors was empty—the outside furniture obviously stored for the winter elsewhere

—and the well-manicured lawn and gardens beyond were free from unexpected shadows. There was nothing to suggest anything or anyone lay in wait.

And yet I was *sure* someone was, even if Nex remained inert.

I carefully pushed the door open and stepped out. The wind stirred around me, freezing my skin even as she whispered her secrets. There were a dozen men up on the roof, though she wasn't able to tell me anything more than that. I had no idea whether that was my lack of training when it came to reading the wind or whether they were protected from observation in some way. Darkside knew Mo was a mage, so it wouldn't be surprising if they'd provided at least some protective measures to their army.

But who was in charge of that army? Was it the presence Nex had so briefly reacted to?

I scanned the night again, then knelt and pressed my fingers against the pavers, splaying them wide in an attempt to capture the signal more strongly, though I had absolutely no idea if it would make any difference.

Her pulse came through, strong and steady, but there remained no indication of anyone or anything in the area around the house. I widened the search parameters, seeking information from the acres beyond this garden, and received the faintest echo of evil.

Nex *had* been reacting to a dark presence, though it wasn't close, and I couldn't immediately tell if it was an elf, a demon, or even a halfling.

My pulse rate leapt at the thought ... could luck be with us? Could it be another incarnation of Winter standing out there?

It was certainly possible. Mo's tracker might have said one of them had slipped back into Darkside, but the nearest of Ainslyn's three gates was only a seventy-minute or so drive away, even in peak-hour traffic. It was perfectly possible that he could be here.

But if it *was*, how the hell had he found us here so quickly? Mo had checked for trackers, but had she somehow missed one?

It was a definite possibility.

And if there *was*, it meant the bastard would run the minute I moved toward him, and that in turn meant I had to be faster than him.

But the people on the roof also meant I couldn't shift into blackbird form—not when my pale feathers contrasted so sharply against the night, presenting an easy target for even a mediocre sharpshooter.

I pressed my fingers harder against the sandstone, gathering as much information as possible about the man up ahead. Then I fixed my gaze on his location, thrust up, and ran.

The earth's pulsing strengthened once I hit the grass. The knives responded, echoing the beat, Nex with hunger and fury, and Vita with warmth and strength.

I leapt over a half-height stone boundary wall and ran on, guided by the trio of powers that now coursed through me.

My quarry was on the run.

I swore and reached for more speed, but he was fast—damned fast. Even with the boost Vita was giving me, there was a very good chance he'd escape. Maybe I should risk the possibility of being shot and just fly after the bastard ... but I'd barely even thought that when, from behind me, came a harsh shout. A heartbeat later, the earth shuddered under multiple impacts, and dirt sprayed into the air.

My heart just about leapt into my throat.

Bullets.

And not just from one gun, but a number of them.

Fuck.

I raised a hand, grabbed the air, and then twisted it around, creating a vortex that wrapped around me so fiercely, all I could hear was its howling. The bullets stopped hitting the ground around my feet; the wind was altering their trajectory.

I leapt over a garden bed, slipped on a damp patch of grass, and went down. I swore and half thrust up, then stopped and instead dug my fingers deeper into the soil, imagining a wave of earth ensnaring my quarry in much the same manner as I had with Winter on King Island. As the earth responded, I ran on.

I was close enough now that I could feel the vibration of my quarry's steps through the ground. I was catching him ... and so was the earth's wave.

From somewhere beyond the delicate pencil pines that lined the fence boundary up ahead, an engine roared to life. I swore. The bastard was *not* going to escape me.

Vita's pulsing increased, and her energy burned through me, lending my limbs additional strength. I was all but flying over the ground, my feet barely touching.

He *wasn't* going to outrun me, even if he was somehow avoiding the wave of earth.

A figure finally appeared on the horizon. He was cloaked in black and wearing a hat, so I had no idea if it was Winter or not and, at this point, didn't care. I just wanted to catch him and find out what they'd intended.

He crashed through the pencil pines and briefly disappeared, but I was only seconds behind him now. I just needed some goddamn luck and he'd be mine.

I plunged through the pines and scrambled over the

fence. A long paddock beyond swept down to a road on which a car waited. The bright gleam of its headlights illuminated the ground between it and my quarry. His hat had been torn off, revealing long white hair that streamed behind him.

Winter.

Running faster than my wave. How that was possible, I had no idea, but the bastard wasn't going to escape. No way, no how.

I grabbed the wind again and flung it forward. It howled across the distance separating us, flattening everything in its path. Winter cast a glance over his shoulder, then reached into his pocket and withdrew what I presumed was a gun. I didn't falter. The wind had protected me once from bullets. It would do so again.

But Winter didn't stop, and he didn't shoot.

He didn't get the chance.

The wind hit him, sweeping him up and around, drawing him ever higher. I released its force and watched as he slammed back down. The wave of earth finally caught him, sweeping over his feet, legs, and arms, pinning him in the position that he'd fallen. He made no immediate attempt to move. I rather suspected that, given the twisted positioning of his earth-covered limbs, he couldn't. His legs and very possibly his back were broken.

The car accelerated away, the squeal of its tires riding across the silence. I paid it no heed, my gaze on Winter. His eyes were closed, and blood seeped from the sides of his mouth, but there was no sense of death coming from the earth.

Not yet, anyway.

I nevertheless approached him cautiously. He might not be moving, but, pinned or not, the gun remained in his hand. He might still be able to pull the trigger, even if he couldn't aim the shot directly at me.

I drew Nex. Lightning flickered around her blade, a pulse that was eager in feel. She remained hungry to shed blood, though I did have to wonder if *she* actually was, or if I was projecting my own desires onto her.

Winter's eyes opened, his gaze flickering from me to her and back again. There was no fear in his expression. There wasn't even pain, though he had to be in a whole world of it. The only emotion etched onto his thin features was acceptance.

He knew he was going to die, and he didn't care—perhaps because there was at least one other incarnation of him out there.

I stopped near his knees and studied him for several seconds. He returned the gaze evenly. I had no doubt he was sharing what he was seeing with his remaining counterpart.

And that's *exactly* what I wanted. I wanted the remaining clone to see my presence at the death of his brother. Wanted him to realize that I'd be coming after him as well. I wanted him to fear that fact even though it was doubtful any of them were capable of it.

"I did promise you all a slow and agonizing death," I said evenly. "The last incarnation of you will be next. And don't forget to tell that bastard I once called brother I'm coming after him as well."

Winter chuckled, though it ended up being more of a gurgle. Blood erupted from his mouth and spilled down his sharp, pale cheeks. He was as broken on the inside as he was on the outside.

"We both know that neither you nor your brother have that sort of courage." His words were a guttural, pain-filled whisper, and I couldn't help but rejoice in that fact. "It's why he gave you to us, and why you will make every effort to save him when in truth he should be dead by now."

I guessed in one respect he was right. Up until very recently, I *hadn't* been willing to give up on my brother. But he'd certainly given up on me. Hell, he'd handed me over to Darkside without any hesitation or qualm, despite knowing exactly what waited for me. In fact, he'd no doubt sanctioned the torture, because he needed to extract everything I knew about his sword and Elysian. His dream—his goal—was far more important to him than the health and well-being of a sister. A twin.

The moment he'd darted me on the bridge, he'd killed whatever remnants of hope had remained within me, and in the process, tightened my resolve to stop him.

And I *would* stop him, no matter what it took. No matter what I had to do.

I smiled, and hoped it looked as cold and as unforgiving as it felt. "I guess we'll find out soon enough which of us is right."

He half laughed, but it disintegrated into another hacking cough. I stepped back to avoid the spray of blood.

"You won't catch him," he said, voice little more than a harsh rasp now. "He knows your grandmother's tricks far too well, and he has the means and the power to counter them."

"Very true." I raised Nex. Lightning flickered around her blade, fierce and white in the gathering darkness. "But here's the thing—he doesn't know mine."

"You have nothing beyond the ability to use the echoes of power that have gathered in those knives over multiple centuries. Your only real worth is the fact you come from a long line of witch kings."

"Really?" I arched an eyebrow. "Then you might advise my brother that even though all my tests for magic came back null, that doesn't mean I have no power. It simply means the testers—*and* the test—were incapable of discovering it."

"You lie—"

"Do I? Then who do you think raised the earth that encases you? Who do you think raised the wave that drowned your counterpart on King Island? And who in hell do you think destroyed both your tunnel and that damn cavern holding those string creatures last night?"

He stared at me, obviously torn between believing and not.

"My brother has seriously underestimated what I'm capable of," I continued, "and his actions on the bridge shattered all restraints of kinship. I'm coming for him."

"And he'll be waiting."

"Good."

And with that, I unleashed Nex's fire and burned the fucker to a crisp. It was a far quicker death than either Nex or I desired, but creating the wave and calling down the air had seriously drained my strength, and not even the warm wash of Vita's energy could completely restore it.

Once his body was little more than a dark stain on the ground, the earth that had caged him collapsed, and her pulse softened to a whisper.

I sucked in a deep breath and then resolutely made my way back to the house, pausing briefly in the cover of the pencil pines to check the situation on the roof. There was no sign of sharpshooters and, at first glance, no indication there'd been any sort of fight.

I frowned, wondering if the shooters had fled and hoping like hell everyone was okay. They should be, given we hadn't been caught by surprise, but Lady Luck had been somewhat fickle with her favors of late.

The closer I got, the more evident it became that first appearances were deceiving. Several ornate windowpanes in the orangery at the far end of the house had been smashed, and there was smoke drifting up from the driveway side of the house. I leapt over the small border wall surrounding the patio garden and ran across to the doors. They opened before I reached them, and Mia appeared.

Her clothes were torn, her hair in disarray, and there were several thick scratches on her face, but her smile was wide and her eyes shone.

"It seems someone very much enjoyed getting in on the action," I commented, amused.

"It's always good to find a legit reason to use my training." She pushed the door open wider and then stepped back. "Mo sent me here to tell you everything is okay and not to panic."

I snorted. "Which generally means there *is* something to panic about."

"Not this time. This way." She turned and led me through the breakfast room. "The mansion's staff are all safe, no one on our team is hurt, and nine bad guys are bundled up waiting for the preternatural boys to come and collect them. Oh, and your Blackbird is here, and looking rather hot, might I add."

Anticipation stirred through me, and it was all I could do not to race through the house. While I wanted nothing more than to be wrapped in the warm solid strength of his arms, we had a whole world of problems to deal with first.

Starting with the fact I'd basically just declared war on my brother and needed to get to him before he got to me.

"So, what's on fire out the front?"

"The van a couple of our attackers tried to escape in. Barney got a little enthusiastic with a stopping spell, apparently."

I smiled. "Care to explain why you have twigs and leaves in your hair, then? Did someone throw a tree at you?"

"Close. I tripped over the protruding leg of a table when I stepped back from a blow and fell into a tree."

I laughed. "I'm guessing you won't be telling your sensei about *that*."

Her smile flashed. "Actually, I will be because I still managed to take the bastard out despite him having the advantage."

"Well done, you."

"Thank you."

Henry appeared as we entered the entrance hall and looked utterly unfazed by everything that had happened. "Dinner has been placed in the warmer, ladies. Would either of you like a drink while you're dealing with the unpleasantness outside?"

I smiled at his polite terminology. "Thanks, but not right now. Mia?"

"I'm good."

Henry nodded and opened the front door for us. The night, I noted with a shiver, was far colder now that the surge of adrenaline had eased and Vita's pulsing no longer warmed my side. I rubbed my arms and wished I'd thought to grab my sweater on the way through the breakfast room.

Mo, Luc, Ginny, and Barney were all standing in the driveway. Behind them were the still-smoking remains of a black van. In front of them, in a somewhat ragged circle, were our nine attackers. Eight were sitting and in various states of bloody disarray. The ninth was lying flat and alternated between groaning loudly and cursing because no one was getting him medical help. None of his limbs appeared broken, so maybe he'd damaged his back. A containment spell looped around them all, though it was Barney's rather than Mo's magic.

We walked across. Luc immediately wrapped an arm around my waist and tucked me in close to his big, warm body. It felt like a homecoming.

Mo glanced at me. "They came here for you."

"I figured as much when I discovered Winter was controlling the attack." I swept my gaze over the nine men. They were all human, no half-breeds. I couldn't help but wonder if they had any idea who they'd been working for. "I take it you've questioned them?"

"Just started to," Barney said. He was a well-built man with silver-gray hair, craggy but handsome features, and kind brown eyes. "But aside from the groaner, they're a closemouthed lot."

"I'm going to fucking sue the lot of you," the groaner shouted. "You're legally obliged—"

"You gave up your legal rights when you accepted an assignment from Darkside," Ginny interrupted calmly. "You'll be lucky to see the inside of a courtroom, let alone a hospital."

"We're not fucking working for Darkside," another man said. "I may be a gun for hire, but I'm not a traitor."

There was something in his expression that made me think he was telling the truth. "Did a man called Winter contract you?"

The second speaker hesitated and then nodded reluctantly. "But not to kill anyone. We were just meant to flush you out."

Me, not the others. "How did you find me?"

"Tracker."

Mo swore. "Meaning I *did* miss one."

"We talking magical? Or physical?" Ginny said. "Because the latter can be microscopic and often need specialist equip—"

"Indeed," Luc cut in. "But this wouldn't be the first time I've had to deal with them. We'll be fine."

"Yes, but I can call in help—"

"No need," Mo said. "Can you, Mia, and Barney keep an eye on this lot and let us know when Jason and his team arrive?"

"As long as all you're doing is removing a tracker and not planning your next course of action," Barney said. "Because this shit is bigger than the three of you. You can't keep going at it alone."

She patted his arm comfortingly. "Trust me, I'm very aware of just how big this shit is, and I know *exactly* what it's going to take to stop it."

Barney's expression suggested he wasn't comforted by her words, and I didn't blame him. But he didn't object when she motioned Luc and me to follow and then strode toward the house.

"Given how thoroughly you checked my body the first time around," I said as we headed into my bedroom, "I'm thinking the tracker is probably in my feet."

"That *is* a favorite location of theirs," Luc said. "Nanotechnology makes it very easy to insert under the skin, and the recipient is rarely aware of them."

"Especially if the insertion area is already battered and bruised." Mo shook her head. "I can't believe I didn't think to check your goddamn feet."

"You might not have found it anyway," Luc said.

"They're very easy to miss unless you know exactly what you're looking for."

He motioned me onto the bed. I dropped down and shuffled back so that only my feet hung over the edge. He knelt in front of me and examined my right foot. After several minutes of gentle probing, he released that foot and repeated the process with the other.

Within seconds, he gave a grunt of satisfaction. "And there it is."

Mo bent and frowned at my foot. "I'm not seeing anything—not even an entry point."

"With the new nanotechnology, you often don't." His gaze rose to mine. "It'll have to be cut out."

I drew Vita and handed her to him. "She'll heal the wound."

"Which suggests the connection between you and the two knives has grown," Mo said.

My gaze met hers. "Yes. And that's in part what I needed to talk to you both about."

"Your tension made it pretty evident there was something you needed to discuss." She hesitated, her expression edged with unease. "What happened in the tunnel after you were captured, Gwen? You never really said."

"Two things—"

Luc pressed Vita's point into my skin, and I jumped, though it didn't actually hurt. He murmured a quick "sorry" even as he dug deeper.

I did my best to ignore it and continued. "The first—and probably the least important—is the fact that, after I'd called on the earth's energy to bring down the tunnel, my lightning flowed via Elysian into the ground and seemed to use my awareness of the demons' weight on the earth to seek each one out and cinder them."

Mo's gaze widened a fraction. "I would hardly call *that* unimportant."

"So the other kings weren't able to do something like that?"

"No—although it has to be said that none of the other kings was also a mage."

"It could be argued that I'm really not, either," I replied, amusement briefly rising. "But they *were* Aquitaines and could not only call and control fire, but also use the might of all four elements via Elysian."

She smiled, though it failed to lift the seriousness in her eyes. "Yes, but none were able to individually target demons in the manner you described. For the most part, they simply unleashed a broad band of elemental energy at the attacking horde."

"Got it." Luc held up what looked to be a tiny microchip. "These things have a battery life of ten days, so it's just as well we found it."

"How can something that small have a life of ten days?" I asked, surprised.

He dropped the chip onto the carpet, then pressed Vita's point into it and sliced it in two. "As I've said, nanotechnology these days is quite sophisticated."

He returned Vita, then sat next to me on the bed, his arm and thigh pressed lightly against mine. It was intimate and yet not, comforting and yet not. It had the connection between us flaring to life, but for once didn't offer a look into his memories or even his fears. It simply offered strength.

Which only made me hope that this wasn't all there'd ever be between us, even as I knew that it might well be.

Because of what lay ahead.

Because of what I needed to do.

"And the second point? Mo asked softly.

I drew in a breath and released it slowly. "The second point is that I felt the presence of the Carlisle gate without having to step into the gray."

Mo stared at me for several seconds, her expression a weird mix of surprise and consternation. "That truly shouldn't be possible. Elysian was never designed to react to the gates in *this* world, only the other. She should be nothing more than a conduit for elemental or even your mage powers outside of the gray."

"But if you actually think about it," Luc said, "her ability to use Elysian as no other king has does make sense. After all, Vivienne not only declared that Gwenhwyfar's fate was tied to the sword, but also that destiny and blood had finally converged in our timeline, with Gwen."

Mo began to pace, her steps long and somehow angry—at the old gods and their plans rather than me, I suspected. "That doesn't alter the fact that Gwen's use of the sword is unforeseen and untested."

"Unforeseen by you and Mryddin, perhaps, but probably *not* by Vivienne." I hesitated. "But in the end, the how or why doesn't really matter. All we need to know is that I can do it and that we need to use it."

She stopped abruptly. "I take it you have a plan?"

I smiled, though it held little in the way of amusement. "I do. I'm going to send Max a message he absolutely cannot ignore."

CHAPTER TWELVE

"By shutting down gates, I presume," Luc said. His expression was calm, but the emotions boiling through our link were a thick mix of acceptance and fear, admiration and anger.

I placed a hand on his thigh, a gesture of comfort I knew would provide none. "Not just any gates. The four London ones."

"That will definitely get both his attention *and* Darkside's." Mo resumed her pacing. "However, there is one tiny flaw in your plan—"

"The fact that the only way to survive Elysian's full power is in the gray," I cut in flatly.

"I would hardly call that a *small* flaw," Luc commented.

"And it's not, but I have no intention of risking death. I'll step into the gray to close each gate."

Mo's expression was suspicious, and rightly so, given I wasn't exactly telling the truth. But all she said was, "That will certainly send them a message."

"Yes, the fact that Darkside placed their bets on the wrong fucking twin."

Mo chuckled. "I meant more along the lines of 'fuck with us and we'll close *all* the gates down.'"

I raised an eyebrow. "I thought you said that wasn't feasible?"

"I don't think it is, but that's not the point. Neither of us know for sure, and they'd be the losers if we actually *could*."

"Just to be the voice of reason here," Luc said. "If you do attempt to shut the gates, they *will* attack en masse. None of us can afford that right now."

"No, but unless they can get the main gate open, any mass attack is naturally restricted by the dimensions of the minor gates. It's probably the only thing that has saved London," Mo said. "Such attacks have been tried in the past, but they were always countered, thanks to the fact that the width of the gates only allows two or three of the bastards to exit at the same time."

"Yes, but there's more than enough of them already in London to make a counterattack on Gwen," Luc said. "Even if the sun forces them underground during the day, there're still the halflings to deal with."

I frowned. "I thought they were slowly being beaten back?"

"The operative word there being 'slowly.'" Luc's voice was grim. "I'd put money on the fact that there's still a multitude of gates that have not yet been properly warded."

My frown grew. "Why would you think that, given the warning went out hours ago?"

"If there's one thing that has never altered across multiple centuries," Mo said, "it's the fact that the wheels of government—large or small—move very slowly. Disaster generally has to punch them in the face before motivation gets real."

"The attack in London would surely have done that, though," I said.

"You'd think so." Her voice suggested she wasn't overly convinced.

"Council action or lack thereof is not the biggest problem with your plan," Luc said. "Historically speaking, closing the gates has always required proximity. That's why the battles between them and us have always been in the fields surrounding the main gate. If closure could have been done from a distance, then surely one or more of the witch kings would have attempted it."

"Just because it's never been done doesn't mean it can't be. And as you've said, I'm already using Elysian in ways no other witch king has."

"Even if we presume you can close gates from a distance, that doesn't alter the fact you can't do four at the same time," he said. "And the minute you close one, every single demon on the ground and in the air will hit you."

"Then I'll close them in an area that's already well protected—the palace." I thrust up from the bed and began to pace. "We *have* to take the fight to Max. *Now*. Before he or Winter can hit us again."

"You won't get anywhere near the palace," Luc commented. "The minute they see you in the sky, they'll hit you with everything they have. You're a target, remember."

"Yes, but while their attention is on me, Mo can surreptitiously track down the last remaining version of Winter and grab him."

"Max won't trade his life for Winter's," Mo said. "Your brother is many things, but romantic was never one of them."

"Whether or not he loves Winter isn't the point," I said.

"Winter is his link to Darkside. They may be using his relationship with Winter to get their hands on the sword and the throne, but Max is well aware of that and using it to his advantage."

His comments on the bridge had made *that* pretty obvious.

"He'll just attack Ainslyn in retaliation," Luc said. "He knows you care about the people there."

"But by the time that happens, her defenses will have been strengthened. And we'll use the map room as a control point and hit any location where we see them gathering, hard and fast."

Luc's expression remained unconvinced. "There are other gates you can close without risking London. Max will still get the message and react."

"Yes, but I need to send a warning as much as a message. Shutting down the London attack will do exactly that. Besides, Winter is in London."

"No witch king has ever been able to shut down an attack by themselves," Luc said.

"No other witch king had mage powers to call on."

"Yours are too raw to be reliable." He glanced at Mo. "You know that."

"Her talents may be raw, but they're also strong."

"It's too great a risk, and you both know it."

"What I know," I said heavily, "is it's a risk that's absolutely necessary to take."

"Bunkering down in Ainslyn makes more sense."

"Do you honestly think the attack on London will cease if I use Elysian to shut down the gates around Ainslyn?" My voice held an edge I couldn't quite control. "The royal family is key to his domination plans. While they exist, he cannot legitimately claim the throne—"

"Which he can't claim anyway, because he didn't draw Elysian," Luc cut in sharply.

"But how many people actually know the sword in the stone wasn't the real one? I'd wager most of your fellow Blackbirds don't even believe it."

"There are some—"

"And if the very people who are historically responsible for guarding the sword *and* the king who draws it won't believe the sword in the stone is fake, why would anyone else? We need to show everyone the truth in a very public manner."

His gaze met mine. I wasn't entirely sure what he saw, but after a moment, he nodded. It was a short, sharp, and extremely unhappy sign of acceptance. "Fine. I'll notify the crew in London to be ready for your appearance. If you're going to put on a show, the palace grounds will be the safest location, but they'll need to patch a variation in the shielding dome to give you access."

"Good." The last thing I needed was to make it to the palace only to be bounced away by the magic protecting the place. "I don't suppose you could also check if there're any spare Blackbirds who could come up to Ainslyn and help?"

He shook his head. "It's all hands on deck in London at the moment, and that's unlikely to change. We're obligated to protect the current monarch, even if Elysian has found a new hand to wield her." Amusement briefly flared in his eyes. "You're just lucky duty and heart have finally crystalized as one in *this* timeline. Otherwise, I'd be there rather than here, and our souls might have been destined to travel through hundreds of more years before they finally got a fitting resolution."

If he thought Vivienne had any intention of making it easy for him in *this* timeline, he wasn't paying attention. Or maybe it was in fact *me* who wasn't paying attention, because his words very much suggested he would still choose duty over love, no matter how strong the pull between us might be.

I pushed the uneasy thought away and forced a smile. "I think my soul would shrivel up and die if it had to wait *that* long for sex."

"Even Vivienne wouldn't be that cruel."

"Oh, I wouldn't bet on that." Mo's voice was dry. "But given she *did* say timelines had finally merged, I'd suggest the only thing standing between you two, sex, and my grandbairns, is your survival."

"Grandbairns *will* have to wait a while," Luc said. "While I have absolutely no doubt Gwen and I will be dynamite in the bedroom, we need to discover if we're actually compatible beyond it."

Mo waved a hand dismissively. "As long as it happens sometimes in this century, I'm good. I *am* rolling toward old age in mage terms, remember, so you can't take forever."

Luc snorted. "To once again steer this conversation back on track—Ainslyn's too spread out to successfully defend. That's the main problem with London."

"The difference here is the fact we do have time to prepare," I said. "Barney can order a citywide evac of humans. When that's done, we draw all witches inside the old city walls and run a shield around the entire place."

"There *will* be a lot of casualties, regardless of what we do," Mo said. "Evacuations are another thing that has been tried multiple times over the centuries, but humans and witches alike tend to think governments are overstating the problem, or that the worst will never happen to them—until it actually does, of course."

"If they believe what is happening in London can't

happen to Ainslyn," I snapped, "then maybe they deserve their fucking fate."

Mo raised an eyebrow. "You don't actually mean that."

I sucked in a breath in an effort to calm the flare of anger and fear. "There's a part of me that does, you know. We're risking our lives for these people, so the least they can do is act reasonably and do what they're told."

"There has always been a minority of people—witch or human—who can stare fact and science in the eye and utterly deny its existence or worth. You cannot abandon principle or duty of care to the majority because of those few." Mo's lips twitched. "Though I will admit it is sometimes very tempting."

"And if everything does go to plan in London?" Luc asked. "What then? Where will you meet your brother?"

"Exactly where all this shit first started—on King Island."

"Why there? Logistically, it offers no great protection from demons, and your presence there will have them flooding the area. It'll make Ainslyn's defense that much harder."

"Yes, but—" I hesitated. "It's Elysian's original home, even if the fake later took her place in the stone. It is also the resting place of the shield. I'm not sure why, but it just feels right to have the final confrontation there."

"But why would Max risk going there after what you did to Winter?"

"He won't believe I was responsible for doing that," I said. "Even if he did, he won't think it possible I could best him in any sort of magical battle, given his years of training. He basically said that to me, not so long ago."

"Vanity has always been one of his major faults," Mo agreed heavily.

I nodded. "It's also vanity that won't allow him to believe I could possibly be more worthy of Elysian than him. He *will* meet me, and he *will* try to take her from me."

"I agree, and that's why you won't be going there alone." Mo's voice held a note that said there'd be no arguing on this point. "Luc and I will be there with you. As you've said already, he won't come alone. I understand the necessity of a final confrontation between the two of you, but that doesn't negate your need to be protected against his treachery."

I hesitated and then nodded. "The High Witch Council will need to be advised of our plans."

"I'll contact them when we arrive on the outskirts of London," Mo said. "At this point, I think it best we work on a 'need to know' basis. Everyone defending the palace would have been checked by now, but we still have no idea how far the wraith infection has spread through the rest of the government."

"If you do manage to grab Winter alive," Luc said, "it'd be advisable to shield him magically while you're transporting him. It's possible he and Max have some means of tracking each other, and they might well hit you before you can get back to Ainslyn."

"Oh, you can be sure I'll be shielding him," Mo said, a glint in her eye.

I raised my eyebrows. "I take it the shielding might be a little unpleasant?"

"It doesn't have to be, but let's be honest here, the occasion does warrant it." She smiled, the glint anticipatory. "I'll update the rest of the crew and get things rolling. You'd better go grab something to eat. We'll fly to London within the hour."

With that, she turned and left.

I sucked in a breath to calm the sudden influx of nerves and then sat back down on the bed, this time facing Luc. "You will be careful, won't you?"

He smiled and touched my cheek, a gentle caress that caused inner havoc. "I'm not the one flying into the middle of a battlefield."

"No, but you might find yourself in one regardless. We can make as many plans as we want, but there's no guarantee Max will react in the way we hope."

"If there're two truths in this whole mess, it's the fact that he wants the sword and that he's spent a lifetime underestimating you."

"I know. It's just—" I hesitated and shrugged. "For all my tough words, for all my determination to put an end to my brother's crimes, I'm worried that Winter is right and I just won't have the courage to do what has to be done."

His fingers slid down to my chin and held me still as he leaned forward and kissed me. It was little more than a gentle brushing of lips, but there was nothing sweet about the storm of emotion that burned between us. It was heat and fire, love and caring, need and desire. We might not in truth know each other all that well in *this* lifetime, but our souls had spent an eternity finding and then losing one another. *This* might finally be our time, but only if we could survive what was coming.

He pulled back and rested his forehead against mine. "You're the most courageous woman I've ever met. You're also the Witch King's heir *and* Elysian's wielder. You can do this. You just have to believe in yourself as strongly as the rest of us do."

A smile tugged at my lips. "That's hard when I've spent almost my entire life believing I was nothing more than a disappointment—"

"Not to Mo, you weren't. Even blind Freddie could see that."

"Well, no, but—"

The rest of the words were lost to another kiss. And oh, this time there was nothing gentle about it. It made my blood roar and my heart sing, and I wanted nothing more than to lose myself in his arms and his touch, to rip off our clothes and feel the press of his muscular and glorious body against mine, the heat and thickness of his erection deep within. But the first time we made love *deserved* time, and we had none of that left right now.

I had to go. If I didn't, we wouldn't stop my brother, though why I was suddenly so certain of that, I couldn't say.

I pulled away reluctantly and pressed a hand against his cheek. "I'll ring when we get to London."

"Good. And good luck."

"You too."

I left without looking back, even though I knew this might be the very last time I ever saw him. Not because he might die, but because it was very possible I would. I wasn't a fool, and I was about to use Elysian in a way that had already been responsible for the death of one witch king.

If such a death was to be my fate then so be it, but one thing was certain—there was no way on god's green earth she would take me before my brother.

The bloody glow of the fires consuming parts of London were visible from a long way out, and were no doubt representative of the disaster happening on the ground.

We flew fast over Watford, following a wide highway of destruction that ran from the gate near the old Priory down

263

into London. But the damage in the outer boroughs wasn't as bad as I'd expected. The demons' target had been London, and they'd simply taken the most direct route to get there, destroying anything and anyone that got in their way, but leaving multiple other areas untouched. There were even streets where destruction was heavy on one side and nonexistent on the other. That was not Darkside's usual method, but given the palace was the key to their plan *and* their main goal, it also wasn't surprising.

We swept over the M25 and into Greater London. Red and blue lights filled the streets below; some screamed through the streets, chased by demons on foot or in the air, while others formed a part of the multiple blockades that spanned many major and minor roads. Each had at least one heavily armed military vehicle on hand and was manned by dozens of people, although from this height it was impossible to tell whether they were witch, military, or police, or even a mix of all three.

While Darkside attacked many of these blockades and ran riot through the surrounding streets and parks, the bulk of the fighting had contracted to the area around the palace. The dome of magic protecting the building and its immediate surrounds pulsed frantically, a sign that the witches who bolstered the power of the old protection spells were nearing the end of their strength. There'd no doubt be others ready to take the reins of control, but the changeover point was always a dangerous one.

Demons were everywhere. There were multiple buildings on fire, monuments were smashed, and bodies lay where they'd fallen, human and demon alike. There was a running battle along Grosvenor Place, tanks mowing down demons along Birdcage Walk and through St. James's Park, and palace guards using the high, wire-topped brick wall near the Mews as a barricade from which to shoot. In the air, squadrons of winged demons targeted the pulsing shield with what looked like energy rifles, while others raged against helicopters or targeted bunkered soldiers on various nearby rooftops.

With a flick of her wing, Mo changed direction, flying across the university area and then on to Southwark. As the glittering and so-far-untouched glass structure that was the Shard came into view, she descended, arrowing hard and fast toward the pyramidal building's open top.

I shifted shape and landed beside her. My heart was beating a million miles an hour, and my limbs were shaking. It wasn't exhaustion. It was fear.

I scanned the sky for any indication we'd been seen, but for the moment we appeared safe. But that would end the moment we flew anywhere near the palace.

I rubbed my arms, but it did little to ward off the gathering chill. "Are you going to contact the High Council now?"

"No. They won't be inside the palace, and they can't help me track down Winter."

I glanced at her. "They could help you capture him, though."

"I've never needed help to grab the likes of Winter, Gwen. Not when I've got their DNA to use. He may think he's oh-so-clever, but he is in the end nothing more than another fucking half-blood with delusions of grandeur."

A smile tugged at my lips, despite the tension that rode me. "Now tell me what you really think."

She nudged me lightly and then retrieved the plastic-wrapped hair from her coat pocket. "While I'm setting up the tracker, why don't you contact Luc and make sure everything is set for your entry into the palace?"

I nodded and made the call.

He answered immediately. "You've made it safely to London, then?"

His voice was filled with weariness, and guilt stirred. Not only because of the responsibility I'd placed on his shoulders, but also on Mia's, Ginny's, and Barney's. Luc had trained his entire life for a moment like this, but neither of my friends nor even Barney had. And yet here I was, placing them on the front line and betting all our lives on the fact that I was stronger than my brother.

What if I was wrong? What if he killed me and claimed the sword, despite the warning on the King's Stone? I sucked in a breath and pushed the doubts away. Truth was, if Max did win, everyone I loved would die anyway. Or be subjected to something *far* worse.

"Have you been able to contact Ricker and the team inside the palace?" I asked.

"Yes. They'll be on standby—the minute they see you, they'll open a portal. It will by necessity be small, so keep your wings close to your body going through."

It wasn't so much my wings I had to worry about but Nex and Vita. In theory, neither knife should respond to the magic in the shield, but given the fickle nature of luck, there was a chance—however remote—that they would.

Of course, I was magic immune and should technically be able to get through the shield without a portal, but I had no desire to risk this being the one time my immunity didn't work. Or even on it working but drawing on too much of my strength.

"How are things going there?"

"If Mia doesn't end up becoming Barney's second on the council after this, I'd be very surprised." His admiration shone through. "She's very good at organizing people."

"Well, she *is* an accountant. They have very organized minds."

"I certainly don't think our plans would be so advanced without her."

"So the exodus of the greater Ainslyn area is proceeding?"

"At a pace. Evac centers have been set up in a number of the business district's more secure buildings, and we've Okoro wind witches stationed at all of them. They'll be able to blow away any demons that do attempt an attack."

"I doubt they will, at least not initially. They'll concentrate on old Ainslyn and the areas immediately surrounding it. How's the shield going?"

"It's in place, but we're raising a secondary one around the old tower and her tunnels as a final line of defense."

"Fingers crossed all this will be over before either becomes necessary. Who's in charge of the map room and communications?"

"Ginny and Barney. I'm heading over to King Island at dawn to make sure there's no demonkind lingering over there."

"Wouldn't it be better if you rested first? We're not going to get back to Ainslyn until later in the afternoon, given we'll have to drive rather than fly."

"I'll rest when you're safe, not before."

"Lovely sentiment, but the last thing *I* want is you collapsing with exhaustion in the middle of battle."

"Pot, meet kettle."

A smile tugged at my lips. He did have a point. "Send Ricker a text. Tell him I'm five minutes away."

"I will." He hesitated. "Come back to me, Gwen."

"I will," I said, and then hung up before I said something stupid.

Something like "I love you", when I barely even knew him.

I shoved my phone back into my pocket and then crossed my arms and watched Mo wrap the final few threads of the tracking spell around the hair. The minute the spell was activated, it began to pulse, the rhythm strong and rapid.

The bastard was close.

I scanned the nearby buildings but couldn't see anyone on their rooftops, and there was no evidence anyone was using a concealment spell.

"He's over the river but moving away rapidly from the main action," Mo said. "I doubt he'd be in retreat, so he's obviously got additional mischief planned. You ready?"

"No." I took a deep, somewhat quivering breath. "Yes."

She smiled and wrapped her arms around me. Though her hug was fierce and strong, it didn't provide a whole lot in the way of comfort. At this point, it was doubtful anything could.

"You'll be fine, darling girl. You just need to believe in yourself as much as an old goddess and I do."

I half laughed. "I'm thinking that old goddess wouldn't be too fazed if her plans go awry. It'd just give her something else to do for the next few centuries."

"She might not be, but I certainly would." She pulled back, her gaze searching mine. "I know what you plan, Gwen. Just be aware of the toll it will take."

I nodded, though in truth neither of us really knew what the cost would be, because what I intended had never been tried before. "I'll be fine. Vita is with me."

"Even Vita cannot stop death."

"I have no intention of dying. I have a gorgeous man

who's promised me days of endless, glorious sex, and I fully intend to hold him to that promise."

Her smile failed to lift the concern and worry in her eyes. "Rendezvous in six hours, then?"

I nodded. Six hours would give me time to recover while still allowing us to reach King Island before dusk.

Her gaze scanned my face one more time, then she turned, shifted shape, and flew away. Leaving me more alone than I'd felt in my entire life.

I gathered the bound knives and resolutely walked over to the edge of the building. Wisps of pink and gold were just beginning to stain the horizon. It was time.

I gathered the unspooling threads of my courage then shifted shape and swept up my knives, one claw over the two hilts, the other gripping the leather binding the blades together. And I prayed, as I leapt off the building and arrowed toward the palace, that gut instinct was right. That not only could I do what no other witch king had, but also no other De Montfort.

This could all go to hell in a handbasket very quickly if it proved otherwise.

I flew on, my gaze on the palace and my wings a blur. But I was a white bird in a still-dark sky and, though small, I was not unnoticeable.

And the winged demons did notice.

They came in hard and fast, their red eyes filled with bloodlust and diamond-sharp claws gleaming wickedly.

I ducked and weaved through their onslaught, missing each attack by the merest fraction. All too soon, the sky was filled with their mass, and the only option I had was to dive. The roar of their pursuit filled the air, and their intent, their hunger, their sheer and terrifying presence as they drew closer and closer swamped my senses ... They'd catch me long before I reached the safety of the palace. It was simply too far away.

I had to attack. Had to.

I briefly closed my eyes, prayed to an old goddess for luck, and then tightened my claw around the knife hilts and reached for the lightning.

For an instant, nothing happened, and my heart just about froze in fear.

Then the blades pulsed and multiple forks of lightning shot from the steel, a sheer, dangerous power that burned away the leather sheaths and left the glowing blades naked. The bolts streaked through the night, hitting countless winged monstrosities and cindering their flesh between one heartbeat and the next.

But not even my lightning was capable of destroying them all.

I arrowed on, my gaze on the small whirlpool now forming on top of the shield protecting the palace. The witches were opening a portal, but it was too small, and I was coming in too fast, and god, it was going to be tight. But I had no choice. I couldn't risk using more lightning without draining the strength I'd need to shut the gates, and the demons were once again closing in fast.

A claw ripped across the primary feathers at the very end of my left wing. I automatically dropped in the opposite direction, glimpsed bits of feather fluttering away, saw the big black monster swinging around for another go.

Then I saw men on the ground with weapons aimed upward.

I swore internally and began zigzagging in an effort to make it as difficult as possible for the bastards to pinpoint me. The screams of the flighted demons grew louder, the shield protecting the palace nearer, the portal wider.

I was close, so close to safety ...

A demon smashed into my body, sending me tumbling out of control, over and over, through the air. For several seconds, I couldn't breathe, couldn't fly, my world nothing more than a whirling press of color, confusion, and fear.

Gravity and my natural sense of balance soon reasserted itself, but flying was suddenly difficult and off balance. I jagged sideways, unable to maintain a straight line or any great speed. It only took a glance at my right wing to discover why—multiple flight feathers had been torn from a good portion of my wing, and the rest were bloody and in a goddamn mess. That I remained in the air and flying was a miracle.

But it was one that couldn't—wouldn't—last for long.

I had to get down into that portal *now*, while I still could.

I tightened my grip on the naked blades and called on Vita, hoping like hell she could help the bird as she'd helped the human so many times in the past.

Once again, energy pulsed, but this time it was internal rather than external. It radiated through my body and out into my broken wing, forming a pocket of energy around the bloody plumage; it didn't heal, but it did allow me to get back onto an even keel and simply fly like hell.

Multiple winged demons screamed in frustration and swung around after me. Others dropped from above, forcing me to once again duck and weave through the forest of their claws. But I was no longer battling them alone. A shout had risen from below, and the guards manning the walls and the soldiers in rooftop bunkers began to target the demons in the air.

It gave me time. Gave me hope.

I kept my gaze on my destination, getting closer and

closer, until the pulse of the shield's power skittered across my senses and filled me with a sense of even greater urgency.

They couldn't—wouldn't—keep that portal open for much longer.

I reached for more strength and simply flew, as fast as I could, toward the opening. Demons came at me from the right and the left, and the air was so thick with bullets it was a rain of deadly silver.

A scream rose behind me. I pumped my wings harder, all too aware of the demon's closeness thanks to the turbulent air striking my body. I had no choice but to ignore it.

The portal was closing. I only had seconds.

I tucked my wings in close and dove down.

Felt claws strike at my tail, felt the rip of quills from flesh. Began to spiral as I dove and didn't care.

The air screamed its warning of another attack. There was nothing I could do. I was too close to the portal now ...

As the demon struck at me, I plunged through the small gap. Magic burned my wing feathers and tore away the shield protecting my broken wing. I tumbled more than flew downward, but somehow found balance at the last possible second, landing on my feet and in human form.

Bits of blood and flesh and gore rained all around me. I looked up, saw the upper half of a winged demon's body sliding down the shield's outside curve, leaving a bloody trail behind it.

Saw other demons hovering, their energy weapons aimed at the still closing portal. Its edges were pulsing frantically, and the rate of closure had slowed. I needed to act, and fast, before the bastards managed to burn their way into the palace grounds.

Footsteps, coming in fast from behind me.

I swung around, Nex and Vita held at the ready, lightning flickering angrily between their blades. It wasn't enemies who approached. It was the Blackbirds, one of whom I knew.

Ricker. Luc's cousin.

"That was some fucking show you put on." He slid to a halt in front of me, his gaze sweeping me and coming up concerned. "You okay?"

"I'm alive. Right now, that's all that matters." I shoved Vita through my belt and then reached back and drew Elysian with my free hand.

The gray rolled away from her blade, and Ricker's eyes widened. "Is that ...?"

"Yes." I gripped her fiercely and strode toward the ornately decorated front gates, the red asphalt under my bare feet cold and lifeless. I hoped the lack of a pulse was simply because I wasn't yet calling on the earth's energy, rather than the multiple layers of stone and brick and paving that lay between me and it being too thick.

Ricker ran after me. "What do you want us to do?"

"If that shield falls before I'm finished, protect me."

"Those orders have already been given," he said. "I don't think those of us who remain would dare go back to the table and face Luc's wrath if we failed in that duty."

"I think Luc's wrath will be the least of your worries if we fail."

I stopped several yards away from the ornate gates. Demons and half-bloods surged forward, pressing against the shield, the sheer weight of their numbers forcing it to bend inward briefly. Others repeatedly, uselessly, fired their weapons. The shield held steady against it all, but for how much longer?

I sucked in a breath and then glanced at Ricker. "No

matter what happens, no one is to touch me until my hands leave Elysian—understood?"

He nodded, drew his own sword, and stepped back. He and the other three Blackbirds formed a circle around me; their blades hissed and screamed, a hunger that was audible despite the din being made by the demons beyond the gates.

I shifted my weight, bracing my feet against the red asphalt, then raised Nex and held her against Elysian's hilt with both hands.

With another of those useless deep breaths, I plunged Elysian deep into the asphalt and followed her down, ending up on my knees. The force of the drop reverberated through my body, and my knees were twin hotspots of pain, but it was quickly washed away by the steady beat of the earth's pulse. I drew in her power, felt it rush through limbs, muscle, and bone, making me more than flesh, more than a being of blood, but something less than a god. Felt a darker response from Nex, a hunger and need to disperse the gathering power.

I pushed the energy back into the ground through my feet, completing the circuit. Deeper awareness surged ... the heaviness of blood staining the ground, the thunderous weight of the demons that ran through nearby streets, the rumbling vibration of the heavy vehicles that chased them. From beyond the immediate palace surroundings came the searing pain of destruction; it raced away in four arrow-like swaths toward the whisper-soft presences that were the gateways.

Once again, Elysian pulsed, and that inner awareness sharpened. Mist briefly blurred my vision, and I stepped into that otherworld, though I remained anchored to this.

A gate stood before me. A gate into which dark forms now raced, desperate to reach the safety of Darkside before dawn fully rose. Not only could I see them, but feel and smell them, even though I wasn't physically there, but viewing it all from the outskirts of the gray.

I tightened my grip on the two hilts. They were my anchor, my connection between the palace, the gates, and the gray. Lose it, and I might well lose myself, just as Cedric had.

As the pulsing of the two blades grew stronger under my grip, I reached for the indefinable energy of the gray. Mist swirled, thickened, briefly blocking my vision of the gate. The tempo of my heart increased, and an odd sort of weariness began to descend. I suddenly realized why using the gray when not wholly within it was so dangerous. It was calling on my strength—my connection with the earth—to interact with this world.

But to permanently close these gates, I had to keep a presence in both worlds, simply because I had no idea how to find individual gates within the gray. Not without physically standing in front of them, as past kings always had when it came to the main gate.

When the mist cleared, the gate was closed. Tendrils of gray clung to its rim and the deeply etched carvings glowed faintly, though whether that was a result of the gray or something else I couldn't say. The demons were screaming in terror, throwing themselves at the door, beating and tearing at it with fists and claws in an attempt to force it open.

I didn't linger to see if they succeeded but moved on to the other gates, repeating the process and closing them down one by one. By the time the fourth gate had been locked, sweat bathed my body, my limbs were shaking, and my heart beat so fast it felt like one long beat of pain.

But the message to my brother wasn't complete. There was one more thing I had to do.

Ignoring the burning in my lungs and the growing ache in my brain, I unleashed Nex. Her power—my power—coursed through Elysian, pulsing down the blade's steel into the earth; from there, it raced in an ever-widening arc, gathering the earth's heat as it arrowed toward the heavy pulse of darkness. This time, it didn't just work its way through cracks in the ground; it exploded. It was a deadly force of heat and fire that swept the stain of Darkside from a huge swath of the area around the palace, leaving only those in the air free.

I didn't attack them. I couldn't.

Consciousness was fading. *Life* was fading.

Somehow, I pried my fingers from the blades and fell back, staring up at the sky through bloody lashes, seeing nothing, hearing nothing beyond the strained pounding of my own heart.

The earth quivered a warning of approaching steps, then a figure appeared in my sightline.

Ricker.

He knelt beside me, his concern radiating from his body as he half reached out and then stopped. "Gwen? Can you hear me? Are you okay?"

"Yes." It was little more than a hoarse whisper, but in all honesty, that was more than I'd expected.

"Well, that was pretty fucking impressive. The way you dealt with Darkside—"

"It was more than just Darkside," I croaked. "I shut the fucking gates. Or, at least, the four closest to London."

He stared at me, his expression a mix of awe and disbelief. "Seriously?"

I half laughed, but it ended up coming out more a

gargled groan, as pain exploded through me. Damn it, *everything* hurt.

"I'm Elysian's wielder, Ricker, and she was designed to close gates. So yes, I'm serious."

He sucked in a breath and released it slowly. The awe didn't leave his expression, but the concern had deepened. "Do you need anything?"

"My knife."

I felt rather than saw his frown. "Which knife? You've two."

"Both."

No one but me would be able to remove Elysian from her sheath of asphalt, but the knives were another matter. While family legend might state only the firstborn female of each generation could use them, given how many other legends had proven untrue of late, I wasn't about to risk a stranger stealing them. The Blackbirds were unlikely to do so, but there were plenty of other people in the palace who might.

Distrust of my fellow witches had definitely sharpened abruptly since my brother's betrayal.

Footsteps vibrated through the ground as one of the Blackbirds gathered Nex. Ricker drew Vita from my belt and then placed both knives into my waiting hand. I closed my fingers around them, but it was Vita's blade I pressed flat against my chest. Her steel grew heated, and her golden glow infused the night's lingering shadows. This time, she wasn't drawing on my strength but rather connecting with the De Montfort healing ability that had lain dormant within me for so long, once again allowing me to do what no other De Montfort had—heal myself. Up to a point, anyway. She eased the dangerous weakness and slowed my unnaturally high heart rate, but I was too weak for the healing to go much further. To fully recover, I needed time and greater strength, and time, for me, was precious and finite.

I blinked away the drying tears of blood and slowly pushed into a sitting position. Ricker remained close, but the other Blackbirds were now looking up, their expressions uneasy. One quick look revealed why—the demons with the energy weapons were slowly but surely widening the portal's gap.

"Why is no one closing that?" I croaked, with a vague wave upward.

"From what comms are saying, those damn energy weapons are somehow feeding on the portal's edges. The more magic our witches pour into the portal to close it, the stronger the weapons become."

"I should have guessed the fuckers would not be easily deterred." I raised my free hand. "Help me up."

He did so easily but didn't release me, holding me steady as my knees threatened to buckle and the world spun crazily around me. I swallowed heavily and tucked the knives into my belt. As the wind stirred across my bare arms and whispered tales of the demons' retreat from other parts of London, seeking unclosed gates before the sun rose, I gathered her force around my fingers and then flung her, as hard as I could, toward the portal and demons beyond.

The surge of air was so fierce, it ripped me from Ricker's grip and sent me stumbling forward. I ended up on my knees again, grunting in pain and blinking back tears as I stared up at the whirlwind I'd created. It sucked up dirt and rubble and tore weapons from hands as it surged toward the portal. As it forced its way through the small gap, I raised a hand and splayed my fingers. The whirlwind responded, expanding rapidly, ensnaring the demons and whirling them around and around, smashing them into each other, shaking loose the weapons they held and then spitting them back out. Some tumbled into buildings, some were smashed into the ground, and others were simply flung toward the brightening horizon.

When there were no more demons left, I released my grip on the air. As the whirlpool disintegrated, the portal finally slammed shut. We were safe.

I sucked in a breath and dropped my head. I needed to move, needed to eat and rest, but I didn't even have the strength to hold my head up, let alone speak.

Steps vibrated through the ground again, then I was gently lifted and cradled against a body that was warm and strong but unfamiliar. Not Ricker. Someone else. An earth witch rather than a Blackbird. He quickly carried me from the courtyard, his weight on the earth light and even.

I blinked. While I wasn't physically connected to the ground at the moment, I was still receiving input from her. But was that so surprising? Mo didn't need to bare her feet to use the earth's energy, so this awareness might simply signify a deepening of the mage skills I'd inherited from her.

But the earth wasn't the only thing I remained linked to. Vita still pulsed, but this time, rather than drawing on the De Montfort healing ability, she was siphoning the energy of the man who carried me. And while it was extremely tempting to broaden the connection and ease the multitude of aches that still remained, it was too big a risk—for him rather than me. I might have closed the four closest gates, but there were plenty of others. Until I took Max out, the palace defenders would need to remain at full strength.

Of course, so did I, but at least Mo could zap some strength into me once we rendezvoused.

I was carried through the palace at speed—which gave

279

me little chance to study the glorious surroundings—and then caught a service elevator down a floor before heading through a dizzying maze of corridors. We ended up in a rather small but neat bedroom.

After lowering me onto the bed, the earth witch stepped back and said, "Would you like a meal brought to you?"

I hesitated, torn between the need to eat and the desperate desire to sleep. "Something hot in four hours would be great."

"I'll make sure it's arranged." He paused. "I'm afraid you're required to remain in this room—for safety reasons, you understand."

He meant the royal family's safety, rather than mine. "And if I need anything?"

He motioned to a small box on the wall. "Use the intercom."

"Thanks."

He nodded and headed out. I pulled out my phone and called Mo. She didn't answer, and though I knew she was probably concentrating on driving rather than answering the phone, trepidation stirred. While she'd been confident Winter couldn't take her down, it was rather odd he'd been on the move just as we'd arrived in London. We might not have any leaks within our small circle, but there were undoubtedly spies in the wider Ainslyn community. It was very possible that the minute we'd begun preparations for the city's protection, Darkside and Max had been notified.

I sent her a text to let her know I was okay and to contact me when she could, then tucked my knives under the pillow and stretched out on the bed. I was asleep within seconds.

A soft knock at the door woke me hours later. I cracked open an eye and watched a thin woman in a blue uniform carry in a tray. She placed it on the nearby nightstand and, after a quick curtsey, hurried back out. An unseen person closed the door behind her; they were obviously very serious about me not wandering about.

I scrubbed a hand across bleary, aching eyes and then swung my feet off the bed and walked over to the nightstand. Removing the plate covers revealed chunky beef stew, mashed potatoes, a ton of vegetables, and a big pot of tea. I poured the latter and took a drink, instantly feeling a whole lot better. Which was undoubtedly an illusion, but one I was going to run with.

My phone rang just as I was scooping up the last bit of the stew. The ringtone told me it wasn't Mo, Luc, or even Max, and the number wasn't one I knew. I hesitated, then hit the answer button.

"Gwen De Montfort speaking—"

"I know who it is" came the sharp, angry reply. "And rest assured, you're going to fucking pay for what you've done."

I tried to ignore the pain slicing through my heart, but it was nigh on impossible. "I don't know what you're referring to, Max, but—"

"Don't play the fucking innocent, Gwen, because I'm not buying it anymore."

"If you're talking about Elysian—"

"I'm talking about Winter. You didn't have to go that far. It could have been just you and me. But now? Now I'm going to fucking destroy every goddamn person you care about. Say goodbye to Mo, dear sister."

And with that, he hung up.

CHAPTER THIRTEEN

I swore and quickly hit Mo's number, but once again it rang out. I thrust a trembling hand through my hair. If Winter was dead, that meant something had gone seriously wrong, but it didn't necessarily follow that she was now in either Max's or Darkside's hands.

His threat could be nothing more than a means of forcing me into a misstep—making me act without proper planning or thought. I *did* have something of a history of that, after all, though I'd like to think I'd grown a little more sensible in recent weeks.

Although, if I was at all honest, acting irrationally was *all* I wanted to do right now.

I sucked in a breath and then hit Luc's number. Even if Max was foxing about Mo, I had no doubt he was about to unleash big-time. Whether that was throwing all his—or rather, Darkside's—resources at tracking down and killing Mo or hitting Ainslyn as hard as he could, Luc and the others needed to be prepared.

The phone rang for what seemed forever and then Luc's deep tone said, "Sorry, Gwen, I was dealing with a couple of tourists who decided today was the perfect day to visit King Island. How are you? And don't give me that 'I'm fine' crap."

I half smiled, despite the tension that continued to rise in me. "I'm bone weary, I've damaged a wing, so I can't fly, and I think I'll need to sleep for a dozen years once this is all over. But I'm alive and upright, and that's probably the best we could hope for at the moment."

"Well, I could personally hope for a whole lot more than that, but maybe that's just me. What's happened?"

"I'm not sure. Max just rang to say Winter is dead and I'm going to pay. I can't get hold of Mo, so something has obviously gone wrong."

Luc swore vehemently. "I'll get Barney to do a locator spell on her—"

"I doubt it'll be successful, because if she *is* alive, she'll have locked down any means of finding her. I'm off to our rendezvous point now, but I thought I'd better give you the heads-up first. It's likely Max will hit Ainslyn hard sometime in the next few hours."

"It won't matter, because they are ready for whatever the bastard throws at them."

"That sounds like you're not intending to be there."

"I won't be." He hesitated. "I've been ordered back to London."

Ice sliced through my heart. "Even after what I just did?"

"Even after." His voice was grim. Angry. "You may wield Elysian, but the Blackbirds' loyalty remains with the crown and the throne. Or so I'm reminded."

I closed my eyes. This was it. This was his moment of choosing. "And are you going to obey the order this time?"

He hesitated. "I swore an oath of allegiance to the

crown, Gwen. *This* crown, not the one that belongs to a throne and a time that no longer exists."

The Witch King's throne *did* actually exist, even if it was nothing more than a historical curiosity these days.

The Witch King's heir also existed, even if she would never sit on any throne, official or not.

"Three Blackbirds are dead," he continued softly. "Two more are seriously injured. I might be able to walk away from duty, but I cannot walk away from them."

I took a deep breath and released it slowly. There was nothing I could—or even should—say or do to change his mind. Vivienne had been plotting the course of our lives for a very long time now, and this decision—this choice—was his alone to make.

But it broke my heart to think that—if his words were to be believed—he was once again choosing duty over love.

"Fine." I scrubbed a hand across my eyes. My fingers came away wet. "But please be careful. The situation here is still very precarious."

"So Ricker has said." He paused again, this time for longer. "What do you plan to do next?"

"Go to the rendezvous point as planned." Despite my best effort to keep my voice even, an edge of anger ran through it. At him. At Max. At old goddesses and their stupid plans.

"Why? Even if Max has Mo, I'd put money on her never telling him the location."

"And I would have put money on him never being able to capture her." I tried my best to ignore the images of what he might be doing to her, even now, but the horror would not be restrained. I briefly closed my eyes and held on to the hope that she was a tough old bird who'd not only survived multiple centuries, but multiple attempts on her life. "Max will know I'll hold to the arrangements made if I can't contact her."

"That old farmhouse is the perfect location for a trap."

"Yes, it is." Because it was in the middle of nowhere and surrounded by empty fields. And arriving in daylight—as we'd planned—wouldn't make one bit of difference to Max if he did plan a trap there. At this late stage of the game, he had plenty of human and witch help to call on.

"Look," Luc said, voice low and urgent. Filled with desperate, frustrated anger. "There's an abandoned barn a mile and a half up from our rendezvous point—stop there and use the earth to check what might be going down at the old farmhouse. I'll get Barney and—"

"No," I cut in. "Under no circumstances are you to send anyone down. I do *not* want to be responsible for anyone else's death, Luc. Besides, this showdown was always destined to be just him and me."

"Weren't you the one who proclaimed it would never be just you and him? That Darkside would always be with him?"

"Yes, but I'm not stupid—"

"I never thought or suggested you were," he cut in, "but Mo's blood runs strong in you, and she's as headstrong and determined as they come. The only difference is, you don't have her years of sneakiness, or even the years of conniving and duplicity that Max has under his belt. *That* might just make the difference between winning and losing this fight."

"Even if I lose, he can't win. He can't raise Elysian."

"That's presuming what is written on the King's Stone is correct," Luc said. "We can't be sure it is, especially given the only man who truly knows has decided to remain in his den."

"Mo believes it, so I'm not about to gainsay her."

"I was just making a point—"

"I know, and I appreciate it, but you're going to have enough on your plate getting to London and protecting the crown to be worrying about me." I hesitated. "Be careful heading out of Ainslyn. It's likely Max has people watching what's going on there."

"They can't watch or follow someone they can't see."

"If he can capture a wily old mage, he can damn well unveil a Blackbird."

"I'll be careful," he said. "Just promise to do the same, Gwen. Remember, Mo's looking forward to grandbairns."

Grandbairns she wouldn't get from him and me. Not if he held to his current course. Vivienne had made past incarnations pay a heavy price for such a decision. I had no doubt she would do the same this time.

I hesitated, and then quickly said, "I love you, Luc Durant."

Because I could. Because it might be the *only* time I could. Because I was walking into a trap that may well take my life. Then I quickly hung up, giving him no chance to reply.

He didn't call back. Maybe he simply hadn't heard. Or maybe I'd misjudged the true depth of his feelings.

I tried Mo again, but she still didn't pick up. I did my best to quell the rising tide of anxiety and pressed the intercom. When a metallic-sounding voice answered, I asked if I could speak to Ricker as a matter of urgency. There was a small pause and then he said, "What do you need?"

"A means of getting out of the palace without being seen."

"You don't want to fly out?"

"I wish I could, but one of my wings was stripped of

flight feathers when I was coming in, and it'll take time for them to grow back."

"Well, that's damned inconvenient." He paused. "We're evacuating nonessential staff over the next couple of hours, so we can include you in that—"

"I'll need my own car."

"Which is doable." He hesitated. "What of your sword? And shoes? You weren't wearing any from memory."

"I'll need to have bare feet for the foreseeable future, but I'll grab Elysian on the way out."

"We're not departing through the front gates." There was a smile in his voice. "They're ceremonial only."

"Then I'll need to grab her before I leave."

"I'll make arrangements and be down to collect you shortly."

"Thanks."

I released the intercom button and then hit redial on the unknown number Max had called from. Unsurprisingly, he didn't answer, but a polite if somewhat metallic voice asked me to leave a message.

I obeyed. Impolitely.

"Brother, I know you're not stupid enough to kill Mo before you have me or Elysian, so let's cut the fucking bullshit and arrange an exchange. King Island, at dusk, tonight." My finger hovered briefly over the end call button before I added, "If you don't meet me, I'll shut every single fucking gate into Darkside. You now know that's not an idle threat, brother, so meet me. Or else."

Still no reply. I hit the end button and then rubbed my eyes wearily. If he'd planned to snare me at the farmhouse, then my demand for a meeting on King Island would be ignored. The question I couldn't answer was whether he'd work on the presumption that I'd realize the rendezvous point would be a trap, and plan accordingly. If he did, this could all go horribly wrong.

Which it probably would anyway.

Someone knocked sharply on the door, and I jumped.

"Yes?" I said, my voice holding just the hint of a squeak.

"It's Ricker, Gwen."

"Come in."

The door opened, and his gaze scanned me. It came up amused. "Not to be rude or anything, but you look like shit."

"A common state of affairs when it comes to me and lack of sleep," I said. "Is everything arranged?"

"Yes. This way." He turned and strode off down the hall.

I hastily grabbed my knives from under the pillow, tucking them into my belt as I ran after him. We moved through a multitude of silent corridors until we reached the service lift, then went up to the ground floor. After walking at speed back through the lavishly ornate rooms, we ended up in the archway that led to the forecourt and front gates.

Elysian remained where I'd left her, upright and half buried in the asphalt. Her plain hilt gleamed in the morning sunshine, and blue-white fire flickered and danced down her fuller. The Blackbird who stood guard over her half bowed as I approached and then stepped back. "No one has been near the blade, my queen."

A smile twisted my lips. "The queen resides in the palace, and that will never change. I'm merely Elysian's wielder."

"Technically, that *does* make you our queen."

"But not the queen you will protect."

His gaze shot to mine. "We cannot break our oath—"

I held up a hand, cutting off the rest. "I know. It's fine."

It wasn't, but there was little point in saying anything

else. The Blackbirds had their honor and their code, and it was too late to change anything now.

Ricker stopped beside me and regarded the sword for several seconds. "I have to admit, I expected something far more ornate."

"That's because most of the paintings depicting her in the hands of previous kings were of the false sword, not the real." I stepped forward, drew Elysian from the asphalt, and then swung the still-cloaked scabbard around and sheathed her. As the gray stole her from sight, I added, "The time of the witch kings is long gone—"

"Because we now have a queen." Ricker's smile flashed, full of cheek. "Or rather, Luc has."

"He may have chosen a queen, Ricker, but it wasn't me." Bitterness rolled through my reply, and I didn't really care. I swung around and motioned to the archway. "My car?"

"This way."

I followed him through another maze of rooms and ended up in a large underground parking area. Ten white passenger vans stood in a single file in front of the exit, their windows blacked out and armed guards standing at the ready as each one was loaded with men and women of various ages. There were three other vans to the right of this line, the back two with a driver and a guard standing at the ready but no passengers waiting. Ricker led me across to the van standing at the front of this smaller lot.

"You'll have to follow the convoy out initially, but once you're over the Thames—"

"The Thames?" I cut in. "Where are you taking the staff?"

"To a secure location outside of London." He smiled lopsidedly. "It's safer if you don't know."

"Safer for them, you mean."

"Yes. As I was saying, once you're over the river, you can leave the convoy. Jan and Mike will follow you for several miles to ensure there're no taggers and then will peel off. Hopefully, you'll be able to get to where you want to go without Darkside's operatives being any wiser."

I touched his arm lightly. "That's brilliant—thank you."

He nodded, opened the van's door, and then motioned me in. Thankfully, it was an automatic, rather than a manual drive, which meant gear changes were at least one less thing I had to worry about when maneuvering the van's bulk through some of London's smaller streets.

"There's a two-way on the passenger seat," he continued. "Mike will let you know when they're sure it's clear. Until then, don't head to your destination."

I nodded and pulled the seat belt on. "Good luck tonight."

"With the London gates closed and reinforcements on the way, we should be fine."

"There're still plenty of half-breeds out there."

"Yes, but will they dare risk attacking us when they can't be sure if Elysian's wielder remains inside?"

"Given my brother wants the queen and her family dead, there's a very good chance they will. Keep alert."

He nodded, his expression suggesting that was a given. "Your actions have at least given our witches time to regain strength. We can hold. Just don't take forever to bring your brother to account."

I couldn't help the bitter laugh that escaped. "Something that might be a bit easier to do if you lot held to your ancient vow to protect the witch king rather than the queen who currently sits on the throne. And hey, let's not forget that doing the former might actually achieve the latter."

He frowned. "Gwen—"

"Forget it, Ricker. I'll do what I can, but I can't promise anything more." With that, I grabbed the door and slammed it shut.

His expression was troubled and he clearly wanted to say more, but, in the end, he simply stepped back and motioned to the guards standing near the exit. The doors immediately opened, and the convoy came to life. I drove up behind the last van in the line and followed it through a long, somewhat winding tunnel, then up a ramp into the street. I had no immediate idea where we were, but I suspected it wasn't close to the palace.

Once we'd crossed the Thames and driven under a rail overpass, I set the GPS for my destination and followed its directions through the streets until I'd crossed back over the Thames and finally reached the M4 motorway out of London. Several miles along, the two-way squawked and a deep voice said, "You're clear of taggers, Ms. De Montfort. We'll leave you to it."

I picked up the device, hit the button, and said, "Thanks for letting me know. Good luck."

"You too."

They peeled off at separate exits, leaving me alone on the motorway. I concentrated on following directions and keeping to the speed limit, while trying not to let fear take hold every time a car or truck remained behind me for too long.

Roadworks and an accident meant the two-hour journey drifted out to nearly three, so by the time I took the Pucklechurch exit, my anxiety levels were through the roof. I drove along a myriad of smaller roads and lanes until I neared our rendezvous point—a small farmstead surrounded by fallow fields. I didn't stop, instead studying the old stone building as I crawled past. I couldn't see anything untoward or out of place, but that didn't really mean anything. If Max and his people were there, it wasn't like they'd be waving flags or otherwise drawing attention to themselves.

I took a deep breath that did nothing for the tension riding me and continued on until I found the abandoned barns Luc had mentioned. Once I'd driven into the largest of them, I stopped and climbed out. Half of the old barn's roof was missing, and the bit that remained had obviously been a roost for multiple generations of birds. The grimy, straw-covered dirt floor was decorated with cowpats, some of which were fairly recent, suggesting it was still used as a shelter for livestock in the more inclement weather.

I looked around for a manure-free area and then dug my toes into the straw until I hit the earth. Her pulse rose to meet me, but held no immediate sense of threat. There *was* the faintest whisper of movement in the distance, but I had no idea whether it was human or animal.

I switched my attention to the breeze that whistled gently through multiple gaps in the building's fabric. Her whispers held little information about the distant movement, suggesting it was inside rather than out. There was, however, a car approaching.

My heart skipped several beats and then raced on. It wasn't beyond the bounds of possibility that Max had seen the van go past and sent someone to investigate.

I grabbed my knives, then walked over to the barn's doorway and squatted in the shadows of roof rubble that lay to the right. It gave me a good view of the road and the driveway, while still remaining hidden.

The inner tension was now so bad my muscles were quivering. Or maybe that was fear. The wind kept me apprised of the vehicle's location, but she couldn't tell me who was driving the thing. If I survived this—if Mo survived this—the first thing I was going to get her to teach me was how to get more information from the whispers of the earth and air.

An old Ford Estate appeared. It stopped briefly and then swung into the driveway. My grip tightened on Nex's hilt, but there was no response from her. As the Estate drew closer, it became evident why—it was Luc.

My heart leapt, and tears stung my eyes.

He'd come here. Despite his orders and the oath he'd made, he'd come here rather than to London.

He'd chosen me. Chosen love over duty.

And suddenly, winning this battle and saving Mo in the process actually seemed possible.

He pulled into the barn and stopped next to the van. I tucked my knives into my belt and then walked around the rear of the vehicle and threw myself into his waiting arms. I pressed my cheek against his broad chest, closed my eyes, and reveled in not only the warm wash of his strength across my senses, but the steady beat of his heart and the tender way in which he held me. I felt safe and loved and utterly secure, and I wished I could simply stay like this forever.

But I had a grandmother to find and a brother to stop, before there was any possibility of *that* happening.

I sighed regretfully and pulled back a little without leaving the circle of his arms. "What happened to London?"

"Nothing. It's still there as far as I'm aware."

I gave him the look. "You know what I meant."

"Yes, I do, and you can blame the crown." He lifted my chin and studied me intently for a second or two. "You look like shit."

"Stop avoiding the question."

A smile tugged at his lovely lips. "Not long after our phone call, the crown and the ring came to life. From what Ricker has said, it happened around the same time as you drawing Elysian from the palace courtyard. It made me remember an off-the-cuff comment an old lecturer once made about Elysian being part of a triad, rather than the sole power that many presume."

"You could have sent Barney or anyone else to deliver them. You didn't have to bring them here yourself."

"I did, but not because of the damn crown or ring or triad of power. You said you loved me, and then you fucking hung up. How could I let a statement like that go unanswered?"

A laugh escaped, even as my heart swelled. "So you drove all the way down here just to give me a response?"

"I had no other option."

And with that, he kissed me. It was heart and soul, love and yearning, the past and the future, all rolled up in one deep, mind-blowing kiss.

"Gwen De Montfort," he whispered eventually, his breath hot and heavy on my lips, "you have stolen my heart and turned my world upside down with your craziness, and I cannot imagine life without you. So you had better survive the battle that's coming, or I'm going to be extremely pissed off."

I laughed and hugged him. He returned it fiercely but all too briefly, then stepped back and pulled his phone from his pocket. "I'm under instructions to report back the minute I arrive."

"Ginny?" I said with a smile.

"No, Mia. As I said, she's swiftly usurped all other members of the council to become Barney's second—a position I think she'll retain once this is all over."

"I wouldn't be at all surprised." Barney had been trying to get younger people onto the council for a while, and Mia had certainly been looking for something new to tackle.

He dialed the number and then put the call on speaker so I could hear it.

"Luc?" It was Ginny who answered, and she sounded slightly breathless. "Everything okay? Is Gwen there?"

"I am," I replied. "Why are you puffing?"

"Been acting as runner between the map room and the forces up top."

Luc frowned. "Why not just use the phone?"

"Because a number of cell towers have been damaged. I'm damn surprised this call even got through."

My gut clenched. "So Ainslyn's under attack?"

"Yes, but at this point, they're not hitting the business district or the port."

"Is the shield holding?" Luc asked. "Are there any casualties?"

"I daresay there are, given the number of folk who wouldn't listen to reason and evacuate to either shelter point. But the shield is holding, and their regular weapons aren't as yet making much of an impact. We've also had word that the military are on their way." Her voice gained an edge as she added, "Of course, the entire situation might change once the dark elves and demons come out to play tonight. You heard from Max yet?"

"No," I said. "And I doubt I will. I think a trap has been set at the rendezvous point."

"Meaning Mo still hasn't contacted you?"

"No."

"That's not like her."

"I know." I drew in a breath in an effort to calm the

angst. "I need you or Mia to tell me what the map says about the area around Pucklechurch."

"Mia!" she instantly yelled, just about deafening the two of us even though the phone was nowhere near either of our ears. "Any demon or half-breed activity at Pucklechurch?"

There was a long pause through which footsteps echoed, and then Mia said, "There wouldn't be demons at this hour, natch, but at least two dozen of those lighter hot spots we think are half-breeds. There's two rings of them, and I would think one is surrounding the farmhouse."

"More than likely," Luc replied. "Ginny, can you take a photo and send it to me? Also, if those hot spots move in any way, can you text us and let us know?"

"Done." She paused. "Don't trust Max, Gwen. Not in any damn way."

The smile that twisted my lips was bitter. "I think he burned away any remnants of trust when he handed me over to Darkside."

"You say that, but he's still your twin, and that's a hard connection to sever. Believe me," she added, "I've attended far too many family disputes that have turned deadly simply because one party held on to love rather than trust their gut and common sense."

Which in many respects was an echo of what Winter had said and a possibility I still couldn't deny, no matter how much I wanted to. But at least I didn't have all that much longer to find out if, in the end, womb kinship was stronger than my love for Mo.

"I'll send the pic through now and keep you updated on movements," she said.

"Thanks, Ginny," Luc said and hung up.

The phone pinged as the image came through. We

studied it for several seconds and then Luc said, "Are you getting any indication from the earth on what may wait inside the house?"

"Not with my mage powers, and I dare not use Elysian in case she sets off an echo in his sword."

Luc frowned. "What makes you think that's possible?"

"When I was on that bridge, just before Max arrived, Elysian and his sword appeared to perceive each other."

"Was she in the gray?"

"Only partially."

"Even so, it shouldn't have been possible." His frown deepened. "What sort of distance are we talking about?"

I hesitated. "Can't really say. Not that far, but I don't think we can afford to take the chance."

"No, I guess not." He scraped a hand across his bristly jaw. "Maybe you should avoid the place and let me—"

"You know that's never going to happen, so why even mention it?"

His cheeks puffed out, frustration evident. "Because every now and again, my protective instincts kick in."

"They should know better by now, especially when Mo is in danger."

"They should, but they don't."

"I'm Elysian's wielder, and I have no choice but to be in this fight."

"I know." He sighed and then reached into the car and pulled out the crown and the coronation ring, handing them to me. "I'll take care of the outer circle of half-demons; you go in through the gate and take out the inner one. We'll meet in the middle and go hard and fast into the house."

My stomach did a series of vicious flip-flops. "You make it sound so damn easy."

"It won't be, and we both know it." He touched a hand

to my face, his fingers oh-so gentle. "But as you said, you're Elysian's wielder *and* Mo's granddaughter. Max has no idea of your true strength."

I half laughed, though it came out a somewhat strangled sound. "After London, he'll damn well suspect."

"When it comes to Elysian and the gates, yes, but he has no clue just how much power you personally wield."

That was also doubtful, given the lightning I'd flung at him on the bridge. But there was little point in saying anything when we'd find out soon enough.

Luc tilted my face, kissed me so deeply that my heart ached, and then stepped back. His eyes were vivid pools of caring and worry. "I'll send a text when I'm near the first of the outer ring's hot spots. We'll hit them at the same time, and hopefully without an alarm being raised."

I nodded even as I suspected neither hope nor luck would play in our favor this afternoon.

He hesitated, his expression briefly conflicted, as if he wanted to add or do something, then he simply stepped around me and strode purposely out the door. The light immediately wrapped around his body and stole him from sight, leaving me feeling more alone and uncertain than I had in ages.

I sucked in a breath, mentally told myself to get a grip, then glanced down at the crown. There was no life in it at the moment, no power, but maybe there wouldn't be until I gripped Elysian. I hooked it onto my belt and then tugged the ring off the chain and slipped it onto my finger. Despite it looking far too big, it fit like a glove.

An old mage's magic, I thought. Or maybe even an old goddess's.

I took a deep breath and then made my way out of the barn and down to the road. The hedgerow was tall enough that I could barely see the farmhouse's red-tiled roof, which at least meant that if someone *had* been watching the road, they weren't likely to spot me. Not from this distance, anyway.

I began the long trek back to the farm, keeping to the middle of the road simply because it was easier on my bare feet. Thankfully, there was no traffic and it was mostly downhill. Once I was close to the old farm, I drew Nex and gripped her tightly. Her blade remained quiet, which at least meant none of the half-bloods were lying in wait near the gate. It *didn't* mean there couldn't be humans or even a magical trap of some kind there, of course. Tris wouldn't have been the only full-blood witch working for my brother.

The hedgerow gave way to a neatly trimmed lime-yellow conifer hedge that led up to an old wooden gate and then lined one side of the driveway that swept around to the right. There was nothing parked in the graveled parking area and no indication the house was occupied. Nor was there any smoke coming from either of the two chimneys on the main section of the house. Although the day had warmed a fraction, it certainly wasn't the sort of weather in which you could forgo a fire.

I studied the open gateway for several seconds but couldn't see any evidence of a trap, be it magical or physical. I should be immune to the former, of course, but I didn't dare take any chances. I moved on cautiously, keeping to the grassed area between the driveway and the well-trimmed hedge to protect my feet. The farmyard was still—the only sign of movement was the line of cows slowly walking toward a stone barn in the field beyond the parking area. But they, like the area in general, were silent.

But it was a silence that held an edge of expectation.

I tightened my grip on Nex's hilt, and she pulsed in response. Ready for action, even if I wasn't.

The conifer hedge came to an end. I stopped, pressed back into the foliage, and studied the old farmhouse warily. It was T-shaped, with the middle section double-story and the rest single. There were no windows on the end closest to me, but the tail of the T was obviously an older barn that had been annexed onto the farmhouse and then restored. A long line of full-height windows ran the length of the building on the side facing me, which meant the minute I went anywhere near that section, I'd be seen. Presuming, of course, I hadn't already.

The map had said there were two rings, but the whispers of the air suggested the inner ring was really three distinct clusters of men.

My phone vibrated against my thigh and made me jump. I quickly dug it out of my pocket and saw a message from Luc. It simply said, *ready when you are.*

My gut churned, and I swallowed heavily, though it did little to ease the sudden dryness in my throat. I sent back, *Meet you at the front door,* then shoved the phone away and squatted on my haunches. The earth pulsed under my splayed fingertips, whispering of the weights that pressed so heavily against her. There was one group behind the barn, a second out of sight at the back of the house, and the third ... Shock froze my breath in the back of my throat.

The third was barely ten feet away, on the other side of the hedge.

I silently swore and plunged Nex into the ground. Lightning rolled through me, through her, and then into the ground, shooting out with deadly force to the five men who silently approached. They stood no chance. The lightning arced from the ground, becoming a deadly web of energy that spun around their bodies, incinerating them in an instant. But their ashes never touched the ground. The wind grabbed them, examined them.

That wind wasn't natural, and it certainly wasn't mine.

Max knew I was here.

The air picked up strength and volume, whipping around me, tearing at my clothes and hair.

There was little point in being subtle now.

I raised a hand, gripped the turbulent air, and flipped it around, creating a wide whirlpool of wind, dirt and debris that roared around me, not only battering away Max's attack, but also tearing apart the gorgeous old hedge.

I didn't wait to see my brother's response—though I could feel it in the air, in the sudden drop of temperature and the thick gathering of clouds overhead. I ripped Nex from the ground and ran, as hard as I could, toward the house.

Men came at me from behind the old barn. I raised Nex, called to the lightning, and flung it at them.

It was bounced away before it got anywhere near them.

Horror surged. Max had found a way to counter my lightning.

I swore, drew Elysian, and ran straight at the five men. I had no idea whether or not they could see me, but they could certainly see the whirlpool of debris that surrounded me. Two slid to a stop while the other three jumped left and right, as if to attack me from either the side or from behind. I flung wind their way, smashing one into the barn wall and tossing the other two high into the air and deep into the field. As my gaze returned to the remaining two men, I saw the guns. I swore, flicked a finger of wind at them, and snatched the weapons from their grasps. As one, they turned and ran.

I couldn't afford to let them escape, if only because they might come back with heavily armed reinforcements.

I snared them with the wind and drew them back into the whirlpool. Then, with a quick flick of the sword, I killed them, slicing their bodies open from neck to toe. As their screams abruptly died and their blood colored the whirlpool, I became aware of the sudden sharpening of electricity and the thick, almost metallic scent in the air.

I swore, let the wind drop, and dove into the barn.

Not a moment too soon.

A bolt of lightning as thick as my arm hit the ground where I'd been standing only seconds before and fused the dirt into glassy black rock.

Maybe Max had decided killing me might be the easier option.

I scrambled upright and, as thunder rumbled ominously overhead, thrust Elysian into the ground, pressed Nex against her hilt, and once again used the earth's awareness of those who walked with darkness to direct the lightning into the ground.

Eight more halflings were ashed. Max obviously hadn't been aware of *that* little trick, because the magic protecting his people wrapped around their bodies but not the ground. He *had* protected the house, however, because I was getting little more than an odd sense of deadness from its entire footprint.

Another warning rumble of thunder. I sucked in a deep breath, silently prayed for luck, and then ran, with every ounce of speed I could muster, toward the end of the house.

Close to the halfway point, I spotted something glinting in gravel and realized it was one of the guns. I scooped it up and ran on. I had no idea how to use one, but I wasn't about to leave it just lying there for someone else to pick up, either.

The end of the house loomed, and the magic protecting the inner walls washed over my senses, a thick slide of foulness that flayed my skin. Horror surged. Not because the foulness told me there were dark elves within the building, but because my skin actually *reacted* to it.

Me, who was immune to magic, reacting to a *spell*.

Fear hit so hard that I stumbled several steps and had to throw out a hand to stop from crashing head-first into the wall. The slimy threads I could sense but not see rolled across my fingers, making them burn and itch. Vita immediately responded and the reaction eased, but it was still a horrifying realization. If they'd found a way to counter my natural immunity then I was in deep, *deep* trouble. At least Vita, for the moment, seemed able to counter the spell's intention, and that meant I had better keep her out of sight and safe.

I swung Elysian's scabbard around and thrust Vita into her. The gray immediately swept her from sight, but her faint pulse nevertheless echoed across my senses. Hopefully, I'd be able to access her if necessary.

I sucked in an unsteady breath, then shoved the gun into my belt at the back of my jeans. I had no idea if the safety was on, no idea if one wrong movement would set the damn thing off, but having it close to hand made me feel a tiny bit safer.

Overhead, the thunder rumbled ominously, and the thick scent of sulfur once again charged the air. But the heavy black clouds weren't gathering above the farmhouse; they were rather racing off to the left. It was only then that it occurred to me—if Max had found a way to protect his forces from Nex's lightning, it was also possible he'd uncovered a means of seeing a Blackbird wrapped in light.

I dragged out my phone and sent a quick warning to Luc. He didn't answer but if he was in the middle of a battle, he was unlikely to. I just had to hope he saw it before that damn storm hit.

With another unsteady breath, I held Elysian out in front of me and padded to the front of the building. A quick peek around the corner revealed no guards, and there was no immediate sign of any other spells. Not that they needed any, given the power in that foul wave.

I took a cautious step out to look at the windows. They'd all been boarded. Max really *had* prepared his trap well, and it was, I suspected, one I'd have to step into whether I liked it or not.

A huge crack of thunder made me jump, and my gaze darted out to the field. Several bolts of lightning struck a stand of trees, and someone screamed—a sound that was cut off by a secondary fork. Fear closed my throat as I stared at the smoking ruins of the trees and hoped—with all my might—that Luc hadn't been standing in them. The scream hadn't come from his throat, but if he'd been attacking the cluster of men hiding there he would, at the very least, have been injured by the strike's monstrous force.

I scanned the fields again, looking for that vague shift in light that indicated his presence. If he *was* out there, I couldn't see him. I sent another text, but wasn't surprised when there was no reply. I hoped it meant he was simply tracking around to the final cluster rather than being injured or worse. Either way, I couldn't wait.

Time was running out for Mo.

The sudden certainty didn't come from fear, but from the earth itself. Perhaps our joint connection was providing me with a sense of her well-being, even if I wasn't getting anything else in the way of information, thanks to the slimy wall protecting the farmhouse's interior and its occupants.

My grip on Elysian's hilt tightened to the point that my fingers ached and my knuckles glowed. Lightning flickered down her fuller, blue-white snakes that struck and hissed at the empty air. She was ready for the final battle. I wished I could say the same.

That same light echoed in the coronation ring's stone.

I glanced down at the crown attached to my belt. It too glowed. The triad of power was ready for action.

I briefly closed my eyes, gathered the thinning threads of my courage, and then softly padded up the stone steps and to the front door. The oily slick continued to roll silently past, and there was no sound coming from within the building. Only the magic suggested there was something untoward waiting within.

That, and the growing sense of elation in the air.

I shifted Elysian to my left hand and then slowly reached out to grip the door handle. The magic slid across my fingers, stinging my flesh for several quick heartbeats before Vita's heat once again washed the worst of it away.

Even so, that brief touch was enough time to understand the slick wasn't, as I'd initially thought, meant to physically hurt me. It had been designed to render me—or perhaps the knives—powerless.

Nex still pulsed, which was at least something, but there was no guarantee that wouldn't change once I stepped inside. I frowned at the door, then stepped back, gripped the wind, and flung it at the both the doors and the windows. Nothing happened. The air's energy slid away from the building like oil on water. The slick magic hadn't only been designed to stop my magic but also elemental.

Meaning I had absolutely no choice but to spring this trap.

Mo's life force was steadily growing weaker. I had no idea what Max or the dark elves had done to her, but I needed to get in there and find out. Fast.

I took one look over my shoulder, uselessly scanning for the man I knew was nowhere near and who wouldn't be able to accompany me even if he was, then turned and flung the door open.

"Well, didn't you take your damn time" came a heart-breakingly familiar voice. "Please don't stand on ceremony in the doorway, dear sister—come on in and close that door."

CHAPTER FOURTEEN

"And why would I do that, brother dearest," I responded, somehow keeping my voice even, "when there are dark elves in there with you?"

"Your magic is stronger than I expected if you can sense the presence of elves over that spell."

Meaning I'd been right in thinking the spell had been designed to restrict my magic. "It's not magic, brother, but rather common old sense of smell. They stink."

He snorted. "Something you'll get used to soon enough. Come in."

"Why don't you come out? Or is the would-be king afraid to face his sister without his guards?"

"If you do not come in," he said, the slightest edge in his voice betraying the anger I could almost taste. "Mo dies."

His threat had my heart leaping, but I didn't move. Though I couldn't see him or the dark elves from where I stood, his voice was coming from the right of the door—no doubt to ensure he wasn't within range of any regular weapon I might be holding.

"And how," I said, voice still even despite the fear and fury roiling inside, "do I know she isn't already dead, given your earlier threat?"

"A fair enough question. I guess asking you to trust me is out of the question these days?"

"Yeah," I said. "It is."

He sighed. It was a strangely sad sound. "Then you shall get your proof. Lads, stand back."

There was a shuffle of movement, then light flared—a round, yellow-white beam that revealed Mo's pale and bloody face. She might have been captured, but she'd obviously gone down fighting.

"How could you do that to her?" I ground out. "She damn well raised you!"

"Yes, and there *is* a part of me that's sorry she was treated so abominably. But she did kill quite a number of my people and it left them with little choice but to take physical action."

"What the fuck has happened to you, Max?" The question was out before I could stop it. "When did you become everything I absolutely and utterly abhor?"

That struck a nerve. I might not have been able to see him, but his emotions were so sharp they could have been my own.

And yet, the one thing I didn't feel in that fierce wave was regret.

He might hate that I hated him, but he didn't regret one single thing he'd done ... or would do.

I'd thought there was no love left in me for him, but I'd been wrong. It had been buried deep, to be sure, but it had existed, praying for a miracle while still stubbornly believing that if I confronted him, I might somehow reach the man I'd grown up loving and believing in.

But this wasn't that man.

This was a stranger wearing his form.

A stranger who *wasn't* wraith infected, because even if he'd drawn a fake, it was still a creation of light rather than darkness. He wouldn't have been able to wield her if he had been infected.

I sucked in a breath and, for the first time since this whole mess had begun, felt free.

Free to do what had to be done.

I studied Mo again, this time looking beyond the injuries and her bruised and bloody state. Her eyes were closed, and there was no indication she knew I was here. She hadn't reacted to the sound of my voice, hadn't moved, hadn't done anything at all to indicate awareness. She breathed, which was at least something, and there was no sign of the shimmer that had indicated the wraith infection in Luc's sister. That at least was good, but it didn't really provide a whole lot of comfort. Something had to be wrong for her to be this still, this silent.

I narrowed my gaze and, after a moment, spotted the magic. It was a dark thread of evilness that not only surrounded her, but also wrapped tightly around her throat. One solitary thread ran off from this into the darkness, and I had no doubt it somehow connected her and Max, and definitely not in a good way.

"What have you done to her?" I growled, my fingers tightening on Elysian's hilt. Energy flickered briefly down her blade, a sharp warning of the fury waiting to be unleashed. "What is the magic that leashes her?"

"That," he answered, "is my guarantee. Kill me, and she will also die."

It felt as if someone had reached in, grabbed my heart, and ripped it from my chest. I couldn't breathe, couldn't think, could only stare at the woman who'd raised me and who meant everything to me.

An ungodly choice now faced me—to stop him, to stop Darkside, I'd have to kill the one person I cared about more than life itself.

"Come inside," he continued blithely. "Or do you need a demonstration on just how effective the spell is?"

"No."

It was a short, sharp bark, and he laughed. "Then move, sister, or else."

I obeyed. As I passed through the spell, fierce heat hit my body, burning across my skin and leaving a trail of itchy uneasiness behind. Neither of the knives reacted, and though I could feel their distant thrumming, their blades remained quiet. Whether that would change if I held them, I had no idea and, right now, no intention of finding out. It was better if Max believed the spell was working.

"Now close the door," he continued.

Once again I obeyed, though my grip on Elysian's hilt was now so fierce her light peeled back the immediate darkness. The crown responded to that energy, shooting thin beams of light into the corners of the room. Multiple hisses filled the air, and the rapid shuffling of steps echoed. The Darksiders, desperate to avoid the searchlight-like sweeps of light.

It was tempting, so damn tempting, to feed more energy into that pulse, but I resisted. I couldn't risk him doing any more damage to Mo. Not until I knew for sure he was telling the truth.

"I see you have the crown," he said, almost conversationally.

As if he had all the time in the world and all the right cards.

From his point of view, I guess he did.

"I did steal it from your people, brother, so why does that surprise you?"

He smiled. It made my heart ache. "I'm just surprised you dared bring it here, but it does at least save me the trouble of trying to find it once you're back in Darkside hands. Now, drop the sword."

My gaze darted his way. He stood half in, half out of Elysian's light, dressed in dark jeans and a natty, three-quarter length dark blue coat, the cut of which was somewhat spoiled by the strap of the sheathed sword that had been slung sideways across his back. Not a position from which he'd be able to draw her easily, but maybe he didn't need to. Maybe he could use the fake without actually drawing her.

"I won't fucking do anything else until I know for sure Mo's not already dead."

"As you said in your message, Gwen, I'm not foolish enough to kill my one ace before I got everything I needed."

"Just because I said it doesn't mean I actually believed it."

His gaze narrowed. "Drop. The. Sword."

"Proof. Of. Life," I echoed, then quickly added, "But hey, if you want to risk a repeat of the London mess, I'm more than happy to comply."

He studied me for several seconds, the silver in his blue eyes shining brightly in Elysian's gleam. It added an edge of coldness to his face—a face that was still as handsome as ever. I really wished it were otherwise. Wished his looks matched the blackness that had consumed his soul.

"Fine," he eventually said, and made a motion with his free hand. It was only then I noticed he wasn't holding the end of that dark thread; it had instead been inserted directly into the veins at his wrist.

Dear *god*, he was siphoning her strength and maybe even her magic.

I took an involuntary half step forward and then forced myself to stop. To remain calm. To watch rather than react, even if that was the hardest thing I'd ever had to do in my life so far.

Energy stirred around his wrist, then some sort of electrical charge ran down the thread and around Mo's neck. Her body jumped and twitched for several seconds and then her eyes slowly opened. For several, gut-wrenching seconds, they were entirely blank. There was no recognition —no situational awareness—within.

Then her gaze focused and came to mine. Love, regret, determination, and most of all pride shone so fiercely in her eyes that I had to blink back tears. She opened her mouth and attempted to say something, but it took several seconds before she succeeded.

"Do," she said, her voice a mere husk of its usual self, "what's necessary."

No, no, no, I wanted to scream. *I can't. I won't.*

But my gaze remained locked on hers, and I nodded, a movement so small I doubted my brother would have even seen it. A smile tugged at the corner of her lips, and the pride and love in her eyes grew.

I wanted to cry.

Wanted to raise Elysian and end my brother's life, right here and now.

But that oily slick and the presence of the dark elves very much suggested that the minute I even attempted such a move, Mo wouldn't be the only one to die.

If that *was* going to be my fate today, I was damn well going to ensure Max got there before me.

The electrical charge reversed, and Mo's awareness slipped away. I sucked in an uneven breath and returned my gaze to my brother. I wasn't sure what he saw in my eyes, but he actually retreated a step before he stopped himself.

"Now," he said, the anger more visible this time. "Drop that sword."

I didn't. Instead, I drove her into the flagstones. "If you want her, you can come and get her."

His narrowed gaze swept me. "Drop your knives."

I tugged Nex free and flung her down. Her point hit the flagstones close to Elysian's blade, but rather than bouncing away, she too slid hilt-deep into the stone. The pulse of her energy echoed through the earth and back into my feet.

The oily energy restricted neither weapon. Not when they were in contact with the earth, at any rate.

I schooled the relief from my features and returned my gaze to my brother. "Anything else?"

"Where's the other knife? There're usually two."

"One was destroyed in London."

He studied me, eyes narrowed. It was obvious he didn't really believe me, but then, he was my twin. We might not share a telepathic link, but we often didn't need to.

"Turn around."

Damn—there went any hope of using the gun as a backup weapon. I once again obeyed, and he chuckled softly. "Do you even know how to use a gun?"

"No, but I figured that if the worse came to the worst, I could beat you over the head with it."

"As if you would ever get that close. Place it on the ground, kick it away, and then step back."

After I'd sent it sliding off to the Darksiders haunting the shadows to the left, I took one step back. No more. No less.

"Gwen, you're being tiresome—"

"If you want the fucking sword, come over here and get it," I ground out. "I have no damn weapons, and dark elf magic scrolls the room. What the hell do you think I'm going to do?"

"Nothing, but recent history has proven it's ill-advised to take appearances at face value."

I snorted. "That suggests you're afraid of me, brother. Or is it more a fear of confirming you are not and never will be the true witch king?"

His anger surged, telling me that's exactly what he feared. But, after a moment, he moved forward. The tension in the air ramped up, and the viscosity of the oily slick increased, burning across my skin with greater fervor, making my muscles dance and twitch. Vita's warmth wasn't countering it, but I made no move to deepen our connection. I just watched and waited.

Max stopped within arm's reach of Elysian but didn't immediately reach for her. The light burning down her blade was fierce, white, and angry, and Max's sword retaliated in kind. The purple-black light I'd noticed on the bridge was stronger than before. Was the stain of the hand that had drawn it forever altering its energy? Sadly, the only person who could actually answer that question had decided abandoning us was the best option for *his* future comfort. If Mo didn't give that bastard a piece of her mind, I certainly would. *If* we both survived, that was.

I continued to watch my brother, my expression passive, even if every muscle vibrated with the angry need to retaliate. After several more seconds, he slowly reached out with the hand that wasn't leashed to Mo. As his fingers curled around Elysian's hilt, she burned brighter, and my heart stuttered in horror. Had the damn warning on the King's Stone been false after all? Or had the fact we were twins voided it?

The pulsing light flickered toward his fingers, but neither rejected nor accepted his grip. Relief flickered across his features as he dropped his gaze to Elysian and tried to pull her from the floor.

I lunged forward, wrapped my hands over the top of his, and pushed us both into the gray. We crossed dimensions so fast, it left me breathless and aching. But at least in this place the oily slick no longer existed and the dark elves weren't a threat. There was just Max and me in an echo of reality filled with ethereal, otherworldly power.

Only that echo now resembled King Island. We were standing within the monolith circle atop of the island's grass-covered ridge, and the stones glowed with the same fierce light that now beat in the heart of the sword, the crown, and the ring.

A fourth power burned to life at my spine and filled me with strength. Vita was here with me.

I raised my gaze to Max's and saw no fear, just confusion.

"How the fuck did we get back to the island?"

"We're not," I said. "You wanted to raise the king's sword, brother. You wanted to know and understand her power. Well, look around. This is what you hungered for. What you betrayed all that you valued and loved for. An empty echo of all that earth is."

His gaze swept across the gray. "But it's not empty. It's far from empty."

It was then I realized he didn't understand that the

cosmic forces that flowed so easily around us could only be used safely with Elysian's aid.

"It's ... amazing." He reached out and touched the nearest power-ridden ribbon. Elysian pulsed under our joint grip, and the ribbon's energy washed through us, sharp, energizing, and utterly, terrifyingly unworldly. Flesh was never meant to contain that sort of power.

Max's gaze widened. He wasn't seeing the danger. He was only seeing the power. The possibilities.

I released one hand from Elysian's hilt, reached back, and called Vita to me.

"Dear god, Gwen," Max whispered. "This is beyond anything I could have ever—"

I'll never know whether he sensed Vita's presence or the subtle change in my stance. It didn't matter either way, because without warning his grip on the ribbon tightened and he flung it at me. It hit with the force of a hammer, cindering my senses and leaving me gasping. Another ribbon hit, pushing me back, all but tearing my grip from Elysian. I somehow caught the end of the cross-guard and clung on, desperately attempting to regain balance.

He growled—a low, almost inhuman sound that echoed across the silence—and whipped around, the side of his boot smashing into my face, tearing my grip from the sword and sending me tumbling backward. Something cracked in my cheek and blood spurted. I swore, but the words caught in my throat, as did my breath. For one brief moment, the force of this place swept through me, tearing at me, pulling me apart, pulling me to pieces.

Then light pulsed from my finger and my waist—the crown and the ring, reestablishing the connection to Elysian, protecting me from the forces that would have otherwise killed me.

A heartbeat later, Vita came to life, her force thrumming through me, sweeping away the pain, but not the fury.

I scrambled upright and ran at him. He laughed, gripped Elysian tighter, and tried to raise her. She moved.

An inch.

Two.

Then she froze. He wasn't the Witch King's heir. He didn't have the right to draw her.

That realization hit him hard, and he screamed—a sound filled with denial and fury. He released her hilt and reached, with both hands, for the gray's energy.

"No!" I yelled and lunged for him.

I reached him the same time as the energy he'd called into his body. It tore through him, tore through me, through flesh and muscle and bone, until once again it felt as if every fiber of my being were being stretched beyond capacity and would surely shatter into a million tiny pieces. But just before the dissolution of all that we were and all that we could be actually happened, the triad reacted, and the shattering ceased. Then Vita pulsed, and energy flowed back into my limbs. She was drawing on Max's strength through my grip on him. Draining him to save me.

I couldn't let him die here, even if I'd brought him here to do exactly that. But that was before I'd felt the purity of this place—the utter perfection of its energy—through every inch of my being. Mo had been right—his death would forever stain the gray.

I took a deep breath, then plunged Vita into his neck, severing an artery—a wound that wouldn't immediately kill him, though he would eventually bleed out unless helped—to strengthen the connection between him, her, and me. As warmth pulsed over the hand holding the knife, I reached for Elysian with the other. The minute my fingers wrapped around her hilt, I pushed us all away from the gray and back into the old farmhouse.

We tumbled to the flagstones in a tangled mess of arms and legs. There was a roar, a rumble of sound, and I became aware of movement, of anger, and magic. Something—someone—pounded at the door, and the oily wave of magic was weakening.

But not quickly enough.

Nowhere near quickly enough.

I pushed free from Max's weight, then rose onto my knees and swung Elysian in an arc over my head. Steel clashed with steel, the sheer force of the blow reverberating down my arms. Light flared down her fuller and peeled away the shadows, revealing thin, pale gray-skinned men with gaunt features and pointed ears.

Dark elves. Ten of them. Max really hadn't been taking any chances.

Movement, behind me. I swept Elysian around and up. Caught the edge of a blade and knocked it away. Reached for the earth, felt her fire respond. It burned through me as the gray's energy had only moments before, but I didn't immediately release it, instead channeling it into the blade and then beyond. Elves screamed as others attacked, forcing me to throw myself down and away. I heard a crash as the door was flung open and saw booted feet run in, accompanied by the unholy screaming of a blade. Luc, wielding Hecate, in the room and wiping out the remaining dark elves in a furious, bloody whirlwind of death.

I hauled the fire back into the blade, back into the earth, then crawled across to Max. He was, unsurprisingly given the wound I'd inflicted, dead. Shock and surprise had forever been etched onto his now skeletal features.

My gaze went past him.

Saw Mo.

No longer surrounded by that dark web of magic.

No longer breathing.

Fuck it, *no*.

I wasn't going to lose her. Not now. Not after everything we'd been through.

I pulled Vita from my brother's neck, then crawled over to Mo and cradled her head in my lap. After tearing open her shirt, I placed a hand under her breast, over her heart, then thrust Vita into the flagstones, gripping her tightly as I made a connection between the earth, me, and Mo. Power surged—the earth's, mine, Vita's—hitting Mo with such force that her spine arched. The red mist of pain descended, and my eyes bled, but I didn't break the connection and I didn't give up. I kept the energy flowing, willing her to breathe, to live.

Time slowed to a crawl, even though my heart raced and a blur of motion and noise surrounded me. I paid it no heed, watching Mo intently, willing her chest to rise, her heart to beat under my fingers.

For far too long, neither did.

Then, with a body-shaking gasp, her eyes snapped open. She sucked in several great gulps of air before her gaze came to mine. Pride shone. Pride and relief.

"My darling girl," she murmured, her voice hoarse and wracked with pain. "You did it."

"Yes," I whispered as bloody tears fell. "I did."

Was the price I'd paid a fair one?

In the end, the answer would always be yes. At least in the cold light of day.

But in the deep silence of the night, when darkness and

regret came out to play? When the heated echo of my twin's blood once again pulsed across my hand and I saw again the shock and reproach in his eyes?

I suspected it was a question that would haunt me for many years to come.

EPILOGUE

From the highest point on top of King Island, the scope of the damage done to Ainslyn was very evident. While the business sector and the new port had come through the attack relatively unscathed, the residential and business areas surrounding the old town wall had basically been decimated. Max might have died unceremoniously on the floor of an old farmhouse, but his forces had taken a while to get the memo.

Or perhaps it had been my brother's last gift to us. A final fuck-you.

I raised my gaze. Dusk was settling in, and the sky was the color of blood. Memories stirred, and tears stung my eyes. I took a deep breath and blinked them away. Despite the doubts I'd had in that old farmhouse, I only had to look at Ainslyn to know the price *had* indeed been worth it, no matter what the night's demons might otherwise whisper. It would take months to clean up the mess in the outer sections of the city and years to rebuild. And while in the end there'd only been a dozen or so deaths here, London had suffered a far greater toll. The grand old city would never be the same, though that in part was not only due to the destruction of her many iconic buildings, but because the High Witch Council had officially been granted sitting rights in the House of Lords. For the first time in centuries, witches would have a hand in the laws governing the land they'd lived in—and at one time ruled—for thousands of centuries.

"You okay?"

The soft question rose from the darkness behind me, and I smiled. "I will be. Eventually."

"Well, that's a definite improvement."

"What is?" I turned and loosely wrapped my arms around Luc's neck. The ragged scar that ran from his left temple to the edge of his mouth was the only visible sign of just how close he'd come to death when Max's lightning had struck that grove of trees.

He wrapped his arms around my waist and pulled me closer to his big, warm body. "I mean you not automatically saying you're 'just fine.'"

I laughed. "Expect a return to form sooner rather than later."

"I'd be disappointed if there wasn't."

"And disappointing you is not something I ever plan to do."

My voice held a smoky edge, and a smile crinkled the corners of his lovely eyes. "Oh, I don't expect you ever will."

"Even when I'm adding your top shelf whiskey to a hot chocolate?"

"Might have to think about that one," he said with a laugh, and then kissed me. It was more than just a long, slow, and utterly delicious exploration. It was a promise of what was to come. Of what lay ahead for us. Not just tonight, but in the months and years and maybe even decades ahead.

A throat was cleared behind him.

"Ginny," I said with a soft groan. "Your timing sucks."

"Doesn't it just," she said cheerfully. "But hey, you've plenty of time later tonight to get hot and heavy. Mo's ready."

I sighed and pulled back. Luc swung around and offered me his arm. "Allow this soldier the privilege of escorting his queen."

I smiled and tucked my arm through his. Numerous people had called me "queen" over the past week—even the true queen had acknowledged my presence, while making it abundantly clear my line had forgone any claim to the English throne long ago—but his usage was the only one that really meant a damn.

I was, and forever would be, his queen.

We followed Ginny back up the path and into the stone monolith circle that surrounded the newly resurrected King's Stone.

A dozen men and women stood around the stone, their expressions so solemn I had to bite back the instinctive need to laugh. Damn it, where were these people when we were struggling to uncover information about Elysian? Why did it take Max's failed coup for them to realize the past was as important as the future and that there were some stories and artifacts that should never be forgotten?

Of course, they wouldn't be now. I'd make damn sure of that.

I took a deep breath and then slipped my arm from Luc's and moved through the circle to the King's Stone. Mia gave me a quick thumbs-up from the other side of the rock, and Barney nudged her lightly with his shoulder as he made a comment too soft for me to hear. From the rather dramatic roll of her eyes, I gathered it had been something about decorum being necessary in what he deemed a solemn occasion.

I couldn't help grinning and returning the gesture. Bugger decorum.

I stopped in front of Mo. She scanned me critically, then nodded, just the once. She, like me, was still recovering from everything that had happened in the farmhouse. We could—and had—healed each other, but only to a point. There were some wounds and some energies that simply needed time.

She raised the elaborately decorated sword and offered her to me. The steel was cold and dead in my grip, the total opposite of Elysian, which remained strapped across my back, but hidden in the gray. We still had a long journey ahead of us both before she could be returned to the concealed depths of the lake on Bodmin Moor.

I intended to close the gates.

Every single one of them.

And while I knew it would take time and the locks would not hold forever—just as the main gate never had—it would give us time to develop a more usable means of confronting and defeating Darkside.

What happened in London, and to a lesser extent here in Ainslyn, must never be allowed to happen again. Even if another heir went rogue and claimed the true sword.

I looked up at the King's Stone. Mo had already placed and lit the short white candles necessary for the protection blessing I'd perform once the sword had been resheathed. While it was traditionally done in the first dawn of the new year, in drawing the sword, Max had shattered its protections.

I took a steadying breath, then shoved my free hand into the hollow smoothed by countless of my ancestors and stepped up onto the rock. The faded warning etched into the stone had not been replaced or sharpened. To be honest, neither Mo nor I saw the need. If was better for all if the public thought this sword was the real deal; it would deter those who might otherwise seek Elysian once she'd been returned to her watery resting place. As long as those who truly mattered—the Blackbirds and the High Council—knew the truth, there wouldn't be a repeat of the mess we'd found ourselves in.

As the dusk settled in, I raised the fake sword to the blood-painted sky. The final rays of the day struck her hilt and, as the golden rose slowly unfurled, I thrust the blade deep into the heart of the stone. Then I raised the vials of sanctified water and slowly moved around the sword's base, calling on the power of the sun and the moon to protect the blade through the upcoming year, to keep it safe from darkness and all else who might wish her harm. As the words ran across the silence, a force sharper and more ethereal than any mere spell rose. I understood what that force was now—it was the power of the earth and the sky.

A shaft of golden light shot from the unfurled center of the rose and fell around the stone, melding first into the blessing and then into the rock. The golden light died, and the rose curled in on itself again.

The sword was safe for another year.

A soft murmur rose from the councilors gathered below, and the curiosity in their expressions suggested they had questions they wanted to ask. Thankfully, we'd expected this to happen, and Ginny, Mia, and Barney firmly ushered them away with a quick "later."

I jumped down from the rock, then stepped into Mo's

waiting arms and hugged her fiercely. She didn't say anything. Not for several minutes. Then she pulled back, caught my face, and kissed my forehead.

"Now go fuck the hell out of that man of yours. Everything else can wait."

I burst out laughing, even as Luc said, "That sounds like a damn fine plan to me."

"I dare say it would, Blackbird. But remember, I want grandbairns. Lots and lots of grandbairns to fill my twilight years with love and laughter. And yes, I already have two I will love and cherish, but I want a brood."

"Define what you mean by brood," I said, voice dry, "because while I may indeed have a very long lifespan, I'm not spending the next fifty years popping out kids for you to spoil rotten."

She pursed her lips, her eyes merry as she pretended to consider the question. "A good even dozen should do. I've already two, so that leaves ten."

Luc laughed and caught my hand. "I'm not sure either of us are interested in a brood that big, but I will promise we'll devote every possible waking moment to perfecting the act of child making."

"Excellent." She made a shooing motion with her hands. "Off you go then. I don't expect to see you for at least three days. Anything less, I'll consider a dereliction of duty."

"Never let it be said a Blackbird is guilty of such a crime," he said, voice solemn.

Then with another laugh, he raced me down the path, over the bridge, and onto his motorbike. But we didn't journey all the way down to his manor house in Somerset.

Instead, we stopped in a quaint little B&B on the

outskirts of Worcester and did exactly what Mo had commanded.

She didn't get her grandbairns. Not that year. Not for several years.

But she did get them.

Six, in fact.

ALSO BY KERI ARTHUR

Relic Hunters Novels
Crown of Shadows (Feb 2022)
Sword of Darkness (Oct 2022)
Ring of Ruin (June 2023)

The Witch King's Crown
Blackbird Rising (Feb 2020)
Blackbird Broken (Oct 2020)
Blackbird Crowned (June 2021)

Lizzie Grace series
Blood Kissed (May 2017)
Hell's Bell (Feb 2018)
Hunter Hunted (Aug 2018)
Demon's Dance (Feb 2019)
Wicked Wings (Oct 2019)
Deadly Vows (Jun 2020)
Magic Misled (Feb 2021)
Broken Bonds (Oct 2021)
Sorrows Song (June 2022)
Killer's Kiss (Feb 2023)

Kingdoms of Earth & Air

Unlit (May 2018)

Cursed (Nov 2018)

Burn (June 2019)

The Outcast series

City of Light (Jan 2016)

Winter Halo (Nov 2016)

The Black Tide (Dec 2017)

Souls of Fire series

Fireborn (July 2014)

Wicked Embers (July 2015)

Flameout (July 2016)

Ashes Reborn (Sept 2017)

Dark Angels series

Darkness Unbound (Sept 27th 2011)

Darkness Rising (Oct 26th 2011)

Darkness Devours (July 5th 2012)

Darkness Hunts (Nov 6th 2012)

Darkness Unmasked (June 4 2013)

Darkness Splintered (Nov 2013)

Darkness Falls (Dec 2014)

Riley Jenson Guardian Series
Full Moon Rising (Dec 2006)

Kissing Sin (Jan 2007)

Tempting Evil (Feb 2007)

Dangerous Games (March 2007)

Embraced by Darkness (July 2007)

The Darkest Kiss (April 2008)

Deadly Desire (March 2009)

Bound to Shadows (Oct 2009)

Moon Sworn (May 2010)

Myth and Magic series
Destiny Kills (Oct 2008)

Mercy Burns (March 2011)

Nikki & Micheal series

Dancing with the Devil (March 2001 / Aug 2013)

Hearts in Darkness Dec (2001/ Sept 2013)

Chasing the Shadows Nov (2002/Oct 2013)

Kiss the Night Goodbye (March 2004/Nov 2013)

Damask Circle series
Circle of Fire (Aug 2010 / Feb 2014)

Circle of Death (July 2002/March 2014)

Circle of Desire (July 2003/April 2014)

Ripple Creek series

Beneath a Rising Moon (June 2003/July 2012)

Beneath a Darkening Moon (Dec 2004/Oct 2012)

Spook Squad series

Memory Zero (June 2004/26 Aug 2014)

Generation 18 (Sept 2004/30 Sept 2014)

Penumbra (Nov 2005/29 Oct 2014)

Stand Alone Novels

Who Needs Enemies (E-book only, Sept 1 2013)

Novella

Lifemate Connections (March 2007)

Anthology Short Stories

The Mammoth Book of Vampire Romance (2008)

Wolfbane and Mistletoe--2008

Hotter than Hell--2008